"Here comes another one," Sapper screamed as he ran along the parapet, then launched himself into the air—

As the grenade exploded off to his left, thankfully along the farthest wall.

Pope witnessed it all in high-definition, real life. You didn't need a remote control to watch this show, only an ass to kiss good-bye.

A long section of the stone-and-tile balustrade exploded into pieces, the debris hurtling at him, knocking him onto his back, Sapper crashing down beside him.

That was grenade number two. The men down below had gotten all creative. They had trapped their prey on the roof and were now lobbing grenades over the parapet. They had crappy aim but decent ordnance. And who knew how many firecrackers they were packing.

Good news was, the absolutely beautiful sound of Night Stalker's turbine was drawing near, the wash already tugging on Pope's clothes.

"Get up you bastards, I'm right here," the pilot barked over the radio.

Pope was about to rise when gunfire from below—directed at the chopper—sparked off the landing skids. If he and Sapper didn't haul ass now, one lucky shot might take down their ride.

By P.W. Storm

The Mercenaries
THUNDERKILL
BLOOD DIAMONDS

Force 5 Recon
DEPLOYMENT: PHILIPPINES
DEPLOYMENT: NORTH KOREA
DEPLOYMENT: PAKISTAN

THE
MERCENARIES
THUNDERKILL

P.W. STORM

HARPER

An Imprint of HarperCollinsPublishers

This is a work of fiction. Names, characters, places, and incidents are products of the author's imagination or are used fictitiously and are not to be construed as real. Any resemblance to actual events, locales, organizations, or persons, living or dead, is entirely coincidental.

HARPER

An Imprint of HarperCollins*Publishers*
10 East 53rd Street
New York, New York 10022-5299

Copyright © 2007 by Peter Telep
ISBN: 978-0-06-085797-4
ISBN-10: 0-06-085797-8

First Harper paperback printing: August 2007

HarperCollins® and Harper® are registered trademarks of HarperCollins Publishers.

Printed in the United States of America

Visit Harper paperbacks on the World Wide Web at
www.harpercollins.com

10 9 8 7 6 5 4 3 2 1

For James Ide

Acknowledgments

· ·

Vietnam veteran and Chief Warrant Officer James Ide, a fellow Floridian with twenty-one years of active naval service, once again brought his considerable experience and expertise to this manuscript. Jim helped me brainstorm and refine ideas and build a working outline. Then he went on to read and respond to every page of this book. His excitement for this series and his contributions have been nothing short of amazing, and much of what you read here is the work of our collaboration. He is a remarkable man.

Major William R. Reeves, U.S. Army, once again helped from the beginning stages, contributing to the outline and the manuscript. He did extensive research on weapons, terrain, communications, and fielded my many questions. He's a continued source of inspiration, and I'm honored to know him.

Many other retired military personnel were willing to speak to me about their work "in the private sector," though understandably, they requested that their names not be listed here. I still would like to acknowledge them, and they all know who they are . . . though you never will.

THE
MERCENARIES
THUNDERKILL

Chapter 1

....

"**B**lackhound One, you got three more, northeast, maybe half a klick!" cried Billy Pope over the radio. "You need to boogie right now. Wait! Two more, directly east your position. Come on, bossman! Move it!"

Michael "Mad Dog" Hertzog heeded Pope's warning and grabbed the ten-year-old boy by the wrist. They took off running along the slope, heading for a stand of trees whose branches were already alive with gunfire originating from somewhere behind them in the morning fog.

"One, this is Two, over," called Alistair Bibby, who was about twenty meters south, hauling his own British ass across the mountainside.

"What now?" Mad Dog asked him.

"Night Stalker informs me the bird is still on the ground. I say again, the bird is still down, over."

"Tell him if he doesn't get that piece of shit airborne, he's fired, out!"

A dozen heartbeats later Mad Dog and the kid reached the trees and crouched behind them. The gunfire tapered off into the faint cries of birds and the rustle of tree limbs.

For a ten-year-old caught in the middle of a firefight, Kwei was remarkably calm, his eyes steady and as jet black as his short hair. Maybe he was shocked into silence, who knew? Mad Dog reached into his ruck, withdrew a big Ka-Bar and leather scabbard. He attached the scabbard to the kid's belt, then withdrew the knife, handed it to him. "Okay?"

Kwei ran a finger along the serrated blade, testing the sharp tip as his face grew even more flush. He bared his teeth, then made a stabbing motion and said something in a fierce tone, followed by, "Okay, I kill!"

"That's right," said Mad Dog, nodding.

Ordinarily, he would never have armed a child, but after what those bastards had done to Kwei—the mental abuse, the sexual torture—he wanted to make the kid feel as though he, too, were fighting back. Just holding the knife might help him release some of the anger.

Off to their right Heverton "Dr. Doolittle" Santiago charged up the hill, and Mad Dog felt a pang of relief as the translator reached them and crouched down to catch his breath. Doolittle was nearing forty, but only the creases near his eyes betrayed that. He had the lean physique of a marathon runner, and his speed was as handy as his language skills.

Mad Dog scanned the bush with his binoculars, then lowered them and regarded the man. "How we doing?"

The translator chuckled sarcastically. "The usual."

"How many?"

"A platoon-size force."

Mad Dog grimaced then raised his chin to Kwei. "Tell the kid not to worry. Just lie, okay?"

"Sergeant, what's with the knife?"

The translator's question struck a nerve. "Forget the knife," Mad Dog said. "Just shut up and do it."

Doolittle sighed and got to work, speaking fluent Burmese, his brown face creasing tightly as he took the blade from Kwei.

"Hey!" cried Mad Dog. He was about to wrench back the knife when he realized that Doolittle was trying to show Kwei how to grip the blade properly.

"Better he doesn't cut himself, right, Sergeant?" Doolittle returned the Ka-Bar and positioned the kid's fingers on the Kraton handle.

"Yeah."

While Mad Dog appreciated that Doolittle called him Sergeant, a tribute to his Force Recon days and their time spent working together as team leader and civilian translator, he didn't appreciate the Brazilian questioning his decision.

And worse, Doolittle wasn't the only one doing that.

Since they had come to Southeast Asia to rescue Kwei from jadeite smugglers and collect their cool million in fees, every one of Mad Dog's men had either openly or through innuendo questioned his leadership. Just the day before, Mad Dog had snapped at Pope: "I had fucking colon cancer, not brain cancer, you asshole! And I beat it! And I will lead this team!"

That was the first time he had spoken openly of his illness, though they knew about it from the reports of old Dan back home at "The Pound" on Cebu Island in the Philippines. The outburst had shocked all of them into silence.

Shit. No wonder he had become a mercenary. His temper was as short as his dick. And after living on this planet for over four decades, he knew he should know better. Didn't. Always let his trap get him into trouble.

Reports came in from Wolfgang, then Boo Boo and Drac. Sapper's report summed up the rest: "Uh, Blackhound One, this is Five. We got about twenty guys coming in from all directions. So we got about twenty seconds to get the fuck out of here. And after that? We got about twenty seconds to live. At least the wait won't be long."

The former Army engineer broke off radio contact and let a few grenades fly, twin booms shaking the hillside behind them.

Damn, these jobs always looked great on paper.

The smugglers had demanded ten kilos of *fei-ts'ui*—kingfisher green—jadeite in exchange for the kid. The estimated value of those rocks? Thirty-eight million.

Kwei's father, Aung-san, owned the mine and had explained in well-practiced English that *fei-ts'ui* jade was the most desirable imperial green jade in the world. The Chinese had named it "kingfisher" to associate it with the iridescent green neck feathers of the Chinese species of the kingfisher bird. Smugglers moved more of the stuff between Myanmar and Hong Kong than the government-controlled jade market; which, of course, Mad Dog knew, explained why the scumbags had kidnapped Kwei and demanded payment in jade instead of cash.

"All of that makes sense," he had told Aung-san. "But it doesn't explain why you're lowballing me."

He was saving the guy thirty-eight million, but the cheap bastard wouldn't pay more than one million for the safe return of his boy.

"Surely, a businessman such as yourself understands something like this."

"What I understand is that your boy isn't worth more than a million. He might be disappointed to hear that."

"Mr. Hertzog, I have five sons."

"Meaning what? You can spare one?"

"I love them all."

"But it's easier to split love four ways instead of five?"

"Mr. Hertzog, if you don't want the job, I'll find somebody else. There are many companies like yours."

The truth hurt. Fact was, Mad Dog knew he owed the job to Mr. Bibby's friendship with Aung-san. During his days with MI6, the British spy organization, Bibby had made a deal with Aung-san. A favor for a favor was how Bibby had put it; he would not elaborate.

And furthermore, the International Philippine Group (IPG), which was Mad Dog's pride and joy—the company he had dreamed of forming—had come under heavy fire from much larger competitors who were stealing all the good jobs based on their size and considerable resources.

Shit. Mad Dog knew he couldn't even squeeze an extra hundred grand out of Bibby's buddy. So screw it. He had taken the gig, had wanted to get back in the saddle, back on the field. A nice, little, million-dollar scrimmage was just what he needed.

What's more, ambushing the smugglers and getting the kid out had gone down by the numbers. The men had come through. But not the chopper. If it wasn't one thing, it was another.

Sapper set off a few more grenades, and Mad Dog took the cue. He signaled to Doolittle and Kwei, and they left the trees, jogging forward along a sharp ridge. The fog remained thick, the moist ground deadening their footfalls.

"One, this is Ten," called Night Stalker, the pilot's voice thin and crackling in Mad Dog's earpiece.

"Tell me you're en route, asshole."

"Negative. Suggest you move farther north, past the LZ toward another clearing I saw during insertion. That'll buy me a little more repair time, over."

"What the fuck? You got no time! Extract us right now, otherwise you're fired."

"Hey, fuck you, Hertzog. Ain't my fault!"

"Bullshit! You told me that helo was a hundred percent before we left!"

"It was! You can't predict this shit. I got the problem ID'd. I'll get back in the air."

"Forget it, asshole. You're done. Walk home, out."

Mad Dog knew the other seven mercs were monitoring the radio, so he added, "All right, Blackhounds, rally north past our LZ to a second clearing. Set up a 360-defense there. If it gets too hairy, we'll shift to Ten's location, make repairs on the helo, and Blackhound Two will fly us back. I say again, rally second clearing, 360 defense, then on my order fall back to Ten's location. This is Blackhound One, out."

Doolittle, who had taken point, thrust a fist in the air, and Mad Dog dropped to his haunches, dragging the kid with him. He put a finger to his lips.

The three smugglers Pope had spotted came up and over a small mound, then dropped onto their bellies, taking up firing positions. They were armed with AKs and grenades, maybe mortars and RPGs, and if your imagination got the best of you, you might think they had Javelin missiles and a hundred other high-tech toys.

Mad Dog crawled up beside Doolittle and whispered, "Idiots don't see us yet. Take left. I got right. Leave the guy in the center. He'll fall back. When he does, I'll drop his ass."

"All right, Sergeant. I'm good," said the translator, staring down the barrel of his Micro-Galil.

Mad Dog raised his M4, the cross hairs of his optical sight floating over the scumbag on the right until they came to rest on his head. *Nice ambush, fellas. But I'm not talking about yours.*

"Sergeant?"

"Yep, on three. One, two—"

Twin shots rang out, yet even as they did, the goddamned kid ran forward—

Right between Doolittle and Mad Dog.

Okay, so two of the three assholes slumped under perfect head shots that were so well-executed, so well-timed, that Mad Dog know no one would believe it when he and Doolittle told the story.

But that guy in the center, the one he had intended to waste with his rifle's attached grenade launcher, had decided to play martyr.

He came running at them, firing wildly, just as Kwei ran directly toward him, the knife jutting from the kid's fist.

It was the stupidest thing Mad Dog had ever seen, but you were talking about an uneducated scumbag kidnapper and an emotionally screwed up ten-year-old who had a jerk for a father and had been raped by his kidnappers.

But fuck, Kwei wasn't just any kid. He was the million dollar boy.

"Kwei!" Doolittle hollered, then added something in Burmese. "Kwei!"

The kid kept running.

Mad Dog bolted to his feet, raised his rifle and sighted the smuggler. *Bang!* Shot to the chest, blood spraying. The guy fell back, still firing, *rat-tat-tat, rat-tat-tat*—

And Kwei went down. *Jesus Christ! He was hit!*

Holding his breath, Mad Dog charged forward after the boy, who was crawling toward the kidnapper. The kid reached the smuggler, drew back his knife, and stabbed the guy in the chest, his hand clenching the knife and not letting go. Mad Dog arrived, seized Kwei's wrist and pried the boy's hand free.

"Roll him over," said Doolittle.

They did, and saw that the boy had been hit in the hip, clean entry and exit but a whole lot of blood. The round could've nicked his femoral artery, but Mad Dog didn't want to speculate on that. No prophet of doom shit yet.

"Fuck, we can't stop the bleeding here," he said as he yanked his knife from the smuggler and stuffed the bloody blade into his ruck. Then he hoisted the kid over his shoulder. "Come on."

The boy grunted and cried as Mad Dog picked his way up and over the mound, past the two dead smugglers, Doolittle just behind, as more gunfire echoed across the mountains.

"One, this is Four," called Pope. "I've found the second clearing. It's about a hundred meters directly north of the first one, over."

"Roger that. Get high and keep it coming, out."

Mad Dog knew that Billy Pope liked being point man—after all, he'd been a Navy SEAL—but didn't like climbing trees. Too bad. Up he'd go. They needed his intel. And they needed Drac, aka "Larry Bowler," the former Air Force combat controller, to help guide Night Stalker into the second clearing. Fire Team Three—comprised of Wolfgang, Drac, and Boo Boo—had yet to report their position. They had better be closing in, he thought, or he'd fire them, too. He'd fire the whole fucking team!

Whoa, doggie. Calm down.

"Right here," said Mad Dog as they descended a few meters into a deep cut in the mountainside, its south side shielded by a large outcropping dotted by shrubs.

They worked as a proficient team, applying a tourniquet and bandaging the boy's wounds. Doolittle jabbed a needle into the kid's arm, giving him a spike of morphine, just the way the team's medic, Vincent Orrello, known as Boo Boo—and whose medical skills were unparalleled on the battlefield—had taught them.

A dumb smile formed on the kid's lips, and his whimpering turned to shallow breathing. He said something to Doolittle.

"What?" asked Mad Dog.

Doolittle's expression grew somber. "He thanked you for giving him the knife."

Mad Dog shrugged.

"We shouldn't move him," said Doolittle.

"No choice." Mad Dog scooped up the kid and off they went, steering around the back side of the mountain and descending through a stretch of muddy furrows.

The first clearing, their original landing zone, lay just ahead, and from their current vantage point, some twenty meters above the valley, Mad Dog spotted the second clearing.

He figured about ten minutes of brisk walking and

they'd be there. Doolittle kept a solid pace, guiding them down into the heavier brush, following the perimeter of the first clearing.

The valley was damper and mustier than the foothills, the humidity already oppressive. Mad Dog's face grew wet, the sweat dripping from his brow.

Wolfgang finally checked in, saying that he and his team had reached the new LZ and were getting set. Bibby was there now, too, having taken a shortcut through the scree lining the mountain's base.

An explosion about fifteen meters ahead sent Doolittle and Mad Dog crashing to the earth, the kid thudding hard onto his side. "God damn it, they see us!" shouted Mad Dog.

"Not for long," said Doolittle as he rose, then caught something over Mad Dog's shoulder.

As Mad Dog turned, Doolittle was already firing at two smugglers who had sprung from behind a row of shrubs. The first went down, clutching his neck.

But Doolittle missed the second guy.

Mad Dog didn't. He had already been reaching for his pistol, his M4 still slung over his shoulder. Two rounds to the smuggler's chest drove him staggering back, then he thudded hard to the deck.

"One, what's your ETA, over?" asked Pope.

"Two minutes," replied Mad Dog, panting into the boom mike. "Stand by, out."

He regarded Doolittle. "Too fucking close, man. I'm tired of this shit."

"Me, too, Sergeant." The translator's gaze turned to Kwei, and the blood-soaked bandage around his hip. "He's bleeding again. We shouldn't be moving him."

"God damn it!" Mad Dog sighed loudly in frustration.

"Aw, hell, let me carry him now," suggested Doolittle.

Mad Dog steadied his breath. "All right. I'm a better shot than you, anyway." He smiled weakly, then helped lift the boy across Doolittle's shoulders. With a nod, he raised his rifle. "Here we go."

"One, this is Ten," Night Stalker called. "You hold 'em off at that second clearing for maybe ten minutes more. That's all I need. Ten minutes, over."

"I thought I fired you."

"Hey, man, if you don't—"

"Ten minutes, meathead."

"Look, don't worry, I'll be there, out."

Mad Dog paused at a tree, waiting for Doolittle to catch up. "You know he's full of shit, right?"

Doolittle nodded. "Ten minutes means thirty to him. They'll be all over us by then."

"And we packed light. We'll run out of ammo before they do." Mad Dog checked Kwei's leg. "The kid's got no time, either. Shit, shit, shit."

They resumed their pace, now soaked in sweat, Mad Dog repeatedly glancing behind them, ever wary of another grenade, an RPG, a sudden rustle as imaginary gunmen whirled from behind trees then opened fire. He swore against the paranoia, willed himself to clear his head, to focus.

No doubt the remaining smugglers would surround them—if the team remained in place. Mad Dog wanted to take them past the second clearing and on toward Ten's LZ. Logic dictated that if they didn't stop moving, they might have a chance.

However, if Night Stalker did get their helo in the air, he'd have nowhere to land. They'd be in dense jungle, and he'd be wheeling overhead, utterly limp-dicked.

But what if he didn't fix the chopper? They'd be sitting in the clearing, firing until they ran out of ammo. Then they'd be on the run with no way to defend themselves.

How much trust should he put in one smartass pilot?

Dick Gallway, aka "Night Stalker," had flown in Somalia and had a front row seat during the Black Hawk Down affair. What he lacked in humility he made up for in skills, experience, and patience, the latter a rare commodity among mercs.

"Blackhounds, this is One. We're nearing your location, coming up from the south, with enemy in pursuit. I need Blackhound Nine right away. Our package is wounded. You hearing me, Nine. I need you right now!"

"One, this is Four," Pope answered. "Roger that. I have you. Nine, get over there. No sign of . . . wait, got two on your tail. Make that three. Seven, do you have them, over?"

"Roger, I do," answered Wolfgang.

"This is Blackhound Nine, I'm on my way, out," reported Boo Boo, his voice gruff.

The clearing was oval-shaped and only about thirty yards across, with tall trees and better cover along the northern side, which was where Mad Dog assumed the boys with the bigger guns had assembled. He was right—

Because as he and Doolittle veered right, following the treeline toward that northern side, a green wall of shrubs sparked to life as at least three of Mad Dog's men belched lead across the clearing.

Then a familiar hissing split the air. Two heartbeats later huge explosions rose to their left, the flashes coming first, the reverberations loud and chilling: incoming

RPG fire, followed by a pair of mortars exploding behind the line.

And then came the gunfire. And the grenades.

Oh my God . . .

The entire clearing erupted into a fire zone as hot as any in 'Nam, A'stan, or Iraq.

Mad Dog crouched down, raised his arm for Doolittle to stop. The translator dropped to his knees, and Mad Dog helped him lower Kwei to the ground, just as incoming rounds tore through the branches overhead, sending shattered limbs and cut leaves crashing down on them.

The ground shook again, with mortars pounding no more than fifty meters away, tearing up the earth, heaving sand and shrapnel that whooshed through the jungle.

Over it all came the voices of Mad Dog's men, cool and practiced. No rookies panicking in the fray. These men were a single defensive mechanism, a cyborg programmed to ward off smugglers, scumbags, and other assorted heathens:

"This is Five," called Sapper. "I got a bead on those mortars. They are mine."

"Roger that," answered Pope. "Seven? You and Eight shift to right flank and answer that small arms fire, over."

"Roger that," Wolfgang responded. "Moving out!"

"See two with RPGs," announced Pope. "I got 'em."

Muzzles winked like stars against the fading gloom, and several more trees caught fire, flames licking their way up toward the sky, gray smoke trailing.

A grenade exploded, followed by a call from Sapper: "First mortar is history! Gonna blow the second back to God."

Not a half second later a rocket launched by Sapper screamed away from the north side of the clearing . . . and *ka-boom*, the jungle directly opposite them turned from lush green to bonfire red.

Sapper barked a victory cry into the radio but cut himself off with a curse as withering gunfire sounded nearby. Something had surprised the burly black man, and he wasn't easily surprised.

A man appeared in the clearing and staggered forward, completely engulfed in flames. He dropped to his knees and was about to fall forward when another of Sapper's rockets struck him dead on, sending flaming body parts tumbling through the air, toward the trees.

"Well ain't it nice to be popular," said Boo Boo, taking one look at the kid and barely flinching as yet another burst from a grenade exploded along the trees to the south.

"You're looking at a million bucks right here, Boo," said Mad Dog. "And not only that, I like the kid. Save him."

The medic scratched his thinning gray crew cut. "No pressure at all." He tore through his supplies to set up an IV, tipped his head toward Doolittle. "Can he stay with me?"

"Yeah." Mad Dog turned to the translator. "Do it."

"You sure, Sergeant?"

"Fucking positive. Do not question me!"

"All right, all right."

Mad Dog stormed off, knees slashing through a thicket, as Pope and the others traded fierce volleys of gunfire with the smugglers, automatic weapons creating a racket so familiar that for a few seconds Mad Dog thought he was back in Afghanistan, fighting the Taliban—

Until a call from Pope ripped him back to reality. "One, we're taking fire from three sides now, over."

Mad Dog froze, glanced back at Boo Boo and Doolittle with the boy. Glanced across the clearing at the muzzle flashes, at another mortar exploding, at the sky filling quickly with more gray smoke and flames. He keyed his mike: "Night Stalker, you motherfucker! I need you right now!"

"Not yet, One. Not yet. Hold 'em off."

"Can't do it!" A round tore through the tree not a meter from Mad Dog's shoulder, sending him flat onto his gut. "Fuck!"

Well, there it was. Night Stalker would not arrive in time. And all they could do now was run with their tails between their legs. Or not. They could stay and fight.

Mad Dog burst up, onto his feet, lifted his rifle and cut loose, targeting the flashes opposite him.

Without warning, a machine gun rattled, and within a few seconds Mad Dog had found its position. He popped the pin on a grenade, let it fly, didn't wait for the boom. He was on his rifle again, shifting and firing.

Then he ran a few meters to the right, paused, raised the rifle, sent off a few more rounds, moved again, fired.

The once cool voices of his men grew tense:

"I gotta fall back!" screamed Pope.

"Lost contact with Seven," reported Drac. "Wolfgang, where are you, man?"

"One, this is Two," called a breathless Bibby. "Intel looks very bad from where I'm sitting. Satellite shows at least another score of smugglers moving in. Let's go."

And when Bibby said it was time to move, you either listened—or you died.

But maybe they could push their luck for just another minute or two.

"Blackhounds, this is One. Shift positions to east and west side of the clearing. Let's see if we can get 'em shooting at each other, over."

"One, this is Four," called Pope. "Can't do it! They have us completely pinned down!"

"One, this is Two. We are out of time," said Bibby, spacing his words for effect. "We have to fall back now—or we will be overrun!"

Mad Dog wove around trees and shrubs, reached Boo Boo, Doolittle, and the kid.

"I've stabilized him, slowed the bleeding," said the medic. "But that femoral artery . . . We can't run anymore with him. We'll be dusting off with a corpse."

Cursing through his teeth, Mad Dog whirled back toward the clearing as the gunfire intensified. Then he faced Boo Boo. "Figure out something. We got no choice."

The medic threw up his hands.

"Sergeant, is it worth it?" asked Doolittle. "They want him alive just as much as we do."

Mad Dog was beginning to lose his breath. "Christ, we can't leave him."

Doolittle's eyes widened. "It's only money."

Mad Dog slapped off the translator's grip. "I don't need this now." He glanced to the sky. "What I need is a goddamned helo!" He keyed his mike. "Night Stalker, you got thirty goddamned seconds! Do you read me? Thirty seconds!"

A burst of gunfire sent all of them to their bellies. Mad Dog faced Boo Boo, who pursed his lips, shook his head, then thrust out his hand. "Well, my friend, it was good times."

Mad Dog would not take the medic's hand. "Screw you, Boo Boo. Let's get off our fat asses and fight!"

The medic grinned and nodded. "Then we'll have bagels."

Mad Dog adjusted his grip on his rifle and turned to face Doolittle, who looked tense, ready to fire. "On three, gentlemen. One, two . . ."

Chapter 2

....

"**B**lackhound One, make smoke, over."

Mad Dog was about to say *Three!* but the voice in his earpiece, strangely thin, made him freeze and hold up an index finger. Doolittle and Boo Boo frowned.

"Blackhound One, I say again, make smoke, over."

Mad Dog pressed the boom mike to his lips. "Who is this?"

"Shut the fuck up and make smoke!"

At that moment another voice—God's voice—rose above the din of gunfire, grenades, and booming mortars, and God sounded exactly like a Huey helicopter, the characteristic *whomp-whomp-whomp* growing louder.

"Blackhounds, this is One. I don't know who the hell is up there, but get me some red smoke on the south. I'll pop green here, over."

Pope was quick to respond: "One, this is Four. I'm on it!"

Mad Dog wrenched open a pouch on his ruck, grabbed a green smoke grenade, and let her fly.

Pope's red smoke would mark the enemy's position, and both colors would help the mystery pilot estimate wind direction and velocity.

Normally, Mad Dog or Drac would have briefed the pilot regarding the LZ's conditions and helped guide him in, but this jock was already swooping down with a door gunner firing madly into the enemy treeline, even as the main rotor clipped a few limbs . . .

And for an excruciating moment Mad Dog thought the bird would roll on its side and crash.

But the pilot leveled off, hovered twenty feet from the ground, then began a slow descent, the helo's chin turret blazing with more fire.

"Blackhound One, this is Night Stalker. I am good to go, lifting off now, over."

Mad Dog smiled bitterly. "You're a little fuckin' late! There's a second helo here. We'll board it. Need suppressing fire on red smoke zone, over."

Night Stalker hesitated, probably wondering what the hell another chopper was doing in the area, then responded: "Uh, okay, uh, roger that! Suppressing fire, red smoke zone, out."

"All right, Blackhounds! Fall back to the chopper! Fall back!"

Mad Dog regarded the kid, then Boo Boo. "We have to move just one more time. Now we roll the dice."

The medic grimaced. "Your call."

"We'll cover you."

Boo Boo gingerly lifted the semiconscious Kwei into his arms, while Doolittle and Mad Dog served up some breakfast encased in brass.

All three paused a few moments, then Mad Dog gave the signal and they bolted for the Huey, quickly engulfed in a choking mixture of red and green smoke driven into their faces by the rotor wash.

Pope, a black bandanna wrapped around his bald head, was already at the bay door, standing beside a door gunner who was probably a local. Both men were hollering, unloading hot brass in the gale, faces ruddy and hard.

Mad Dog and Doolittle reached the bird, then helped Boo Boo slide Kwei on board.

At the same time, Drac and Wolfgang came charging from the treeline on the opposite side of the chopper. *Boom!* A mortar went off behind them—

And they hit the dirt as shrapnel flew overhead and pinged across the chopper.

The pilot, whose face was concealed behind a black helmet and opaque visor, screamed something inaudible, probably, "Move your fucking asses!"

Drac sprang to his feet and began climbing aboard the helo. Mad Dog turned back toward the trees, still pinpricked by muzzle flashes. He reared back and lobbed a grenade. Then he lobbed a second and was about to leap into the bay when he saw Wolfgang still lying in the dirt, unmoving.

"He's down!" shouted Mad Dog.

Drac's lean, birdlike face screwed into a knot: He couldn't hear a goddamned thing because Mad Dog hadn't keyed his mike. But Mad Dog pointed as he scrambled into the bay, crawled across it, and then jumped out the other side.

Drac was right behind him, and together they lifted Wolfgang, drawing a spate of fresh fire that was as quickly halted by the chopper's door gunner. They reached the bay and slid the fallen Wolfgang inside.

"You're hit!" Mad Dog screamed, eyeing blood on Drac's neck.

"No!" he hollered back. "Got cut on a tree!"

Bibby was already on board, too, and he pulled Drac up and into the helo. Mad Dog would be last on. The landing skids were already leaving the ground as he set off a last grenade from his rifle's launcher, watched the explosion, then took Pope's hand and was hoisted aboard.

As they lifted off, Night Stalker arrived, the rocket pods on his own Huey blazing. Lines of billowing white smoke cut across the sky like chalk across a green board, then . . . the entire south side of the clearing blossomed into mushrooms of fire. Secondary explosions shone between the dark pockets of red smoke and rings of burning trees.

Mad Dog glanced at Boo Boo, who was holding Kwei's IV bag in one hand, his expression grave.

Wolfgang, who was lying against the back of the empty copilot's seat, blinked hard while Drac checked him for wounds, though Mad Dog suspected that the former Army master gunner was perfectly fine, at least physically.

Wolfgang had been going through a funk for the past year, and one night he showed up at The Pound sans ponytail and long beard, sans all body hair, to "get clean." Weird.

An RPG screamed across the Huey's windshield, missing them by about two meters, maybe less. The pilot cursed, banked hard right, then brushed the treetops, jostling everyone hard before they finally cleared the zone.

Night Stalker, meanwhile, was still laying down rocket fire, and he was assisted by Bibby, who raised his middle finger at the enemy. The Brit then leaned over and shouted in Mad Dog's ear: "Bloody mess, this was! Two birds next time. Always two!"

Mad Dog nodded.

"Ladies, I think we have now reached the friendly skies," began the pilot over the radio, "and the pucker up sign has been turned off."

Mad Dog snickered. "Pilot, your voice is sounding more familiar. I don't even want to ask."

The pilot threw up his helmet's visor . . .

And *he* was most definitely a *she*.

Lean, mid-thirties, with supermodel cheekbones framed by blond hair, their mystery chopper jock was the kind of woman other women wanted dead because no one deserved to be that beautiful—and that smart.

No shit, she was the most stunning thing he had ever seen, jumpsuit and helmet notwithstanding, and he was thrilled to be near her again—and not just because she had saved their asses.

"Oh, fuck," gasped Mad Dog, hamming it up. "Not you."

"Yeah, it's me," she replied, mimicking his disappointed tone. "A bitch and her bird. It's all about timing, huh?"

"You must have a crush on me."

"You, old man? Come on. Why I'm here has nothing to do with you, believe me. Don't flatter yourself."

"Then this is an amazing coincidence."

"Not really, given our line of work. We'll talk later. You're buying, of course . . . "

Pope's eyes narrowed. "Yo, bossman, you know her?" he asked over the radio.

"Yeah, she wanted to work with us," Mad Dog replied.
"And he turned me down."

"That's right. And hey, you guys can call her Fraulein
Hemorrhoid."

The pilot glanced back, caught Mad Dog's broad
smile, smirked, and keyed her mike. "Hey, Mr. Mad Dog,
you won't be smiling when you get my bill."

"Hey, we didn't ask to be picked up."

"Then maybe you'd like to get off?" She threw the
stick forward, taking the chopper into a steep dive, drawing shouts from everyone on board.

Mad Dog grabbed one of the door straps. "Jesus, all
right! We got wounded, you crazy bitch! What do you
want?"

Dom's Beer Bar
Soi 7, Central Pattaya, Thailand
2130 Hours Local Time

What she wanted was obvious . . .

Two days after the debacle in Myanmar, Mad Dog and
his savior were drinking beer and playing pool on a table
that wasn't exactly flat, so it was like hitting balls on a moving ship. As a matter of fact, the game room was so tight
that twice Mad Dog had to ask a few of the bar girls to shift
around so he could make a shot. Still, the place was intimate, well off the beaten path, and quiet enough for them
"to talk," as she had put it. Of course, he wanted to take her
to one of the nearby hotels, get a room, and "talk" there.

"You know, the only reason I saved your ass," she said,
"was so I could kick it at pool."

"Are you a man hater or just horny?"

She eyed him salaciously, taking a year off his life.

Katharina Kugelkerl—"Kat" for short—had exploded into Mad Dog's office in Cebu a year ago, just before he began his chemo treatments, asking for a job.

Her résumé was impressive. In fact, too impressive. She didn't need IPG or the money. She had already established herself as a well-respected VIP bodyguard. The way Mad Dog saw it, she wanted to join them for kicks.

"Fuck you," was his response, and he kicked her out of his office. But goddamn, she was hot!

And now she was back in his life. Was it fate? he wondered. More likely it was some kind of celestial bowel movement . . .

She lined up for her next shot. "How's the boy? He make it? He didn't look good."

"My medic's an ace. The kid made it."

"So mission accomplished, huh?"

"By the time I get done paying the bills for that job, I'll be lucky to make a nickel."

"Then why'd you take it? Don't you analyze a job before you bid on it? You could look at computer models, the whole fucking ball of wax. That's what I do."

"Computer models? I'm a simple guy. The job wasn't far from home, and I don't know, I wanted to get out and do something."

She called her shot, took it. He winced and could almost feel her boot connecting with his rump. "Look, I know you've had a tough year."

"Oh, yeah?"

"I've been there myself."

Mad Dog set down his beer. "Probably not."

"Think again. I had Hodgkins lymphoma when I was only twenty-three. Knocked the crap out of me, but I beat it."

"No shit. I guess that's not something you put on your résumé. God knows it's long enough."

"But you hardly know it all," Kat said.

"Yeah, like why you were flying around Burma."

She made a face. "I got myself hired to babysit the American ambassador on a human rights fact-finding mission. We were near Bhamo when I started picking up chatter about a firefight involving some Americans. I actually found your band and homed in on you."

"I'm supposed to believe that? I like my original theory better."

"You would. Anyway, I told the ambassador I needed to drop him off in Bhamo and go help you guys. He said if I did that, I was fired."

"Why would he fire you?"

"Because I said you guys were mercs, and he didn't want his name associated with mercenary activities—even if you were Americans."

"So now you're broke, living in a refrigerator box."

"Yeah, which brings us to my next request."

She finally missed a shot, and Mad Dog studied the table. "Come on, we've been down that road."

"You really think I'm here for fun or to show up some macho assholes? I got enough money to buy a thousand refrigerator boxes . . . "

"Then tell me why. Make me believe."

"I'm sick and tired of catering to the snobs. I came from the bottom, just like you. There's more out there for both of us. We can make money and actually help people along the way."

"Well, you've come a long way from the bottom, but come on, Kat, you don't need me or my company to get away from the snobs or to satisfy some do-gooder guilt trip. Find another employer. Fly charters. Donate to charity. It's a lot safer. Hell, I might have some charter work for you, but that's it."

"Come on, that's not the same."

"You mean no adrenaline rush, huh?"

"Yeah, that's part of it. Bottom line is, I'm looking for work. I'll complement your team. I'll gather intel much more discretely than they can. I'm not afraid to shake my ass and tits to do it."

"Would you fuck a guy for intel?"

"I don't know. What do you have that I need?" she asked, and stood tall to show off her body.

Johns Hopkins Hospital
Baltimore
1720 Hours Local Time

Mad Dog had dozed off in the examination room, his thoughts focused on long legs, blond hair, high cheekbones, and a silky voice that repeatedly cooed, "Mr. Mad Dog, oh, yes, Mr. Mad Dog, tell me what I need to know."

When the doctor entered and shook him by the shoulder, his throbbing hard-on was tenting up his gown.

The doc must've noticed, too. She cleared her voice, spoke in an uncomfortable tone: "Uh, Mr. Hertzog, sorry to keep you waiting . . . "

"It's okay." He sat up, embarrassed, pulling at his gown to cover Mad Dog Jr.

The doctor removed her glasses, revealing deep wrinkles around her eyes. She was in her mid-forties, his generation, a kindred spirit. "Well, you're doing terrific, you know that?"

"Cancerwise, yeah."

"You're one of the lucky ones."

"I know."

During his chemotherapy, most of the individual "bays" were wide open, and he couldn't help but over-hear conversations: spouses consoling their partners after learning chemo wasn't working.

He learned a great deal more about bravery as he watched a fourteen-year-old girl come in each week, alone, with the most positive attitude in the world. He saw others led to private rooms in despair. He listened to stories from individuals who were undergoing their third or fourth chemo regimen because their cancer had come back as many times.

In his world, the enemy was always tangible, but this cancer was like a spirit, coming and going as it pleased, haunting you day and night. And you couldn't get a fix on its position, couldn't set up for a sniper shot, couldn't send in mortar fire or call for air support.

These folks, the young and old, they knew an enemy much worse than the ones he usually dealt with, an enemy who moved much more slowly than a bullet but killed just as unmercifully.

Mad Dog shrugged. "Well, is that it? See you in three months?"

She came to him, held his hands. "Probably not. You'll see someone else."

"Really, how come? I thought we liked each other."

She smiled weakly. "You've heard of the fireman whose house burns down, or the cop whose house gets robbed?"

"Or the oncologist who gets cancer?"

"They told you?"

"No, but I can hear it in your voice. I've been around that voice a lot lately."

She pursed her lips. "I just found out last week, and it's so hard to tell people. They think it's contagious or something."

He returned her grin. "Living hurts, I know. But it sure beats death. You're a fighter, Doc."

"I told you that."

"I listened."

He hopped down from the table and, awkwardly at first, gave her a hug.

But then it was a real embrace, kindred spirits consoling each other.

"Now it's your turn to prove it to me."

Safe House
Outskirts of Angren, Uzbekistan
2140 Hours Local Time

"No, please, we beg you! Don't do this!" cried the soldier, his mouth twisted as he struggled against the handcuffs, his naked body covered in gooseflesh.

They were standing in the backyard before a large metal tub brimming with oil. Two of TK's men threw more logs on the fire below the tub, and oil bubbled even more.

Tohir Khodjiev was thirty-one, lean because he lived on a diet of roasted pigeons and squirrels and whatever else he and his men could steal or scrounge up, and he was perpetually angry because as a child his parents had been murdered by the army for being "religious dissidents," for being Muslims, for practicing their faith outside of government-controlled mosques. They had been killed before his eyes.

TK had exacted revenge upon that same army over a dozen times in the past, so it was with no great sense of justice that he was about to boil alive these two prisoners: a lieutenant and a major, who had been captured by his men.

These victims would, however, serve a purpose: their deaths would send a powerful message to Alisher Atayev, the country's newly elected president. If Atayev continued the campaign of murder against Muslims the way his predecessor had, then TK's group, the Jihad Union of Uzbekistan, dubbed by the media as the J-U2, would strike back, and many more men would die. Not only that, capturing and killing Atayev's bodyguards proved that TK and his men could infiltrate the president's security forces—demonstrating that no one was safe, ever.

Although they numbered just five hundred men, TK believed that by year's end their numbers would be in the thousands. The recent sentencing of a sixty-two-year-old woman to six years of hard labor for possession of unsanctioned religious literature had fueled a public outcry and served as a recruiting message for the J-U2.

TK's younger brother, Maruf, twenty-four and second in command, came outside with two others, Amal and Nasim, who carried digital cameras. They would photograph and videotape the executions and deliver the images to the media.

"If you spare us, we make a deal," said the major.

Maruf went up to the man and spat in his face. "We will deal with the president."

"Easy, Maruf," said TK, slapping a palm on his brother's shoulder. "Let them beg. It's only human."

Amal and Nasim began snapping pictures and shooting video, flashes like lightning glinting off the dull gray
metal tub whose bottom glowed a deep red.

Another of TK's men, the old man Sherzod, limped up
to TK and whispered, "They are here to see you."

"I thought they weren't coming until tomorrow."

Sherzod threw up his hands. "They're inside."

"Tell them I'm busy."

"I did. They won't wait."

TK exhaled loudly in frustration, shouted to his men
to hold up the execution.

The two soldiers dropped to their knees and began
thanking him for his mercy.

"Get up, you dogs," he told them. "You're still going
to die." TK gestured to Amal and Nasim to stop taking
pictures and drag the prisoners to their feet. Then he
went into the house, where the two well-dressed men
were waiting.

"I'm busy right now," he told them, speaking through
his teeth.

"Not too busy for us," said the taller one. "Or for what
we offer."

TK checked his watch. "You have thirty seconds."

The man thrust a suitcase toward TK, who set it down
on a table and opened it. There, inside, he saw American
dollars in small denominations.

"Ten thousand," the man said. "But you only move on
our orders."

TK shook his head. "You want me to kill him for ten
thousand?"

The man smiled. "We have nine more suitcases in our
car. One hundred thousand, plus another one hundred
thousand when the job is complete. All American. Do

you know what this money will do for you and your people?"

"Who will replace Atayev?"

"That's not your problem."

"Yes, it is. We could change this president's mind. He could stop this war against us."

The tall man snickered. "You're not that naive, are you?"

"Why do you want him dead?"

The shorter man stepped up to TK and lowered his voice. "Asking too many questions is dangerous."

"Shame and guilt and disgrace are much harder than death to face," said TK, quoting an old Uzbek proverb. "Who sent you? Moscow Center?"

The taller man thrust a satellite phone into his hands. "We will be in touch. We will give you instructions. Take this money now, and begin to arm yourselves. We will help with that, too."

The two men started for the door.

"Wait, I want you to see something," TK called to them.

They turned around and followed him to the back door, then out into the yard.

The tall man muttered something, then whirled to leave, but found himself staring at a pistol held by Maruf.

"My brother would like the honor of your company," Maruf told him.

"I should remind you that we have friends who are watching us right now," the tall man said. "Look . . . " He pointed to Maruf's forehead, where a red laser dot had appeared.

TK glanced to the rooftop across the street, saw a figure lying prone there. Something flickered across his chest. He looked down, saw another red dot squarely over his heart.

"Who are you?" he cried.

The tall man smiled. "Friends. And we all want the same thing. Now, if you'd like us to stay for your little show, that'll be fine."

TK stood there a moment, unsure whether to proceed or attempt to kill these men and take their money. But they were obviously powerful, had men set up around the area, and were in communication with men whom he assumed were even more powerful.

A chill fanned across his shoulders. "Maruf? Throw the first one in."

The lieutenant began screaming. Maruf pistol-whipped the man, then, with Nasim's help, carried him up onto a pair of crates. From there, they rolled him into the tub, the fire flashing as oil heaved over the sides.

The lieutenant cried out, the sounds inhuman, like nothing TK had ever heard before. His cries lasted only a second.

The tall man nodded to TK. "My bosses were right. You are a monster. Just the man we've been looking for."

Chapter 3

....

Dr. Galina Saratova sat at her desk, reviewing a dossier. She repeatedly flipped back to the various photographs of a man with a sandy gray crew cut and penetrating eyes. Mr. Michael Hertzog was a fascinating individual, and his recent exploits in Myanmar added more to his intrigue. For the past month Saratova had been looking for a mercenary like him, and based on all of her intelligence, it seemed that Mr. Hertzog and his company would make a perfect fit.

Hertzog was her age and assumedly as cynical and difficult to impress as she was. He wouldn't take the job easily, so she knew she had to be well-prepared. Her argument would contain the facts, of course, but she felt certain that his decision could be swayed by a strong emotional appeal—and that's where his experience as a

U.S. Marine and the evidence from Uzbekistan would come to her aid. It was a difficult mission, more difficult than either of them could possibly imagine.

And she knew it might spell the end of everything for her.

Dr. Galina Saratova, née Galina Sinitsyna, was born in Kalinovskaya, Chechnya, in 1965. She was the love child of a Russian army officer and his Chechen mistress. At twelve, she was shuffled off to Moscow with scores of Internally Displaced Persons from Chechnya and North Ossetia.

Young, quick to learn, and intelligent, she came to the attention of individuals charged with the protection of the Rodina—the "Motherland"—and was sent to "special" schools where she was taught English, tradecraft, and given a whole new identity.

At eighteen she was "granted" a visa to study in the U.S., and arrived as an exchange student majoring in political science at Harvard University, where she was quickly spotted by CIA recruiters. She defected, and under the tutelage of the CIA, continued her education, ultimately earning a Ph.D. in Asian Studies.

Twenty-two years later she had become the director of the Asia Desk at Langley.

Her career was remarkable, and she had grown to love the United States of America, the land of opportunity.

Yet now she must do as they asked, no matter what they asked, no matter the risks. Ties of blood could never be ignored.

She removed a compact from her purse, checked her graying red hair and her lipstick in the mirror. At the very least, Mr. Hertzog should find her desirable. Though she had lost her Russian accent, she considered turning it back on for him, speaking in a smoky, sexy voice. He would tremble, want her. Yes. That would make her feel better.

She rose, called her secretary, and said she was on her way out for lunch.

During the brief walk to her Lexus, her eyes burned and her mouth grew painfully dry. She thought, I can't go through with this, then fought to remember what was at stake and reminded herself who she really was.

In the end, they were all soldiers.

Che Valentino's Italian Restaurant
I Street
Washington, D.C.
1210 Hours Local Time

Mad Dog had a feeling Ms. Galina Saratova would be a looker. Her phone voice suggested that, but sometimes you could be wrong. Most phone sex operators were obese Midwest housewives, according to Sapper and Wolfgang, who claimed to be experts on such matters. Experts, indeed . . .

As Mad Dog sat at the elegantly appointed table, stealing glances at her boob job and bright, green eyes, his lust was tempered by thoughts of Kat. But he and Kat weren't even a couple. What the hell was the matter with him? He should go with the flow, drink in Saratova's redheaded beauty, enjoy life for God's sake. Yes, sir!

Her hand had been as warm as her smile, and her accent cast a powerful spell. His people had run their background checks on her, and everything seemed to check out. She had an impeccable record and was even being groomed for promotion.

"Well, you're terribly handsome man," she had begun. "And I am terribly bold. I guess my problem is worse, eh?"

"I guess so." He'd grinned and taken a seat.

Now, as he pondered the menu, she spoke slowly, cautiously. He let the words sink in for a moment, then set down the menu, took a sip of water, and said, "Well, it does sound like you have a real problem there."

"Mr. Hertzog, we can't do this ourselves. We need you and your company—"

"For plausible deniability. I get it. The op goes south, you blame it on mercs."

"That's not the only reason we need you. Our field agents in the region are very good, but the men who work for you are some of the most highly skilled soldiers in the world, with much more experience in unconventional operations."

His lip twisted into a grin. "It's clear you haven't met them."

"Don't be humble."

"Oh, trust me, I'm not being humble. They're pretty good. But you're talking about getting into Uzbekistan, finding a guy who has his own small army and doesn't want to be found, and killing him before he kills the president. That's way out of our league."

He was lying, of course, to drive up the price. No rocket science involved here. It was always best to take the job with great reluctance and wheelbarrows full of cash.

"It has to be done." She handed him a manila envelope. "I don't want to ruin your lunch, but inside are photographs and a video iPod with a clip you must watch."

Mad Dog slipped one of the photos out, held it under the table and took a peek. Two bodies, swollen and red, floated in a metal tub. The image made him grimace. A caption identified the men as bodyguards of President Atayev. "Oh, I'm sure the video is even more fun than these pictures," he said darkly.

Saratova went on, "Tohir Khodjiev, who is called TK, is a brutal murderer, and the J-U2 is linked to many groups, including Hezbollah and the Taliban."

"They're all linked. And they're all scumbags. And I'd love to wipe 'em all from the face of the earth. I can't. Especially there. That place is locked up tight."

"Please, listen to me. There is much at stake here. Atayev has sworn to reopen the K2 air base to the United States. You were in Afghanistan. As a Marine, you understand the importance of support and resupply in the field. When we lost access to that base, we lost a lot. Marines—your Marines—need you."

"I understand that. But I'm not a fool."

Saratova sighed deeply. "It is vital that Atayev remains in office and that Tohir Khodjiev is removed. Without TK's leadership, the J-U2 will fall apart. This is in the best interests of the Corps and the United States."

"Ms. Saratova, this is all very interesting, even dramatic. And you've done a fine job attempting to pull on my heartstrings. I think you're sincere—which may be naive on my part—but what you're asking is impossible. You got the wrong guy. I don't have the assets to take on something like this. You need a much bigger dog."

"No, I need a Mad Dog. That is what they call you, is it not?"

"Yeah, and with all due respect, I'd have to be more than mad to take on this job."

"I wouldn't waste your time if I didn't think you could accomplish this mission. We've studied your organization. I've been authorized to hire IPG because you work as a small team. We'll help with intelligence if necessary. The rest will be up to you, but I know you can do it."

"You got a lot of faith in a guy you just met."

She raised her brows. "I've been studying you for a while . . ."

The waiter came over, took their orders, then Mad Dog smiled self-consciously at her. "I like your necklace."

Her hand went reflexively to her neck, to the band of translucent, emerald green beads. "It's *fei-ts'ui* jade."

"Really." His gaze turned suspicious. "That's, uh, interesting. I know somebody who mines jade."

"I know you do. I read about your work in Myanmar, and I don't know what came over me, but I thought it'd be nice to have something like this. I had to go to San Francisco to buy it, but I just love it. You wouldn't believe what I paid, but really, it's the only nice piece of jewelry I own. And I thought we could talk about jade, if all else failed."

He considered that, considered the loneliness that had seeped into her words. "It is a beautiful piece. And you're a terribly handsome person yourself, if not a little nutty. I'm sorry I've wasted your time. Maybe you can give Blackwater or Sandline a call. I bet those guys would take the job in a heartbeat."

"We simply don't want them and all of their loose ends. Mr. Hertzog, we haven't talked numbers yet."

"That's the thing. I doubt the Agency would authorize what I need. No chance of backup or support. Lots of cash wasted. Not to mention gear we'll have to dump. I have a C-130. Is the Agency prepared to replace it if we have to ditch?"

"Name your price."

He chuckled. "You're kidding me."

No, she wasn't. She raised a perfectly tweezed brow.

"Ten million," he blurted out.

It was her turn to chuckle. "Let's be serious. I've been authorized for up to five million."

Mad Dog kept his poker face, even though he wanted to gasp and cry out *Holy shit!* then jump at the offer. He took a deep breath. "Five million? All right. I want all of it up front." He regretted that immediately. He sounded like a meathead merc. He should've said half up front.

"Two up front, which you will keep despite the outcome. Three upon completion."

Mad Dog swallowed. "You *are* serious."

She thrust out her hand. "Do we have a deal?"

When they left the restaurant after lunch, before they said their good-byes, she came up behind him and rubbed his aching shoulders. "When you get back, I'll be waiting for you."

He sighed into her hands. Yes, they did have a deal.

That night, Saratova emailed a single word "Сделано!" (Done!) to ashcroftandanderson@aol.com, the first of eight server blinds that eventually terminated at Moscow Center. Those server blinds would relay her message and make it impossible for it to be traced.

The sleeper from Kalinovskaya was awake and on the job.

But that sleeper could hardly live with herself. Unbidden, painful memories of her childhood in Russia flooded her thoughts. One word, *chornye,* stung repeatedly; it meant "black," the cultural equivalent of nigger, the name Russians used for all Chechens. But she had moved past that, learned to exploit those bastards . . . until now.

She poured a glass of Stolichnaya vodka straight from Irkutsk, felt the tears come, then threw the glass across her kitchen. She thought of all the friends and colleagues at the Agency whom she had just betrayed, thought of all they had done for her, and whispered, "I'm sorry. But I am a solider."

Then she thought of Hertzog, who had no idea that he had just been hired by Moscow Center to do their bidding.

"The Dog Pound"
Talisay City
Cebu, the Philippines
48 Hours Later
0900 Hours Local Time

"Hey, Dan? You coming to this or what?" Mad Dog asked as he stood near the entrance door of the guest house.

Gunnery sergeant Daniel M. Forrest, III, USMC, retired, hobbled across the living room, raised a hand and muttered, "Yeah, I'm coming. Don't rush me. But I'm not sure I should dignify this job with my presence."

"You got a problem with us working for the CIA?"

"You're fucking right I do!"

"Look, they're not all like Agent Moody," Mad Dog argued. He winked. "Only nine out of ten of them are assholes."

Dan nodded, raked fingers through his snowy white

crew cut. "Well, you know how I feel about this. You can't trust the fucking CIA! You just made a deal with the devil!"

Old Dan, the Marine who'd been like a father to him, was battling with diabetes, a bad memory, and a fiery hatred for the CIA because a year ago Agent James Moody, aka "Jimmy Judas," had hired some terrorists to kidnap him so he could blackmail Mad Dog. Dan was saved, but had been shot.

Mad Dog couldn't blame him for wanting James Moody dead and to nuke Langley, in that order—or simultaneously, he didn't give a fuck.

"Dan, me and the devil go way back. I'm not worried. So far, so good. Bibby's already confirmed the deposit, IPG, London, from an untraceable source. She kept her word. We're up two million and we ain't done shit yet."

He helped Dan down the stairs and they started along the paved brick walk, toward the main house. "Ever think about leaving it at that?" Dan asked.

"You mean take the money and screw them over? You know that taking it has already locked us in. They could threaten our contacts, create a whole lot of fear, and put us out of business."

"You should've thought of that before you sat down with that bitch."

"I did. And I'm thinking we can pull this off. Bibby's got a lot of tricks up his sleeve. He's calling in every favor from every James Bond he knows at MI6."

"Well, your men will need that kind of help. But as for you, stay home. You're still recovering from cancer, for God's sake. The big C."

"I wouldn't send them out there alone. Not for something like this. I'm going. No discussion."

"I figured. Just don't let your battleship mouth overload your tin can ass!"

Mad Dog laughed. "I won't. And hey, thanks for all your research. Wait till you see what Bibby's done with it."

"Whoa," the old man groaned sarcastically. "I can't wait."

Billy Pope was tearing into a blueberry bagel loaded down with cream cheese as he listened to Sapper give them the 411 on their new lady merc, who had yet to arrive for the briefing:

"So the bitch is hot."

"That's some remarkable intel you got there," said Boo Boo, wearing a smirk. "I did not know that. In fact, when she unzipped her flight suit and her tits popped out, I wasn't looking. Nope, not me."

Sapper waved him off. "Let me finish. Now, okay, how 'bout this shit: She was Secret Service, working for Clinton. Turns out he groped her."

"Oh, you're so full of shit," Boo Boo cut in again.

"Nope. I got this from an inside source." He turned to Pope. "Bagel boy over there helped me."

"That's right," Pope said with a full mouth. "He ain't shitting. We dug up a lot on her."

Sapper's eyes grew wide. "Now, listen up, boys. She slapped the motherfucking President of the U-nited States right across the face."

"Bull . . . shit!" cried Wolfgang.

"It's true! After that, she left the Secret Service, went into freelance VIP protection, made friends with some Arabs who financed the living hell out of her."

"Financed? You mean they f—" Pope began, but cut himself off because he was choking on his bagel.

"I mean she traveled the world, knows a bunch of languages, martial arts, she's like a freaking Barbie doll on steroids, a goddamned video game chick who kicks ass."

"Didn't know people like that really existed," said Wolfgang, nervously massaging his shaven head. "But I still think you guys are yanking our chains."

"She's got sailboats, powerboats, yacht club memberships. She's a pilot, and a damned good one. That Huey? She owns it, plus another helo, an MD520N. Owns some other aircraft. We heard she's worth over twenty million."

Alistair Bibby came over, sipping tea. He cocked a brow, pushed his glasses farther up the ridge of this nose, then said, "If you'll cease this pathetic gossip and take seats, we'll begin shortly. And until then, I'll remind you that I've known our new hire for nearly ten years now, and while she'll need to earn your respect, she already has mine."

"No shit?" said Pope. "Why didn't you tell us you knew her? We're over there doing background checks on her."

"No one asked. I was the one who suggested she apply for the job. Unfortunately, Mr. Hertzog doubted her intentions. I think, though, he recognizes what a valuable asset she'll become."

"I think he recognizes what a hot ass she has, too," said Sapper, chuckling through his words. "And hey, Bibby, you tap that ass or what? Come on, she probably got turned on by your accent. You tapped that, didn't you—"

"Take a seat—before I silence you forever," Bibby said, then whirled away and headed to the front of the living room, where he had set up a computer projector and a large screen.

Pope washed down his bagel with some coffee, then took a seat next to Wolfgang on the large leather sofa. "You eat?"

"Not hungry."

"You're losing weight."

"I was fat."

Pope lowered his voice. "You'd better talk to somebody. If not me, then somebody. 'Cause I think you're fucked up."

"Feeling's mutual."

Mad Dog and old Dan entered the living room, went right to the food and began filling their plates. Pope glanced around, saw everyone save for their lady merc. Was she planning on making a grand entrance?

"All right, now that we're all here, let's begin."

"Uh, two things," said Sapper, rising from his chair and digging into his mouth with a toothpick. "We're not all here. And shouldn't we send her off before we get started?"

Sapper lifted his chin at one of the maids, dressed neatly in black and white, who was standing on a chair and dusting off a long window treatment at the opposite end of the room.

"All right, Kat, your point's been made," said Bibby, directing his words to the maid, who climbed down from the chair, strode toward the group, removed the pins from her hair and let her gorgeous blond locks flow freely.

Not one of them in the room had even noticed her.

"Oh, I think so, too," she said. "No matter how horny or keen-eyed they are, they never notice the help—which is where I come in handy. And no, Sapper, Mr. Bibby did not tap this ass."

Sapper winced. "Sorry, ma'am."

"No shit, sweetheart," said Boo Boo, impressed.

"Name's Kat, remember? With a K? As in I'm a *kick* your fuckin' ass? But don't mind me, right? I'm just overcompensating because I'm a woman."

"Damn, I can't handle all these mind games," said Pope, throwing up his hands and grinning broadly. He liked Kat, mainly because he immediately saw her as an equal and, truthfully, he didn't want to screw her. That would just mess it all up.

"Kat, would you please join us?" said Mad Dog. "You'll finish dusting later."

That drew laughs all around.

"Don't doubt that I will. You need to talk to your help. That's some damn sloppy work!"

Bibby cleared his throat, hardly amused by the banter. "Let's get down to business, then, shall we?" He moved the wireless mouse beside his laptop, and two images appeared on the portable screen. They were side-by-side satellite photos of the Aral Sea in Uzbekistan. The one on the left, dated July-September 1989, showed a large, thriving lake. The one on the right, dated two months later, revealed the massive depletion of water and an increase in dry lake beds.

"Someone was thirsty," muttered Pope.

Bibby tipped his head toward Dan, acknowledging the man's research, then explained that the sea had shrunk dramatically because the waterways that fed into it had been diverted to assist in cotton production. Uzbekistan was the world's second largest producer of cotton.

"Ironically, it's those dry lake beds that are now threatening production." He read from his screen: "'Growing concentrations of chemical pesticides and natural salts are blown from the lake bed and contribute to soil salination, desertification, and many health-related problems.'" He glanced up. "Basically, the Soviets raped the ecosystem and even dumped radioactive waste in the Aral. That waste is now threatening the entire populace."

Bibby then showed them photographs taken from reconnaissance helicopters. Bleak-looking plains stretched out into nothingness, the ground cracked, forming massive mosaics traced by weeds and other resilient foliage, with berms scattered here and there, breaking up the horizon.

Wolfgang raised his hand, as though he were still in grade school.

"Yes, Mr. Wolfgang?" said Bibby.

"What's with those mounds we're seeing every so often?"

Bibby clicked to an overhead shot of a fishing trawler canted on its port. "There's your mound, sir."

Wolfgang shrugged. "So it's a boat in the middle of the desert, left there by UFOs."

"Left there by greed."

Bibby brought up more photos of stranded boats. Some amounted to just a mast and the top of a pilot house jutting up improbably from the sand. One was of the stern protruding from a mound, its thrust bearings, thrust plates, shaft, and propeller salvaged for some other boat. Two shots showed two different boats with holes cut in their sides and a ladder from the ground to the keel. Several families were living in the rotting wooden hull.

"Uh, excuse me for interrupting," said Pope. "But as I understand it, we're supposed to go in, take out this TK guy, and then haul ass back home."

"I'm getting there, Mr. Pope. And I'm well aware of the attention span of lower primates such as yourselves, but indulge me. Please."

"Okay," Pope said, winking at Sapper. "But we monkeys are waiting."

"He's talking about our cover, you knuckleheads," said Kat. "Let him finish."

"As we're all painfully aware," Bibby began again, "we can't just fly into Uzbekistan as tourists armed to the teeth and expect to move freely. But the environmental problems associated with the Aral Sea have provided us with a unique opportunity. We're going to pose as a French Algerian agricultural survey team and fly into the K2 base at the invitation of Gulomov Erkinovich, the minister of Agriculture and Water Management.

"We have a ninety day mission to travel to and from the Aral Sea area and any other exposed lake bed areas to take soil samples, climatological data, etcetera, to determine practical ways to combat ongoing soil contamination and protect/preserve the Uzbek cotton industry as well as the local citizens. Our documentation will allow us freedom of movement."

Wolfgang raised his hand. "Mr. Bibby, maybe Doolittle over there can speak French, but the rest of us—"

"It's a multinational team, so a few Americans among us shouldn't raise too many eyebrows. Doolittle, you'll need to brush up on your French because you're our survey team leader."

The translator nodded, glanced at Mad Dog. "Will I also be in charge of the entire operation?"

"I don't doubt you could do it," said Mad Dog, appearing to tense up. "But it's my party, as usual."

Doolittle nodded. "Of course, Sergeant."

"We're in the process of acquiring some survey equipment to complete the illusion," Bibby added. "Mr. Hertzog?"

Mad Dog shifted to the front of the room. "We'll be packing two helos aboard the C-130. Kat has a 520 she's volunteered to pilot, and we've just purchased a new MD600. Seats up to seven. One of the safest, quietest helicopters in the world. Both should be good for those short hops."

"You mean you don't want to bring the Huey?" Night Stalker asked from the back of the room.

"Why? You looking to get fired again? We'll be leaving that piece of shit home, thank you. Besides the birds, we have the usual toys, some new small arms, and a couple of AT4s."

"AT4s?" Kat asked.

"They're recoilless rifles that shoot an 84mm high explosive antiarmor warhead," answered Mad Dog. "Good for taking out LAVs, choppers, anybody else who gets in our way. Uncle Sam loves 'em."

"Sweet."

"Ms. Saratova at the CIA will be providing us with up-to-the-minute intel on TK's whereabouts," said Bibby.

Drac, who sat near Night Stalker, cleared his throat and stammered a bit, a tic all of them had grown so accustomed to that they hardly heard it. "Uh, excuse me.

But, uh, I, uh, don't see finding TK too difficult. If he wants to kill Atayev, then you just track the president, and your target should be close."

"That's true," replied Bibby. "But tracking the president is a challenge itself. However, we do have an important lead." The Brit reached for the mouse and brought up a page of thumbnailed images of an ancient city in the desert, like something out of an Indiana Jones film, with madrassas, mosques, and minarets of remarkable beauty, some with ornate carved wooden columns.

"Where are we now?" asked Pope. "Cairo?"

"No, we're still in Uzbekistan," answered Bibby. "Gentlemen, this is Khiva. It's more than twenty-five hundred years old and the only walled city in all of Central Asia that has survived. They call it an open air museum and a tourist attraction." He glanced down at some printouts in his hand. "Let me read: 'There are great mud-brick walls divided by four gateways, and within is the old town with narrow medieval streets and the palace of the former Emir of Khiva, including tiled reception rooms, a mint, a harem quarters consisting of over a hundred tiny rooms, and even an open-air theatre.'"

Bibby displayed a map of Uzbekistan that pinpointed Khiva about 150 miles directly south of the Aral Sea, which was located in the northwest portion of the country. The map also identified Urgench, just twenty miles northeast of Khiva; the K2 air base, which was 445 miles southeast; and Termez, located far south, near the Afghanistan border.

"We'll be flying into K2. From there we'll refuel and greet Erkinovich. Then we'll proceed to Urgench, where we offload the choppers for our supposed trips up to the

Aral Sea area. But, of course, we'll never make it there."

"We're going to Khiva?" asked Wolfgang.

"You, sir, might become a scholar some day," said Bibby. "President Atayev has been invited to Khiva by a man whose name should be familiar: Phillip Steinberg."

"Are you serious?" asked Pope.

"Yes, he's directing an action-adventure film that's being shot on location there. Atayev is a big film buff, and it's during this visit that our client believes TK will strike. There's a lot of security on movie sets, but also a lot of confusion and make-believe, and I'm sure TK will exploit that in every way possible. Kat?"

"I've worked for a lot of VIPs in Hollywood, and my contacts came through for us. Doolittle and I will be entering the city, posing as field reporters for *Entertainment Tonight*. They've even scheduled me for an interview with both Atayev and Steinberg. I'll be as close to the president as possible. He does travel with a team of National Guardsmen who serve as his personal bodyguards. I'm assuming that TK will pose as either one of them or try to become part of the film crew."

"In theory, this should all work out," said Bibby. "However, there are still many variables. Weather could halt film production, thus canceling Atayev's visit. A host of other things could come up. But for now we stick to plan A."

"What's plan B?" asked Pope.

"Well, that involves once again finding Atayev and coordinating with the CIA to find TK."

"Okay, if we eliminate the target, what's our plan to get the hell out of Dodge?" asked Sapper.

"We load up the choppers at Urgench and fly from

there directly to A'stan," said Mad Dog. "Pretty straight run, hopefully under cover of darkness."

"Any chance of backup?"

"None from the CIA," said Bibby. "I'm working on a few other possibilities, but negotiations are, in a word, tenuous right now."

Pope had already done a little research on the Uzbek military and thought it time to chip in a few words. "Well, I hope we can firm up some support, because Uzbekistan has Central Asia's strongest armed forces. We're talking about nearly fifty thousand troops, an air force of over ten thousand, and they've been building those forces steadily to fight their war on terrorism. If they get on our tails, we'd better know which way to run."

"Gentlemen, do you have any questions?" asked Mad Dog.

The C-130 pilot, Gerald Styles, along with his copilot Denny Zito, and his loadmaster Kenny Wilcox, all retired Air Force guys, had taken seats up front. Styles was about to turn sixty-three, the others a bit younger, mid-to-late fifties. All three had hardly looked up from their plates. It was all about the breakfast. Styles raised his hand.

"Yes, Gerry, what do you got?"

"Oh," he said, glancing around, embarrassed. "Just wondering if we have any more bacon."

Later, Kat drove Mad Dog to the open field behind the house to show off her chopper and give him a little ride. The bird impressed him, but not as much as she did. They took off, flew over Cebu Island, the view spectacular both inside the cabin and out. After a long moment of silence he asked over the headset, "So . . . what do you think?"

"I think this isn't a simple assassination, and neither should you."

"Simple? That's the wrong word. Fucking complicated is how I'd describe it."

"Our so-called friends in Langley want TK out of the picture, and what I'm saying is, their agenda is not that simple."

"We're still digging up everything we can on Saratova. So far, though, she checks out."

"Keep digging. And you might do yourself a favor and study the relationship Uzbekistan has with Russia. Two big powers at play here, Moscow and Washington, trying to manipulate the little guy."

"You take me up here to give me second thoughts?"

"Nope. I'm a realist. I read the labels on everything I eat, and I like to know exactly how deep every rabbit hole goes."

"You don't like surprises?"

"They come no matter what you do. Like right now." She banked so hard that Mad Dog's stomach felt as though it were splayed across the landing skids.

"Don't do that again."

"What's with you men? Never any time for foreplay."

"You're just a tease. Take me back. We still have a lot to do."

"All right," she cooed.

"And hey, you sure you still want to work for me?"

"You kidding? You're nuts. I like that in a man. But seriously, you need to prepare yourself for what's going to happen."

"Lady, I've done this a few times."

Her voice turned grave. "I mean, you'll be lucky if half of us come back alive."

"Luck's got nothing to do with it."

"Luck or Fate or God or Murphy, yeah, I know. But I'm guessing this is the big one for you. The most dangerous so far. You're not up against some half-assed militia in Angola."

"We'll be ready."

She didn't respond.

"You don't believe me?"

"I didn't say anything." She leaned forward and rapped a knuckle on one of her dials. "Oh, shit."

"What? We got a problem?"

"Yeah, I mean, no. But if we did, would you go to Heaven or Hell?"

Mad Dog resumed breathing. "Damn it, bitch, don't screw with me like that!"

"So, where would you go?"

"Heaven, of course. All Marines were permanently kicked out of Hell for misbehavior. What about you?"

"I don't believe in anything. I want to believe in something, but I haven't found it."

"When you got your cancer—"

"No, I didn't get religious. I got pissed off. Then I got serious about my health, my diet, the whole nine. You know what I want to believe? That doing this, helping people, making a difference—that that's going to help me find God."

"Does that mean *I'm* going to help you find God?"

"In a way, yes."

"Damn, woman, talk about performance anxiety! Now I'm supposed to introduce you to Jesus? You're a trip, baby, a real trip . . . "

"No, just you're average everyday woman of sinister beauty, modest to a fault, sarcastic beyond belief, and a little too cynical for her own good."

"That sounds rehearsed."

"Unfortunately, it is. You'll help me rewrite it, okay?"

He reached over and put his hand on hers. She didn't shrink away. "Okay."

Chapter 4

....

Karshi-Kanabad (K2) Air Base
Former Home of Camp Stronghold Freedom
Khanabad, Uzbekistan
120 Hours Local Time

Located smack in the middle of a flat, sandy desert that made anything approaching easy to spot, K2 offered about as much eye appeal as an aging trailer park in rural Texas.

Tents, Quonset huts, and the like were laid out in a grid, with streets that had been named for the thoroughfares of New York. About a thousand or so U.S. troops had worked on the base, with many more passing through. Other large transport aircraft, along with maintenance trucks of every kind, were scattered across the base, the perimeter lined with concertina wire and small guard towers. Before Atayev's predecessor had kicked them out, American troops had breathed new life into the otherwise dismal and remote confines.

A couple of squads of Uzbek Army regulars were waiting for Mad Dog and his men on the tarmac, rifles at the ready. Doolittle went down the ramp with their IDs and documents in hand. He spoke with the head monkey in French, who looked bored as he went through their documents, muttering in his native tongue, probably not understanding a word from Doolittle.

Mad Dog hit the tarmac, took in a deep breath—

And nearly gagged. "What's that smell?"

"I hope it ain't lunch," grunted Pope.

"It's coming from that trench behind the tents," said Bibby, who was at his side. "Don't worry about it. We won't be here very long. And that's fortunate. This place is heavily polluted. I read a report of soldiers finding black goo in the ground when they dug. There's no telling what the Soviets have buried here, including chemical waste. There are high levels of disease, including TB."

"Which of course is why you can't win a trip here on *Wheel of Fortune,*" Mad Dog quipped, but Bibby's face was stone. "Let's get set up for refuel."

Doolittle finished up with the officer, then nodded and shouted something in French, adding in English, "We are clear. They're going to search."

The soldiers moved into the plane, but Mad Dog and his pups had hidden every piece of ordnance in the custom-made and cleverly concealed compartments throughout the craft. No self-respecting mercenary would do anything less. It would take a hell of a lot more than some third-world airport security force to find their toys of doom and destruction . . .

Or that sexy blond pilot who was also hidden in one of the compartments so she could later prance around with her microphone, asking silly questions to celebrities. Still, a pang of fear wrestled with Mad Dog's spine at the thought of her being discovered.

They had painted the C-130 camo and adorned the tail with the Algerian flag, which was split equal parts green and white. Green was closest to the pole. A red crescent and five-point star was centered on the split between the colors. It was amazing how many times the bird had been painted and repainted for missions, but she took a licking (and painting) and kept on chugging.

"There's the welcome wagon," Mad Dog said, pointing to an up-armored Mercedes with dignitary flags, along with three olive drab utility trucks, old Russian UAZs whose engines sounded like they had bronchitis. A few soldiers were getting out of the trucks, slinging AKs over their shoulders.

Mad Dog felt stupid in his button-down shirt, wool jacket, and loafers. The only things missing were his pocket protector and specs pieced together with Band-Aids. Pope, Sapper, Drac, Boo Boo, and Wolfgang looked equally ridiculous—or respectable, depending upon your point of view—in their survey team garb. Pope had even donned a pair of glasses, as had Sapper. "We badass survey motherfuckers," Sapper had said, staring over the rim of his specs like an NBA star turned maniacal Catholic school teacher with a sailor's mouth.

Gulomov Erkinovich looked thinner than his photos, which were dated nearly six months earlier. He had a thick shock of white hair receding in a widow's peak that suggested Transylvanian vampire might be in his blood, though he appeared amicable enough. He said something in broken French that sounded like he was introducing the translator.

Erkinovich grinned slightly and gestured to a lean, dark-haired man of about forty who spoke quickly to Doolittle. After that, Doolittle introduced them, using their bullshit cover names, to which Mad Dog paid close attention because he couldn't remember whether he was Maxell, Jefferson, or Harris. Oh, yeah, he was Harris. Whatever.

After a few more excruciating smiles and equally painful pleasantries, Doolittle turned back to Mad Dog. "He wants to inspect our cargo himself. He also says he's dubious of our entire mission because the country seeks to lessen its dependence on agriculture while developing its mineral and petroleum reserves."

"Oh, that's interesting," whispered Mad Dog. "Tell him we don't give a fuck."

"Of course."

Doolittle called out to the minister, his translator, and the minister's escort, and they all moved up the ramp and into the C-130, even as the airport security force moved out, the officer exchanging a few words with Erkinovich.

About two dozen crates of various sizes, all labeled in French, English, and Cyrillic, were lined up along the walls of the plane. Erkinovich gestured to them and spoke to the translator, who turned and relayed the message to Doolittle. Mad Dog surmised that the minister wanted to know exactly what was in the crates.

In fact, the soldiers had pried opened a few of the larger ones, revealing some of the survey equipment, and Doolittle showed them to the minister.

"My French isn't what it should be," said Bibby, drifting over to Mad Dog's shoulder. "But he's describing our mission to the minister right now."

Doolittle was, according to the plan, discussing how the team would utilize two mobile weather stations, while pointing out an anemometer, barometer, hydrometer, and rain gauge. He took the minister to two narrow, eight-foot crates and was saying—or at least Mad Dog thought he was—that they contained gas-driven core samplers.

The minister did not look impressed. He muttered a few more things to the translator, his eyes narrowing more each second.

Doolittle's tone turned a bit urgent. Then he excused himself and came up to Mad Dog. "We got a problem. This guy is smart. He says none of these crates appears big enough to contain sufficient add-on segments for deep core samples. I don't even know what that means. What do I tell him?"

Bibby jumped right in: "You tell him that we only need twenty-five- to thirty-foot samples since our area of interest concerns the geophysical changes occurring since the diversion of the two rivers. And make sure you tell him about how we're going to use the two mass spectrometers for detailed chemical analysis of rock and soil samples."

"Oh, no problem. My French is that strong." A nervous Doolittle shook his head and headed deeper into the hold, toward the minister, who was having two of his troopers pry open yet another crate.

"Hey, buddy?" Mad Dog called. "See if his translator speaks English."

"Okay."

"I'm not sure that's wise," said Bibby. "Our friend Doolittle is a little more even-tempered than you are."

"I know, but these fuckers are wasting our time. And if this gets too far out of hand, we'll have to pull out our surprise sooner than I thought."

"That's up to you."

They did, in fact, have a surprise waiting for the minister in the cockpit.

Doolittle waved over Mad Dog and Bibby. As they neared the minister and soldiers, Erkinovich's translator said, "I can translate into English if that will help?"

"Oh, great. Thanks."

"The minister says that this project sounds very similar to the survey the Americans did about eight years ago, before their State Department started telling other nations how to live. In fact, he says, as he looks around, the whole atmosphere feels American to him."

"Well, it should," said Mad Dog. "We're standing in an American built plane with the finest portable equipment in the world, thanks to our space program."

Bibby cleared his throat and added: "Minister, you should know that Algiers is reaping the benefits of the Middle East Partnership Initiative. The U.S. provided $3.5 million to Algiers for economic and political development programs. As a requisite for MEPI funding, Algiers Atmospheric Survey Project shares its findings worldwide via the National Oceanic and Atmospheric Administration."

After listening to the translator, Erkinovich nodded at Bibby then frowned at Mad Dog. "I thought all American hate French?"

"Not true."

"Why this helicopters?" he asked.

Mad Dog made a fist. *This is getting fucking annoying.* "Uh, Minister, we have nearly twenty-five different sites to survey, starting in the north at the Aral seabed, moving southward while crisscrossing the country to other dry lake beds."

After hearing out Mad Dog, the minister rattled off something in Uzbek, translated as: "I insist you use our helicopters and our pilots."

Well, that one caught Mad Dog with his pants down. He figured no one in a piss poor country would be volunteering their time, equipment, and manpower for the survey.

"I'm sorry, Minister, but that just can't happen," said Bibby, his words echoing in the translator's mouth. "Our helos are equipped with highly sensitive air samplers embedded in the skin that sample and continuously record atmospheric chemical content along with the bird's position while in flight. These data are vital to the survey. The data quantifies the amount of contamination being circulated by the prevailing wind patterns. This is one of our most vital samplings."

God damn, that Bibby was a Bullshit Artist Extraordinaire, Mad Dog thought. There were no air samplers embedded in the helos. He'd pulled that one out of his most proper British arse.

The minister thought a moment, then conferred with the translator, who finally regarded them and said, "Under the circumstance, he'll allow it. But he doesn't like it, and his staff will be monitoring you closely."

Pointedly ignoring the minister's obvious threat, Bibby added, "In short, Minister, we'll take core samples at the source in the Aral Sea—call it a kind of fingerprint. Then, by taking core samples at all the other sites, we'll track that fingerprint throughout your country to determine where the winds are carrying it and in what quantities."

"And you can add that we're trying to identify the problems of nuclear waste and contamination," said Mad

Dog. "We aren't just some scientists digging in the sand for fun. The Soviet Union poisoned this country, and we're here to help."

The translator nodded and got to work, and, when he was finished, Erkinovich's expression softened, if just a little. He spoke slowly, in broken English. "Okay. You can help. But I leave three men with you. For security."

"It's okay," said Doolittle. "We have." He gestured to Pope, Sapper, and Drac, standing near the ramp.

"No, no. I insist."

Doolittle spoke rapidly, and as he did, Bibby leaned over and said, "I think he's telling him we don't want soldiers around, drawing attention to ourselves."

"No go," said Doolittle, turning to them. "Unless we take his escorts to Urgench."

Mad Dog exchanged a look with Bibby and Doolittle, then nodded. "Okay."

They'd deal with their "escorts" later. The in-flight movie would be canceled, replaced by a live action performance so realistic you'd swear that three men had been abducted, and perhaps killed.

"If there are no other questions then at this time, Minister," began Bibby, "I believe Mr. Harris has a project of special interest for you in the forward section of the plane."

Mad Dog smiled broadly, then waved the minister over, leading him up into the cockpit, where he was greeted not by the flight crew but by two Filipino hookers. The girls seized the minister, threw him into the cockpit, then slammed the door behind them.

Mad Dog winked at the minister's bodyguards, who burst out laughing and reached for their cigarettes. Mad

Dog shooed them off. "No smoking in here! Outside, away from the plane!"

Bibby, whose expression appeared far more relaxed, raised his brows. "I still disagree."

"With what? Getting him laid?"

"It raises too much suspicion."

"No, it raises something else—but that all depends on the minister."

"This isn't funny."

"Just breathe easy, old chap. It's just the way these people do business. Trust me. He won't bust our balls as much."

"Sometimes, I must question your logic."

"Question it all you want. But if I were that old man, I'd be thinking . . . well, then again, I wouldn't be thinking about too much."

Bibby sighed. "Blasted Yanks."

"It's going down by the numbers. Keep saying that. Make it come to pass."

They headed outside, after the minister's men. Styles and company were outside complaining about the loss of time due to slow wing-top gravity refueling because of incompatible single point mating connectors.

Mad Dog nodded his way through the technobabble then told them to gas up—or else.

Either Mad Dog had a very sick sense of humor or he was trying to send some message to her.

Because the compartment in which she lay hidden was so close to the cockpit that she had to endure every squeal and groan and labored breath coming from there.

Oh, God, it was horrible, like a rhinoceros trying to mate with a pair of Siamese kittens.

Kat closed her eyes, covered her ears.

Mr. Michael Hertzog, payback is a bitch. And you're going to find out the hard way!

Nikolai Tikhon lowered his binoculars and told the young solider driving the truck to move on. He had seen enough of the C-130 and the men outside to know that the Americans had arrived at their refueling stop. He reached for his satellite phone, made a call back to Moscow Center, to a man he knew only as Petrov, a man he suspected answered directly to the Russian president.

"They have arrived."

"Good. Mark their departure time, then you will follow them up to Urgench."

"Four of my men are already there, waiting, and two are working with the group. We're in."

"Excellent."

"Yes, but I will need more money."

"The negotiations are already over."

"They are never over. I can put a stop to this entire operation. You know that. Moscow Center knows that."

"How much do you want?"

Tikhon unscrewed the cap of his vodka, took a swig, then grinned. "Double."

"Ridiculous. Mercenary scum like you are lucky to be paid . . . "

Tikhon chuckled under his breath. "Then consider me twice as lucky." He hung up, leaving Petrov to consider the threat. He handed the vodka to his driver. "Keep it."

"Thank you, sir!"

"I'm not an officer anymore. Now take me back to my plane. I'm leaving now."

* * *

Mad Dog got word from Styles and his crew that refueling was complete and that they wanted to return to the cockpit. One of the two Filipino hookers called to Mad Dog, saying they would need help with the minister. He smiled and headed into the plane, only to find the old man sprawled out on the cockpit floor, his underwear bunched up around his knees.

"Jesus Christ, what did you do, kill him?"

"No, no, no, no, no," cried the hooker. "He's still breathing. But he's very tired now. Very satisfied, I think."

Mad Dog called to Pope and Sapper, who came up and carried the man out of the pit. Doolittle was there, along with the minister's very embarrassed translator, who helped his boss get dressed.

The translator spoke rapidly, even as the minister spoke very slowly, slurring his words. So the hookers had gotten him drunk first. It happened.

"The minister thanks you for your hospitality," said the translator. "He also requests your complete confidentiality regarding this matter."

"Tell him he has our promise."

The minister grinned weakly, shook hands with Doolittle and Mad Dog, then rose slowly to zip up his pants.

"I'm pleased that my life has come to this," muttered Bibby, who'd come up behind Mad Dog. "Bribery, prostitution, and assassination."

Mad Dog grinned. "Could be worse. You could add constipation."

Bibby rolled his eyes, then gestured to the back of the hold.

They started away, and the Brit asked, "So what plans do you have for the minister's men?"

"Well, they come with us for a ride up to Urgench, then we just tie them up and leave them in here while we go play."

"But I'm sure they'll need to report in. How will their lack of reports not set off an alarm?"

"So they'll have to make those reports. At gun point."

"We'll need to leave someone here to cover that."

"Styles and his guys can do it."

"I wouldn't leave it to them. I suggest we post a security man."

"And you have someone in mind, don't you?"

Bibby pursed his lips, nodded.

"Wolfgang, huh? But he won't like it."

"But he likes money. And he's best left behind. I don't trust his emotional state. I was surprised you let him work with us in Myanmar."

"He was okay, up till the end. But you know, you're right. That boy's got a lot on his mind."

Within an hour they were back in the air, kissing K2 good-bye, that godforsaken outpost for the poor and poisoned.

Mad Dog gathered all three of the minister's men into the passenger compartment, where Pope, Sapper, and Drac disarmed them in a matter of seconds. They were cuffed, and Doolittle assured them they would not be hurt so long as they complied. They were young, and only one man, the ugliest of the group, gave them any attitude, which resulted in Pope pistol-whipping Mr. Pockmarked Face into silence. Mad Dog could see that the other two would fall in line, as evidenced by their ashen faces.

Kat was still glaring at him, but he, unaffected, kept winking at her from across the cabin. He had sworn that he hadn't realized she'd be in such close proximity to the minister's sexual exploits. Well, maybe he was full of shit, too. She liked to unnerve him while flying her chopper; the least he could do was return the favor and place her in an equally uncomfortable position.

"You wanted to talk to me?" asked Wolfgang, taking a seat beside him.

"When we land in Urgench, we'll need you to hang back, stay here, run security, and make sure these knuckleheads report back to the minister."

Wolfgang's tone darkened. "What the fuck?"

"Hey, buddy, this is what I need from you."

"So, you've been talking to Pope or what?"

"I've been watching you. I don't know what's going on, but work it out. I don't have time for this. And I don't work with people who are anything less than a hundred percent—'cause it's my ass we're talking about, and I'm pretty fucking fond of my ass, thank you. So you stay here with the plane, and that's that . . . "

"I don't speak Uzbek. How am I supposed to make sure these clowns are reporting back?"

Shit, he had a point. Where the hell was Mr. Bibby when he needed him? "You'll manage."

Wolfgang rubbed his eyes, palmed his sweaty and shaven head. "You're wasting me back here, you know that?"

"Look, you've become a hell of a sniper, and I didn't even hire you as one. Thought you'd make a good heavy armor man, artillery guy, what have you. And it's been good. Let's keep it that way. Doolittle?"

The translator climbed from his seat and started over to them, stifling a deep yawn. "Yes, Sergeant?"

Mad Dog pointed across the cabin, indicating the prisoners. "We need those guys to report back to the minister. They need to say everything's okay, that we're in Urgench, the usual bullshit. Can you write up some scripts for us, then Wolfgang will have these meatheads read 'em?"

"Yes, I can do that. I'll get to work on it right away."

"Thanks." Mad Dog leaned over to Wolfgang. "So now you'll manage, okay?"

"Whatever. You want me to babysit three fat old air force farts, that's up to you." Wolfgang stood abruptly.

"Hey, Wolfgang, things get really slow, you can always have a little fun with the girls."

He made a face. "I'm sure Styles and his buddies will keep them busy. Anything else?"

Mad Dog shook his head and watched Wolfgang shuffle back to his seat.

Suddenly, Kat was in the chair next to him. "We're all set on my end," she said. "I just got off the phone with the studio people, and they'll be expecting Doolittle and me."

"Good. Which means I'm getting a bad feeling in my gut. Usually something goes wrong a lot earlier than this."

"What do you want to happen? Engine trouble with the plane? We figure out there's a traitor among us? This isn't exciting enough for you?"

"No, that ain't it. I just got no luck, is all."

"Uh, excuse me, Mr. Hertzog?" called Bibby, staring at the laptop on his knees. "I have some new information from Langley." His tone sounded ominous.

Mad Dog raised his brows at Kat. "See, what'd I tell you?" Then he looked to Bibby. "What do you got?"

"Atayev has moved up his schedule. He'll visit the movie set tomorrow night."

"We'll ain't that a bitch."

"He needs to be back in Tashkent for some kind of a conference the next day."

"There goes all our prep time." Mad Dog rose and addressed the entire group. "Gentlemen, when we land, we'll need to get set up right away. We now have fifteen, maybe eighteen hours if we're lucky."

"If we're lucky," repeated Bibby.

"I'll let them know on the set that we'll be coming early," said Kat, reaching for her satellite phone.

Mad Dog nodded, then drifted back to the main hold, where the choppers and crates lay. He stared at them for a long time, as the big plane's vibrations worked up, into his gut.

"Hey, Zog, what're you doing?" asked Boo Boo. "They sent me back to get you."

"Oh, just thinking about the old days."

The medic's hair was as gray as Mad Dog's, his face just as creased. Yes, he knew all about the old days, too, and all he needed to do was smile and nod, a tacit understanding among men in their line of work.

"Hey, if it makes you feel better," Boo Boo said, "I promise not to die."

Mad Dog palmed the man's shoulder. "I'll keep you to it."

"All right, you smelly bastards, this is the captain speaking," began Styles. "We'll be setting down in Urgench in about fifteen minutes."

"Oh, gee," groaned Boo Boo. "I can't wait."

Mad Dog sniffed his armpit.

"Don't worry, Zog, she don't think you smell."

Mad Dog raised a finger. "Don't start any rumors."

Boo Boo's lips curled. "We already have."

Chapter 5

....

Urgench Airport
Uzbekistan
1450 Hours Local Time

Mad Dog supervised the unloading of the crates, while Night Stalker and Kat instructed Pope, Sapper, and the rest in how to get their choppers prepped for flight.

Security at the airport was a joke. Far less than what they had faced at K2. Two airport policemen greeted them, and one gave a perfunctory glance at their paperwork.

Doolittle spent a few minutes going over the scripts with a dour-faced Wolfgang, while Zito and Wilcox went to see about getting the C-130's tanks topped off.

Night Stalker soon gave the word that he was set to lift off. He, Pope, Sapper, Drac, and Boo Boo would first run some aerial reconnaissance of the city and its environs, noting any potential strongholds or safe houses in which TK might be holding up until Atayev arrived. Once noted, they would land and begin to clear those areas and buildings. All of them would be dressed like tourists, brandishing cameras, pistols hidden in calf holsters and tucked in the back of their pants.

Meanwhile, Mad Dog, Bibby, Doolittle, and Kat would head directly to Khiva. Kat and Doolittle would meet with her contacts on the set. Mad Dog had purchased some professional video equipment for Doolittle and instructed the translator turned videographer to get some footage of the production because they were all fans of Steinberg's action/adventure films, and what the hell, they might as well grab a souvenir.

Bibby and Mad Dog would pose as film crew members and work to clear buildings and mark potential ambush sites. Kat had even procured baseball caps emblazoned with the name of the film: *The Perfect Target*. All of them would remain in close contact via discreet radio earpieces and microphones hidden beneath their clothes.

They were in for a very long night.

Wolfgang watched the two birds take off, raised a pair of middle fingers at them, then turned back for the plane.

"Why you so mad?" asked one of the hookers as she examined her long purple nails. Wolfgang had already forgotten her name—like it even mattered.

"Back in the plane. I told you not to come outside."

"You're an asshole, you know that?"

Her English wasn't great, but it didn't have to be. She knew enough to piss him off. She gave him the bird, a glossy purple bird, then whirled on her sandals and marched up the ramp, white shorts riding up her bony ass.

Styles, who was in the throes of some safety check or

some other bullshit inspection, broke off and came up to him. "Shouldn't you be guarding the prisoners?"

Wolfgang looked daggers at the man. If he had some, he would have thrown them.

Styles shook his head. "Young man, you got an attitude problem, and I *will* fuck you up into next week."

"You just gave me a chill, Grandpa."

"Just do your job, dickhead. Do your job."

Snick . . . snick . . .

There it was again, that fucking sound in his head. Kept coming. Wouldn't go away. Like a metal latch on his brain snicking shut.

He was going crazy. And it had all come on quite suddenly, back in Angola, when he'd been unable to raise his rifle and take out one of Kisantu's men. He had been trembling, unable to focus.

He'd attributed his stress to lack of sleep, but the feeling kept coming back, every time he got in a high risk situation. He couldn't shake it, had tried to clean himself of it, clean his body, shave everything, but the feeling persisted, and then, during the past few months, the sound, that damned snicking had come out of nowhere, like the feeling.

Strangest fucking thing in the world. Some days he would panic, not know what the hell was happening to him. Other days would slip by, and the fear wouldn't cross his mind.

But now, out in the field, all he could think about was screwing up. And the others had recognized it, penalized him for it. He stomped into the passenger compartment, where all three of the minister's guards were seated, eyes closed, sleeping.

He wasn't sure what came over him, but he couldn't

control the anger. His arms stiffened, his hands clenched into fists. He would make sure these assholes knew who was in charge, make sure they didn't fuck with him one bit. Time to put the fear of God in them, and *he* was god! He reared back—

"I don't think so," came a voice from behind him.

It was Styles, who seized his wrist. Damn, the old pilot had remarkable strength. He twisted his arm behind his back, then shoved a pistol into his ear. "Beating the prisoners ain't part of the job, got it, asshole?"

Styles shoved him forward, loud enough to wake the men, who, seeing the confrontation between their two captors, began talking and chuckling.

"Stupid American," said the pockmarked one. "I hope you kill each other."

"Oh, so you understand some English, huh?" Wolfgang said. "Learned it from watching American porno film? So, asshole, it's time to call your fat, old, whore-mongering boss, tell him everything's A-okay." He withdrew the papers from his breast pocket. "You're going to read what's on this paper. You say anything else, and I'll blow your fucking brains out."

The guy bore his teeth and said, "No speak English."

Wolfgang widened his eyes. "Fuck you."

Pockmarked man narrowed his eyes. "I want girl first."

"You get nothing."

Zito was calling from outside to say he needed a hand with something.

"I don't give a fuck about that. When's our fuel coming?" Styles demanded.

"Some kind of delay," answered Zito. "They say soon."

Styles swore again then raised an index finger at Wolfgang. "Kid, I have work to do. You're wasting my time."

Wolfgang nodded. "I got this. You go bye-bye."

"You know, they didn't do me any favors by leaving you. And now I know why you're here."

"Shut up."

Styles's eyes bugged out, then he looked at his pistol, as though deciding whether to shoot him.

"Why don't you try it?" Wolfgang suggested.

"Don't test me."

"Why not? We'll see who's faster. I'm betting I can relieve you of that pistol—and your life—before you take another breath."

Styles grinned darkly, then turned and walked away. "I'm keeping an eye on you, asshole. A sharp eye."

Wolfgang froze, looked around. What the hell was he doing? He was a man, a professional. He'd been given orders. He just needed to follow them. He'd been doing that all his life.

Snick . . . snick . . .

"Gentleman, our friend in Moscow has agreed to double our pay," said Nikolai Tikhon.

Two of his better hired hands, Gorlach and Mykola, sat attentively in the backseat of the truck parked about a sixty meters away from the C-130, alongside a small hangar. "That's going to buy a lot of vodka, a lot indeed!"

The men laughed heartily.

"But no more talk. We are late."

The men hopped out of the truck, moving quickly into the hangar, carrying two long cases and several shorter ones.

Tikhon took his time getting out. He lit up a cigarette,

glanced across the tarmac at the plane with the Algerian flag on its tail, and smiled.

Inside the hangar lay a small office in the rear, where his men were already going over their equipment: rifles, C4, remote detonators, the usual accoutrements for a grand party, Russian mercenary style.

"Nikolai, are you going to stay and help?" asked Mykola, whose wispy hair dangled in his eyes.

"No, I trust you to take care of one big, fat American plane. You are a young man, but if you prove yourself tonight, you will not be so young anymore. Do you understand?"

The twenty-year-old shrugged. "You are a good teacher. How long were you a solider?"

"Too long, Mykola. And never paid what I was worth." He walked over to Gorlach, who would be in charge of planting the explosives. He was slightly older than Mykola, but a lot more high-strung. He was the wild card Tikhon feared, but it was Gorlach's very nature—his unstable mental condition—that made him so valuable and so deadly.

"Remember what I said, Gorlach. We are getting paid double now. That means there is an even slimmer margin for error."

"According to you. And they expected to pay double, so don't be too proud of yourself."

Tikhon stiffened. "You'd better get the job done. That's what I expect."

"Don't worry, old man, I'll blow up your plane. You should worry more about those fools in Khiva. This job will live or die with them. And if we fail, you know what Petrov will do to you. You know."

Tikhon blew smoke in Gorlach's face. "No mistakes."

With that, he left the hangar, climbed back into the truck, and began the drive out to Khiva, along the "old silk road" that wended its way between Europe and Asia, an ancient path beaten by mercenaries and merchants alike for hundreds and hundreds of years. The terrain was barren, and as the sun began to set, Tikhon reached for his satellite phone, stared idly out the window, and dialed a number.

The man on the other end, Ivanov, spoke breathlessly. "We heard Atayev is coming tomorrow night!"

"Are you sure?"

"Yes!"

"Where is TK now?"

Ivanov hesitated before answering.

Veteran pilot Gerald Styles was well aware that the preferred method to ground refuel a C-130 was to utilize a single point control panel situated in the aft side of the wheel well fairing. That was for pressurized fueling. Method B involved access ports atop either of the wing facilitates for gravity fueling. Once the six wing tanks were full, the fuel could be transferred to the auxiliary fuselage side bladders.

Back at K2, those barbaric Uzbeks had told him that their fuel line fittings were incompatible with the single point fueling station fittings and that they had to gravity fuel at the access ports atop each wing. And so they had.

Now, as the Urgench airport refueling crew arrived to top off their tanks, Styles used clumsy hand gestures to remind them about the incompatible fittings.

One man with wispy hair and an odd light in his eyes

smiled and nodded. "Yes, we know all about this problem."

"Wow, your English is pretty good."

"My father taught me. He did a lot of business with the United States."

"Well, that's a relief."

The kid winked, flashed a thumbs-up. "So we refuel from the wings."

Wilcox called from the ramp: "Yo, Gerry, hurry up! It's the kid! Come on!"

"All right, coming." Styles smiled at the fuel guy. "Go ahead and fill us up."

"Okay," said the young man. "Don't worry. We know exactly what to do."

Kat set them down in a makeshift landing zone established by the production company for their three helicopters. The zone lay just outside the northern gate, Bukhara-Darvaza, a great stone affair with little windows cut into a great block of stone spanning the entire gateway. Two towers whose upper quarters were covered in ornate, turquoise tiles glistened in the sun. You swore you were entering the gates of some awe-inspiring, ancient fortress. No wonder Steinberg had chosen to film in Khiva. She was already impressed.

Several police officers in ruffled uniforms who'd been hired by the production team asked for their identification, and Kat got them through without incident. Doolittle even cracked a joke and had the cops laughing and staring wide-eyed.

"What did you say?" Kat asked him.

"I told them that the president was really coming to see you," said Doolittle. "They agreed."

Damn, maybe she was showing a little too much cleavage, but she enjoyed the spell a simple pair of C-cup tits cast over men. She sighed, then crossed onto the long dirt road leading toward the Dost-Alyam Madrassah on their left.

"Whew, look at this place," said Mad Dog. "Big buildings, narrow streets, literally hundreds of places to hide. Tomorrow night we'll need everybody up on the rooftops."

"Probably," said Kat. "Today, they're shooting a scene inside one of the newer buildings, a museum up on the right." She checked her map. "It's called the Matpanabay Madrassah."

"All right, you and Doolittle go hook up with them. Stay in touch. Mr. Bibby and I will do a little scouting and take a lot of pictures."

"Okay, remember the production schedule for tonight has them right below the big minaret, Islam-Hadji." Kat pointed at the towering structure, the most recognizable and obvious feature of the entire city. The minaret loomed over two hundred feet, its bands of tiles like multicolored rings slipped over a massive finger of stone growing wider toward the base.

Bibby and Mad Dog hustled off, digital cameras in hand, clipboards tucked under their arms, Bibby with his small laptop stowed in a backpack. Kat grinned. They still looked rather goofy in their ball caps.

"Lead the way, boss," said Doolittle.

"You might be my favorite," Kat said.

The translator smiled and muttered, "You don't know me very well." He spoke Portuguese, his native tongue, not expecting her to understand.

But Kat surprised him with her reply, though in English: "Let's hope we're both full of happy surprises. Come on."

Wolfgang was leaning over the ramp and puking his guts out. He wasn't sure what the hell was wrong. He had never been airsick before, and he had eaten food brought from home on the plane. Couldn't be food poisoning.

The minister's men had refused to read the scripts and were willing to die first. But he knew he couldn't kill them. He had orders to make them talk. And once he'd begun screaming at them—and delivering a few punches while Styles was outside—he had grown so frustrated, so stressed out, that suddenly he couldn't breathe . . . felt like he was drowning . . .

Then the nausea came in a great swell, and he was running toward the ramp, nearing it, and then . . .

Oh, God, he hated throwing up.

"Why don't you go sit down over there," said Styles.

"I'll be all right."

Snick . . . snick . . .

"No you won't." Styles eyed the prisoners. "Did you get 'em to report back?"

Wolfgang just looked at the man.

"You asshole!"

"I need to call Mad Dog. One guy has a satellite phone that's rung twice already. He needs to answer it."

"Simple little job like this, and you can't even handle it. Son, I think you need to rethink this career."

Wolfgang was about to curse him out when another wave struck. His cheeks caved in as he leaned over, closed his eyes.

*   *   *

Pope made sure that everyone on board the chopper had taken another long, hard look at the intelligence photos of TK, photos supplied by the CIA. He knew that TK would no doubt have disguised himself, but at least a base image of him was a start. Tohir Khodjiev was unremarkable: dark-skinned, with a short beard, medium build, and a forgettable face that only added to his prowess and ability to blend into his surroundings.

Night Stalker had put them down in a clearing outside a small town about a quarter klick south of Khiva. Other than the hotels and the excavations and desert citadel of Toprak Kala, this unnamed village was the only other place of real interest. If TK was not in the town or in any of the hotels, then he was already holed up inside the city, waiting for his moment to strike.

Night Stalker hung back with the chopper, voicing his paranoia about something going wrong with the bird based on his streak of bad luck in Myanmar. He would perform all of his systems checks and inspections, ensuring that when the time came, they'd be airborne in a heartbeat and hauling immediate ass back to Urgench.

Pope and Sapper paired up, as did Boo Boo and Drac. Pope reminded the men to "look less intent."

"What do you mean by that?" Boo Boo asked.

"Try not to look like you're on a reconnaissance mission, for God's sake."

"Gee, I didn't realize I look like that," said the medic. "I guess I got recon written all over my ugly face."

"Just relax your shoulders. Try to look more stupid, more like a tourist, actually interested in this fuckin' hole."

"Do this," said Sapper, gaping at the village, then pretending to trip because he was so enthralled by the view. "See?"

"Both of you guys are idiots," grunted the medic.

Drac said nothing, but he held his camera at the ready. He followed Boo Boo away, toward the east side of the village, while Pope and Sapper headed west.

Just a dozen or so small buildings in ill repair, and a small, central marketplace lay before them. A thick layer of dust blanketed everything and seemed to smother time itself. Two dusky-skinned men wearing dress pants and short-sleeve dress shirts stood behind long tables in the shadows of one building. One was much older than the other, probably a father and son. They were selling white, blue, and emerald colored ceramics; wood carvings; puppets; miniature painted boxes; slippers; chess games; and *telpaks*, which Pope recognized as the traditional hats worn in the region. The *telpaks* looked like wigs and were made from wool of the Karakul sheep.

The men came around their tables to stare at Pope and Sapper, their gazes focusing mostly on the baseball caps. They muttered a few words to each other, then the older one said, "Hello. You here to make movie?"

"That's right, Chief," said Pope. "We're thinking about coming here. We're scouting some new locations. Maybe we'll use your shop in a few scenes, huh?"

The old man scratched his balding and sun-weathered pate, revealed a broken and yellowing smile, then shrugged.

Pope spoke through his own grin. "You don't understand a fucking word I'm saying, Chief. But that's all right."

"Special price for you today," said the old man. "Everything for special price."

Pope nodded, then turned away, called to Boo Boo for a report. The medic told him: nothing so far.

Mad Dog listened to Styles bitching and moaning about Wolfgang's failure to get the minister's men to talk. Then he told Styles to simply make it happen. No time for bullshit.

He tucked the satellite phone into Mr. Bibby's pack, then took out his retractable tape measure, extending it across a wall, as though measuring for a supposed shot or camera angle or whatever the hell it was those movie set people did. Kat had told him to do that.

According to the map, they were in a place called Tash Hauli—the khan's palace—standing in the courtyard of the harem, though they would be hard-pressed to find any real harem women there—mostly fat tourists with cameras wandering along the walled-in area, clicking off shots of the elaborate tile work. After a while all that turquoise became a blur, and Mad Dog found himself just standing there, imagining the film crew present, the cool, night air chilling the scene, harsh lights on the dirt, cameras rolling, the president standing there—

Then TK leaped down from the fifteen-foot-high veranda and fired an RPG while still in midair.

The rocket whistled, struck the ground a few inches from Atayev's well-polished shoes.

Mad Dog gasped.

Atayev was torn into a dozen ragged and flaming pieces, the entire assassination caught on film by Steinberg's cameramen.

"I said, is everything okay back at the plane?"

Oh, Bibby was talking to him. "Yeah, they'll work it out. I'm not too worried."

"If the minister chooses to alert the local authorities or the military—"

"Yeah, I know, I know. But let's give Wolfgang the benefit of the doubt."

"Or enough rope to hang himself."

Mad Dog swore, rubbed his eyes, took another look around. "We got one hell of a place to secure."

"But it is somewhat predictable."

"Yeah?"

"If this is the location that President Atayev will be visiting, then I argue we have one of two scenarios. TK or one of his men will set up for a sniper shot. Or, he or one of his men will infiltrate the film set, posing as a crew member. Perhaps they already have."

"Kat's already working that."

"Indeed. It's quite simple. TK gets close to Steinberg and Atayev, then simply draws his weapon and fires point-blank. He would, of course, be martyring himself, knowing he could not escape."

"What about RPGs, mortars, IEDs, grenades? Kill everyone around Atayev, and maybe you'll get the man, too. Keep a distance."

"That's a possibility, but it's rather sloppy. The intel I've studied indicates that Mr. Khodjiev likes to slip in and out, which is why Atayev's forces have been unable to capture him thus far. He's quite cunning, likes to make a powerful and intimate statement, so bombing the set might be a last resort. I would not be surprised by a single shot, a surgical removal of the target. Or the martyr route. And furthermore, as I told you earlier, I suggest he's only brought a small group, perhaps a dozen men at most, all serving as observers."

"Anything more from Saratova?"

He shook his head. "TK left the city of Angren. He's here, somewhere, no doubt."

Mad Dog glanced up at yet another balcony. "Yeah. The bastard could be watching us right now."

Kat had already met both of the lead actors at a cancer benefit in Century City, Los Angeles, so she was hardly star-struck. Tina Rosalie was an overpaid bimbo with surgically enhanced lips and one too many tattoos. Chad Schmidt was a chain-smoking alcoholic with a million dollar smile that should've been given to someone else. He had the personality of a toad—one that had been flattened by an SUV.

She blew them off with precision, focusing instead on the crew, trying to get every member to look into the camera and say a few words to the folks at home. She planned on speaking to everyone, over 100 people on the set, even craft services.

Doolittle followed her around, working the camera like an expert, his patience infinite.

But not hers. After speaking to nearly fifty crew members over the course of several hours, she was growing frustrated. She had a clear picture of TK in her head, and no one matched. She had the pictures of a few of his closest confidants, including his brother, Maruf, but they, too, were nowhere around.

"It's a fucking needle in a haystack," she told Mad Dog over the radio. "But I'll keep looking."

She went over to a few of the extras, locals hired to pose as vendors inside the museum. She studied their faces intently, then one man rose from his chair, his closely cropped hair gray at the temples, his jaw square. "Can we be on American TV?" he asked in a thick accent.

Kat sighed deeply. "Sure, what's your name?"

"My name is Nikolai."

"And what is your occupation?"

He reached into his breast pocket for a pack of cigarettes, offered her one. She refused. "I would like to be movie star. Maybe bad guy, huh? I could be Russian mercenary."

"That's terrific. But what do you do here in Khiva? Are you a real vendor, basically playing yourself in the film?"

"I'm playing myself. You could say that, yes." The man's cell phone rang. "Oh, I'm sorry. Excuse me."

In Urgench, Wolfgang had convinced himself that the only way to get his prisoners to talk was torture.

But again, Styles and his cronies would have none of it. They stood outside the C-130, at the base of the ramp, just out of the prisoners' earshot.

"This whole op will go to hell if these jackasses don't report in," Wolfgang heatedly told the pilot.

"Then let's make a real deal with them." Styles regarded the prisoners and shouted, "Hey, assholes, what do you want?"

Pockmarked Face grinned. "I want to fuck you up."

"You see?"

"I just won't have it," Styles said to Wolfgang. "I won't have you doing that shit on board my aircraft."

"*Your* aircraft?"

"As matter of fact, I've pumped some of my own money into this bird."

Wolfgang rolled his eyes, beat a fist into a palm. "Wait a minute. Think about it. We're on the same side as these guys. Why don't we just . . . tell them the truth?"

Styles laughed. "Now you're really losing it."

"I'm serious."

"They'll never believe you. Don't waste your time."

"Like you got a better idea?"

"You know what we're going to do? You're going to sit there, and you're going to listen to the way that guy speaks. And when that phone rings, you're going to answer it, and you're going to read the script."

"And then, when I'm done, I'm going to tell those guys that we don't need them anymore, that they're just taking up space. And then I'll screw on my silencer."

"Yeah. Then they'll really believe that you're going to kill them. And who knows, maybe then they'll talk."

"Okay. Follow me."

"What now?" Styles asked.

Wolfgang marched into the plane, went directly to his ruck, removed his pistol and found the silencer.

He screwed on the silencer then went up to the first prisoner, the youngest of the three. He put his gun to the man's head, and said, "Watch this!"

Thump! He executed the man right there. Head shot. Down he went.

Styles began screaming, reached toward Wolfgang, but he was too late. Wolfgang shot the second prisoner in the heart.

The hookers came running down from the cockpit, also hollering.

Wolfgang leaned toward Pockmarked Face and screamed: *"When that fucking phone rings, you're going to answer it!"*

The guy turned white and nodded.

Wolfgang realized he'd been wrong. Torture wasn't the way to get them to talk. That took too long.

Murder, on the other hand, was brief. Effective.

As Styles ripped the pistol from his grip and wrapped an arm around his neck, Wolfgang relaxed, felt faint for a moment, then said, "All right, okay. We're good to go here. Good to go."

And as if on cue, the satellite phone rang.

Wolfgang, still held by Styles, glared at the remaining prisoner. "Ready?"

Chapter 6

· ·

Central Intelligence Agency
Directorate of Operations
Asia Desk
Langley, Virginia
0410 Hours Local Time

Dr. Galina Saratova was on a secure line with her father, Boris Sinitsyna, an NKVD colonel and political
officer working at the Russian embassy in London.

Saratova had kept in touch with him over the years,
called at least twice per month, visited him during the
Christmas holidays every year since her mother had died
five years ago. Papa openly wept every time she saw
him, and for a generally stoic man nearing retirement
after a long and distinguished career as a solider, this
was a great embarrassment to him. Yet he told her he
could not help it, that he wished they could make up for
lost time, that he wished things had been . . . different.
He said he had softened with age, which made Saratova
feel even more guilty.

"Galina, it must be so early there."

"It is."

She had never fallen asleep, and once the tossing and turning became unbearable, she'd risen in the middle of the night, showered, and gone to work, because there was nothing else on her mind.

"Galina, are you there?"

"Yes."

She was literally trembling as she sat at her desk, staring at the photos of family friends, at the degrees on the wall, at the life that was . . . or the life that had never truly been?

"What is it, Galina. Tell me."

"I've been asked to do something terrible. And I thought I knew where my loyalties lie, but I'm not sure anymore."

"What happened?"

"Papa, I can't tell you. But I want you to do something for me. Don't go back to Russia. Ever. Leave there. Leave the embassy."

"What are saying, Galina?"

She lowered her voice to a near whisper. "I want you to defect."

He raised his voice. "Galina, what happened?"

"I can't say."

"Do you know what you are asking?"

"Yes, I beg you. If something goes wrong—"

"Tell me!"

"If something goes wrong, they might come for you . . . use you against me. So you have to leave. Please, Father, do this for me. Please . . . "

"Galina, I want to know what happened. I thought you were doing well there."

Her eyes burned. "Papa, I'm not who you think I am."

City of Khiva
Uzbekistan
1810 Hours Local Time

Mad Dog had booked them several rooms in the Malika Khiva Hotel, a decent-looking, three-star place whose architecture mimicked the tall walls and spires of the ancient city. The rooms were simple and clean, with brilliant red bedspreads and antique-looking phones. The restaurant had a dining area that afforded views of the city and the great minarets.

He, Kat, Doolittle, and Bibby were seated in the restaurant, near the windows. They had just ordered dinner and were comparing notes. Mad Dog shared news from the plane: Wolfgang had killed two of the prisoners, but the third was now cooperating. Styles had asked what they should do with the bodies and he told him to keep them on board for now. Better that than taking the risk of dumping them, only to have airport police or some other meatheads stumble upon them. Understandably, Styles was concerned about the smell. Mad Dog explained that he told him to stuff the bodies up into the wheel wells, if that would help for now.

Then it was Kat's turn to report. "Well, I spoke with most of the crew, still have a few more, but I've come up with nothing," she said. "I mean, absolutely nothing. If TK is here, then I either somehow missed him or he's got something else in mind. With the president coming tomorrow night, you figure he'd already be in place."

"Maybe he already is," said Mad Dog. "And if I'm right, then he's one smart son of a bitch."

"After dinner I'll check mail," Bibby said. "We'll see if Langley has anything else to offer. My friends back in

London should also be checking in. They have several people in Tashkent who can confirm Atayev's itinerary."

"And what about Saratova?" asked Mad Dog.

"She's still clean so far, but they'll keep digging."

"Sergeant, there was one man who bothered me," said Doolittle.

"Do you mean that guy Nikolai?" asked Kat.

"Yes, him. Not many of these local merchants make enough money to carry around cell phones, but this man had one."

Kat's gaze narrowed. "Yeah, you know, now that you mention it, there was something about him . . . "

"He's working as an extra, but he didn't seem as excited as the others." Doolittle handed a flash memory card to Mr. Bibby. "I took a picture of him."

"And he had no problem with that?" asked Bibby.

"No, but maybe he realized he had no choice. If he refused, that would be odd. The other merchants around him were asking me to take their pictures."

Bibby nodded. "I'll run it, see what we come up with."

"So I was wrong," said Kat. "We found nearly nothing. And this guy could be harmless, but that's about all we have so far. And now I'm pretty damn concerned."

"Yeah, and Pope's team is still out there," said Mad Dog. "They checked out a little town, came up empty. They should be here in about an hour, then . . . "

His words drifted off as he glanced out the window. A half-dozen camels with colorful blankets thrown over their backs had been gathered by their owners to offer rides to tourists, but just behind them, three military trucks were pulling up outside the city gates. "Oh, shit. What do we got here?"

"I recognize those uniforms," said Bibby.

They all rose just as the waitress arrived. She told them their dinner would be out in a few moments. Mad Dog shoved his credit card into her hand and requested that the food be delivered to their room. They had a small emergency.

Nikolai Tikhon lay back on his bed in the Asia Khiva Hotel, stealing a few moments' rest. All of the driving and air travel he'd done had taken their toll, and though exhausted, he couldn't sleep. There was far too much on his mind.

His men reported that several of the Americans had come into the town, pretending to be members of the film crew. They had scoured the place, questioning merchants about the movie and about the arrival of other strangers. Then they climbed back into their chopper and flew away.

At the moment, though, their movements concerned him less than those of Tohir Khodjiev. Tikhon had two men among TK's group, and both were late making their reports on the terrorist leader's movements and location. Their silence worried him, and if they did not check in by nightfall, he would have to charge some of his men with finding the others and TK, which would be a horrible waste of time and assets. Such a search would leave them with their guard down, and leave fewer eyes on the Americans, who were the priority.

Damn frustrating, that's what it was, because the mission was, at least at the outset, simple: allow TK to kill Atayev, and prevent the Americans from interfering. Ironically, he and TK were on the same side. At least on paper.

However, Moscow Center wouldn't be paying him so much if the mission didn't have a catch: The Americans were, at first, not to be harmed. Moscow Center wanted them alive until—repeat, *until*—Atayev was murdered.

Though Petrov had never confirmed it, Tikhon had a good idea what their plans were. The Americans had to put on their big dog and pony show. They must appear to be aiding and abetting TK. Atayev's men had to report that there were Americans on the scene at the time of the assassination.

After that, it was up to him to make sure the Americans and TK were taken out, either by his forces or the president's bodyguards.

The way Tikhon figured it, the Americans would be blamed for the murder, and TK would be identified as a terrorist who worked for them, a terrorist hired by the American CIA to do their dirty work, when, in truth, TK was being hired by Moscow Center, and the Americans were being set up by Moscow to have their reputation ruined in the region.

As the Americans would say, everyone was screwing over everyone, but in the end the Russians would win.

Exactly how Moscow Center intended to prove the Americans were involved in the payoffs was beyond Tikhon. Perhaps they would create bogus bank transfers or offer some other kind of physical proof. He wasn't sure, but it didn't matter. He had been a military man long enough to recognize what was happening, and his gut confirmed it.

Earlier, Gorlach and Mykola back in Urgench had called to confirm that the explosive was in place. If the

Americans managed to escape Khiva and reach their plane, they would lift off, then Gorlach would activate his remote.

Tikhon closed his eyes.

The sky flashed. The colossal plane plummeted, and seconds later the earth rumbled as a fiery flower blossomed in the desert, a flower grown in American blood.

Tikhon opened his eyes and smiled broadly. Those pathetic cowboys were doomed.

His phone rang. It was Ivanov at the gate, posing as a local policeman. "Trucks here. National Guard, I think. Something's happening."

"Coming." He rose from his bed, grabbed his pistol and watch.

A look at the bottle of vodka proved to be a mistake. He hesitated, grabbed it, took a long swig, then headed out, grumbling about the aches and pains in his joints, about how much he hated surprises, and about how much he just wanted to get drunk.

And then another surprise occurred. The pistol he kept tucked in the back of his pants slipped inside, into his briefs, and he paused to reach back and fish it out just as a maid pushed her cart on by and stared curiously at him.

What else could he do but grin?

TK lowered his binoculars and turned to Maruf. "If Atayev is scheduled to come tomorrow night, perhaps his men have arrived early to begin setting up their security team?"

"I don't know, brother."

They were atop the Islam-Hadji Madrassah, hiding on

the roof as they had all day, receiving reports from Amal, Nasim, and the other eight men posted throughout the city.

Just then, the two men whom TK believed were spies, probably for Moscow Center, swung over the railing and came forward. "You wanted to see us?" asked the taller one.

"Did you go to the hotel as I asked?"

"Yes, but there was no one there."

Maruf moved up behind the men while both were focused on TK. "I'd forgotten how beautiful it really is." He glanced to a sky washed pink and orange and deep blue.

"You called us to admire the sunset?"

"Yes. Why don't you have a look?"

The taller man snickered.

"Why don't you have a look—for the last time."

With that, TK withdrew the blade tucked into his belt, near the small of his back.

His victim glanced down, gasped.

But the blade was already penetrating his heart.

And TK was already grinding his teeth, hissing through them, tensing every muscle in his body for a few seconds.

Then he wrenched the blade out.

At the same time, Maruf wrapped piano wire around the other man's throat. The traitor fought for a few seconds, his face growing flush, fingers digging at the wire. Then his eyes rolled up into his head and he went limp.

TK's victim fell onto his rump, clutched his chest, and glared at him.

"I know who you are," said TK. "I know what you are. And Russia will soon learn that no one looks over my shoulder. No one."

The spy opened his mouth, but his gaze went blank and he collapsed.

"I wouldn't have guessed," said Maruf. "Everything about them, all the background checking we did . . . What gave them away?"

"I knew who they were from the first day they joined us. And when Moscow Center came to us, I knew why."

"Are you mad! Then why did you let them get so close for so long?"

TK chuckled under his breath. "I was curious."

"Tohir!"

"No, seriously, I knew something would happen. I knew there would be money involved. A lot of money. And soon we'll have it."

"Maybe not, now that they're dead."

"I don't think so. They expected us to kill them."

"Expected?"

"Think, Maruf. They've been with us for three months, meaning this operation has been well-planned by Moscow Center—but even Moscow Center cannot hire experts all the time."

"They're running out of money."

"That's right. They've resorted to mercenaries, and that's what we're dealing with. But the time has come to shut down their communications. And we have. Call for help. We'll dump them in the desert."

"All right. Good. The filming will start again soon. We can use the distraction. But what about them?" Maruf gestured to the trucks below, just outside the gate.

"I'll call Amal and Nasim. See what they know. Otherwise, we don't move until I say."

"Brother, what if Atayev is not coming? What if this is a trap?"

"We're being used, of course. But I don't think it's a trap. The Russians want Atayev dead. He's coming. And we will kill him. But after that? Yes, they will want to kill us—but we'll be ready for them."

TK had not eased his brother's fears, and that fact suddenly angered him. He seized the young man by the shoulders, shook him, and whispered, "You are strong!"

Maruf nodded. "Yes, all right. I am strong."

"We both are."

"Anything?" Mad Dog asked Bibby, whose finger was gliding over his laptop's touchpad.

"Nothing updated. Atayev still scheduled to come tomorrow night. He probably sent a squad or two here to do some reconnaissance, radio back what assets they'll need for security purposes."

Mad Dog glanced idly around the hotel room, considering that. "You know something? I think he's coming tonight."

"That would be foolish. He should secure the area first, unless he's just a fool."

"He's securing it right now."

"With what? A squad or two of guardsmen? He's hardly securing anything."

"I'm telling you he's on his way. He's going to make a surprise visit tonight—when everyone thinks he's coming tomorrow night. And when everyone first thought he was coming two days from now."

"I see," said Bibby. "The surprise, unannounced visit

gives his enemies less time to prepare. And the confusion regarding his exact arrival day and time adds to the . . . well, general sense of confusion."

"We need to move into position and assume he's on his way. If he doesn't come, then we'll consider this a practice run."

"I understand. And I assume he'll be coming by air."

"He could fly directly here or land in Urgench and come by ground. Big Booty should be able to get us some eyes on this area, in case our intel from Langley isn't all that it's cracked up to be."

Big Booty was Mad Dog's special friend at JSOC, and they had shared their own Joint Special Operations in a hotel room bed. Okay, so she was Oprah before the diet, but she always knew how to make him laugh. He could see the big woman now, bullshitting her way into getting satellites aimed where he and his dogs needed them.

"Great minds think alike," Bibby said. "It's already done. I'll check with her again."

"You're the man. I'll talk to Pope. Let him know."

"Mr. Hertzog, with less time to prepare, TK might resort to something sloppier than I've anticipated."

"Bomb?"

"Perhaps. If he doesn't plan to martyr himself—"

"Then maybe he'll get one of his meatheads to wire up and blow everyone back to God."

"But he wouldn't get onto the set, not with all that security," said Kat.

"Unless he's already got access, and you missed something," Mad Dog countered.

She twisted her lip.

Mad Dog returned the ugly face. "You'll need to get back to the set. Where are they again tonight?"

"Right below Islam-Hadji."

He frowned. "Oh, that helps."

Her eyes widened. "Hello, the big minaret?"

A knock came at the door. Dinner had been sent up.

"You mind if I stuff my face for a minute?" asked Kat.

"I'm eating," said Doolittle. "Then we'll go. The president is not here yet."

"All right, you got a hundred and twenty seconds to stuff your faces," said Mad Dog.

"You stand there and count," said Kat, though she already had a huge piece of bread jammed into her mouth. She added something unintelligible, lost in all that dough.

Mad Dog swung around, incredulous, shaking his head at Bibby. "You believe this? You know, if this were a Marine Corps operation, you'd work dirty, tired, hungry, and you'd beg for more."

Just then Mr. Bibby shoved his laptop aside, raised his chin at the kid from room service, then practically dove for the food cart. "I believe, Mr. Hertzog, that you owe this young man a tip."

Mad Dog shrugged and reached into his pocket. He handed over the bills. The kid wasn't happy, muttered something, left.

"What'd he say?"

Doolittle shook his head. "You don't want to know."

"Bossman says we got National Guardsmen in the city now," Pope told the others. "He wants the area cleared and wants us in position right now." Pope craned his head toward the pilot. "Night? You stay with the helo. Be ready to boogie."

Night Stalker sighed. "It's what I do. Sit around and jerk my stick. What a life."

"Just be ready, big guy." Pope pulled a duffel bag from the chopper, dropped it on the dirt before Boo Boo, Drac, and Sapper. "Come get your scopes."

They were fielding a new toy, a radar scope about the size of a VHS videotape. The scope would "see" through twelve inches of concrete and detect movement as small as breathing. They could now prioritize what rooms to enter and have an advantage over their enemies.

"This thing says I'm dead," said Boo Boo, holding the scope up to his own chest.

"Then it's working," said Sapper.

"What?" cried the medic. "You don't like my sparkling personality?"

Sapper grinned and held the scope up to his groin. "Wow, this thing says I'm huge."

Pope swore under his breath. "Let's go, assholes."

Drac came up beside him. "Uh, yeah. All we got are these little sidearms and the sniper rifles in these cases. This is, uh . . . what I'm trying to say is, uh, I would like a big fucking machine gun, thank you."

"I know, Drac, but our enemies aren't packing much, and their aim's not worth a shit." Pope patted the H&K PSG1 semiautomatic sniper rifle inside Drac's case, a case marked LIGHTING and bearing one of the studio's logos.

"You're a bad liar, Pope."

"Ah, who cares? This makes it more fun anyway."

Pope was, indeed, a bad liar, and he knew he'd be lying if he said he wasn't chilled by the prospect of trying to take down an elusive terrorist with a team armed like street cops instead of soldiers. Well, the rifles would help, once they got into position on the rooftops. But it was all too quick, too haphazard. Oh, he was just getting old. Quick and haphazard used to be his middle names.

He thought of the Barbie doll in his backpack. They all knew about it. No one had ever said anything except Rookie, who . . . Pope didn't want to think about it, about death right now. Not the time.

He was a brother who still carried around his sister's doll because he would never let go.

He was a son who had grown up hating the water because he blamed himself for his sister's drowning.

He was a former Navy SEAL who had decided to confront his demons and take on the water in a way that most mortal men feared.

And now he was a mercenary finally at peace with the past, but his future looked pretty damn uncertain.

"All right, motherfuckers," he breathed over the radio. "I want to see happy faces. We're so happy to be in the middle of this shit-ass desert, taking pictures of this friggin' city for our famous boss, Mr. Steinberg, okay?"

"Hey, you seeing that?" said Sapper, hustling back to him. "Two guys there with the police. Looks like they're closing up the whole place."

"That doesn't happen till ten."

"Maybe the president's really coming after all."

"All right, get your IDs ready," Pope said again over the radio. "And remember, we're all glamorous, whacked out, big fucking movie people."

"Two out of three ain't bad," said Sapper. "Two out of three."

"Yeah," Pope muttered, wishing they had their very best shooter with them to ease his nerves with a little crass humor and over-the-top bravado.

Wolfgang was being wasted back at the plane. When Pope heard that the guy had executed two of the prisoners, he wasn't surprised. Men like Wolfgang—men like him—were too hard on themselves, but they had to be. Par for the course.

Wolfgang, you dumb fuck. I could use you now.

Back at the C-130, Wolfgang wasn't having one of his proudest moments. "I don't care, give me that fucking bottle!" he screamed, wrenching the whiskey from Wilcox's hand.

Snick . . . snick . . .

"Does Mad Dog know you got that?"

"I don't give a fuck if he knows or not!"

"So, you've decided to get drunk in the middle of an operation," said Styles, marching into the plane's hold.

Wolfgang plopped into one of the mesh troop seats along the wall, threw back his head, raised the bottle, toasted the two assholes, and took a big, fat swig.

The burn. Ah, the burn.

"We have to do something," said Wilcox.

"You're the loadmaster, huh?" asked Wolfgang. "Guess you got a load of me, huh, motherfucker?" He laughed.

Copilot Zito joined Styles and Wilcox, and all three farts wore big pusses, hating him.

"See my bestest buddy there?" asked Wolfgang, feeling the numbness wash up to his lips. He was pointing at the ugly son of a bitch, the one he'd let live. "He's a good fucking boy now. Does what I say. Says what I say. Does what says I and says you, too. You want me to say that again?"

"He's already drunk," grunted Zito.

"Fuck 'em," said Styles. "We'll get the hookers to keep watch through the cockpit windows. We'll stand guard outside. We'll leave this sack of shit here."

"Nope, I guess I ain't such a likable guy after all, eh, Grandpa?"

They took their scowls outside. They didn't get him. They had no idea what it was like to be fucking perfect one day, then feel all this shit the next. Stupid really.

Snick . . . snick . . .

I am not weak. I'm going to find out what you are, you fucking noise, I will. I am not weak. I will take control. I will beat you.

But what am I forgetting?

Kat was still on the set, pumping everyone willing to talk for information. She learned that Steinberg was in one of the trailers, discussing a scene with star Tina Rosalie.

No one else knew anything about President Atayev arriving soon, so Kat figured she'd go to the top. Atayev might well have called Steinberg to announce his arrival. Rumor had it that they'd spoken often on the phone since the director began filming.

That Kat thought she could get Mr. Celebrity Filmmaker to cough up such information was a testament to her strong will and unwillingness to take no for an answer.

In a perfect world, her tits and ass would have nothing to do with that, either.

But she hadn't expected to have the door slammed in her face before opening her mouth.

Steinberg's assistants took rudeness and cruelty to a new level, but instead of groaning over the fact, Kat decided to try a different approach by wandering over to the head of security, a heavyset black man standing a few yards behind one of the cameras. He had a Bluetooth headset in one ear, a radio headset in the other, and a walkie-talkie in his thick grip. She whispered to Doolittle to keep watch and call her if needed. He nodded and backed away.

Kat approached the distracted ape, proffered her hand, and gave him a look usually reserved for those watching her remove her bra and panties. "Hi, I'm—"

"I know who you are." He didn't bother to look at her, placed a hand on his ear, listening to a thin voice.

"I was wondering if I could ask you—"

He raised a finger. "No."

"I mean before the president arrives. Just a few questions."

"Lady, he's going to be here in ten minutes. I don't got time for this."

Kat raised her brows. "Neither do I. But thanks anyway."

He gave her a funny look as she turned and practically ran back to Doolittle. "Atayev will be here in ten minutes!"

She was at once thrilled by having tricked the security guy and anxious over the lack of time.

But most of all she was proud that she had gathered the information they needed, the information Mad Dog needed. She had a sudden and crazy need to impress him. Strangest thing. They weren't in competition. And yes, she wanted to prove herself as a team member, but this was different. This was about him and his reaction to her work. It was suddenly very, very important to her. She wanted him to like her, admire her, and maybe, though she was scared to admit it, she wanted more.

"Well, Kat, I have a good idea," said Doolittle, wearing a crooked grin. "I think you should call the sergeant and let him know."

"You mean Mad Dog?"

His eyes bulged. "Yes!"

Jesus Christ, she was like a schoolgirl with a crush, her breath gone, her thoughts flying in wild orbits. She pulled out her headset, slipped it on. "Okay, okay."

Chapter 7

....

City of Khiva
Uzbekistan
1930 Hours Local Time

Mad Dog ran breathlessly through the hotel, rattling off orders into the radio, trying to get Pope's team into position near and around the minaret. He was barely looking up, dividing his gaze between the map and the hallway. "So I need those sweeps like yesterday, understand?"

"Yeah, I do," Pope answered. "We'll get started, but you understand, our goddamned pants are down. We need more time."

"Just do it. Blackhound One, out!"

At the same time, Bibby, who was jogging behind him, was saying something about intel, about how there was no sign of any motorcade or chopper flights or anything that might indicate a presidential arrival.

"So what that means," the Brit added, "is that Atayev is already here, probably came with the security team, maybe even disguised himself as one of them."

"Yeah, that's right. Make it look like he sent people ahead to recon when, in fact, he's part of the recon team. It ain't genius, but it might've worked."

"If his people learned of a possible assassination attempt here, smuggling him in would make sense."

Mad Dog grunted his agreement. "Guy wants to stay alive. Can't blame him for trying."

"But he's brought a small security force. That's a calculated risk." The Brit slowed, began to lag behind.

"Come on!" Mad Dog cried, then charged through the hotel lobby, drawing stares from the concierge and bellboy.

"Wait. There's one more thing."

Mad Dog paused, let Bibby catch up. The Brit reached him, breathless and bleary-eyed.

"I don't want any more bad news. Not now."

"Not necessarily bad. Possibly terrible."

"Jesus Christ."

"Then again, it could be nothing."

"Well, then it can wait! Come on!" Mad Dog pushed through the doors and jogged outside, working his way parallel to the building, running toward the main gate, near the minaret looming like a nuclear containment building turned into art.

"Blackhound Six, this is Blackhound One, over," Mad Dog called to Kat.

"One, this is Six, go ahead."

"Where are you now?"

"Just below the minaret, right on the set. They're setting up for an action shot here, gunfire. Don't like that. And I still don't see Atayev, over."

"All right, I want you out of there," said Mad Dog.

"You and Doolittle back to the chopper, in case all this goes south."

"Uh, I'm looking at Steinberg right now. He's like within spitting distance. If Atayev is coming, I'll be as close to him as anyone. You take me out of here, you're making a big mistake."

"Blackhound Two and I will there in a couple of minutes."

"You won't get as close as me without raising flags."

"I don't want you close."

"In case of a bomb? Look, just shut up. Blackhound Two can fly my bird. Have him stand by there and keep her warm."

Mad Dog slowed from a jog into a walk as he neared the gate and the two guards posted there. He looked back at Bibby and realized that Kat was right. "Go back to the chopper and wait there," he said. "Keep gathering intel. And have her ready to fly."

"I wish we were better organized," snapped the Brit. "And so do my feet!"

"Wait, that thing you wanted to tell me?"

"Let me confirm first. Off I go to the chopper, oh fucking joy!"

As he bolted away, Mad Dog called Kat, told her to stay on the set but keep a "safe" distance.

"Define safe," she countered.

This time he told *her* to shut up.

Funny. She had second-guessed him—even challenged him—and that hadn't sent him into a rage. In fact, she'd been right, and remarkably, he was okay with that.

Damn, was he just mellowing out or letting her get away with it because, well . . . he shuttered off the thought.

Mad Dog showed his ID to the men at the gate, adjusted his ball cap, then entered the city, just as the film crew's bright lights turned the gloom of Khiva into pale neon, a harsh glare beaming off the minaret's tiles.

He ran hard and fast down a dirt road. No one around. A ghost town. Yes, they had closed for the evening, sent the tourists back to their rooms. That was good. Less civilians to get caught in a cross fire.

To the northeast of the minaret stood the madrassah, a square building with a large, open courtyard, five stories of ledges, and a broad rooftop from which a hundred snipers could set up and exact hell upon unsuspecting dignitaries and Hollywood icons. It was a complicated and generally fucked-up place to secure. At least a few of Pope's men should be inside by now, he thought. They'd better be.

To the west lay the Pakhlavan-Makhmud Mausoleum, yet another multistoried affair with central courtyard, domed roof, and ancient stone tombs, some crumbling into excellent perches for snipers and other assorted assholes.

The streets and alleys between both buildings were dark and narrower than the rest of the city. Even if they cleared both the mausoleum and the madrassah, he knew there was still a good chance that TK or one of his cronies could move unseen through those dark passages, slipping from alcove to alcove.

As Mad Dog reached the film set and spotted Kat, he got back on the radio. "Hey, Six, you there?"

Kat responded quickly, "Yes, what?"

"I told you to keep a safe distance. Was I ordering Chinese food or giving you a fucking order?"

"Uh, you want combination platter with egg roll?"

"Don't play games, sweetheart."

"Don't 'sweetheart' me."

Mad Dog slipped up behind her before she could answer and whispered, "You got a problem with authority figures."

She jerked back her head. "No, just you."

Then she turned and looked at him.

Her expression turned weird. She looked . . . nervous? He wasn't sure.

He shrugged. "What?"

"Uh, I was just thinking—"

A small group of people suddenly moved behind them, gaining Mad Dog's attention. He scrutinized the men and women, most wearing ball caps identical to his own, saw one man dressed in jeans and a sweatshirt with the studio logo. Gray sideburns. Familiar eyes. Wait . . .

"That's him!" he stage-whispered. "It's the president, right there, dressed like the crew, going up to Steinberg!"

Pope's radar scope told him there were two men inside the room. He looked to Sapper, ready to burst inside.

They were on the third floor of the madrassah, and the window inside the room overlooked the entire film set. It was a sniper's dream come true. That window called out to Pope—so while Drac and Boo Boo had gone across the street to the mausoleum, he and Sapper obeyed the siren's song of mercenaries, a song whose lyrics included the phrase: "check out that fucking room, you meathead."

A wooden door that might be a hundred years old, maybe older, stood in their path. Pope had wondered if they should try the latch, kick it in, or just knock. If they tried the latch and it was locked, they'd be tipping off the occupants. Knocking would do the same but make them appear less threatening.

"It looks too thick. Can you break it down?" he whispered to Sapper.

Though Pope's tone had been neutral enough, he knew Sapper would interpret the question as a challenge.

And challenging Sapper's physical prowess was akin to calling him a Republican.

With his teeth flashing, he moved back, ran at the door, launched himself into the air—

And his black Nikes made contact.

Holy shit. That big piece of wood snapped in two like it was a panel of balsa used to make toy airplanes.

Even as the pieces crashed to the stone floor with echoing thuds, Pope spotted two figures near the window. They were illuminated by a small kerosene lamp, the light filled with dust motes, the odor enough to make him gag. Sweat. B.O.

The silencer was already on his pistol, so when one figure turned and something metallic flashed in his hand, Pope's SEAL training kicked into high gear.

There was no doubt or delay—only a bullet streaking right toward the figure's head.

As that guy fell, Sapper was up on his feet, throwing himself forward again, snagging the second guy's ankle.

Pope fired once more, hitting mystery guy number two in the ass, a deliberate, nonlethal shot.

Good to keep one alive. Get him coughing up what they needed to know.

The man went down. He was dark-skinned, somewhat familiar. As Sapper crawled forward and pinned him to the floor, Pope brought over the lamp, and his jaw dropped.

He reached into his pocket and studied the intelligence photo. "How fucking easy was this! We got him! Fuck, Sapper. This is him! This is TK!"

"God damn, we took him alive. Props to me for a job well done. Props to you for not fucking up."

"You arrogant asshole. Blackhound One, this is Blackhound Four, over."

"Go ahead, Four."

"We got him, One. The tango is ours. And he's alive, over."

Silence. Probably stunned silence from Mad Dog. Then, finally: "Roger that. Where are you?"

"In the madrassah, third floor, the room with the broken door, over."

Mad Dog told Kat to stay on the set, keep her eyes on Atayev, while he and Doolittle went to Pope's location to check out the prisoner. He'd believe they had TK when he saw the man for himself. As he and the translator shifted past one of the big lights, Steinberg cried, "Action!"

Mad Dog couldn't help but turn around and watch the chase scene, one man pursuing another, both firing submachine guns while small "explosions" erupted around them and squibs burst along the walls, simulating the gunfire. It all looked pretty damned real; perhaps too real.

But Atayev was right there next to Steinberg, huddled over a video monitor. Three big VIP bodyguards stood behind them, and a glance up to the ledges and rooftops revealed nothing.

With a chill working up his spine, Mad Dog trotted off, hoping they had just earned another three million bucks the staggeringly easy way.

It was Doolittle who reminded him of the obvious:

"Khodjiev is very, very good. He would not make a mistake like this."

Bad things happen to good mercenaries. "Good" mercenaries? Well, yes. Good in the sense of efficiency, in the sense of occasionally having a conscience, in the sense of—

Oh, Bibby, shut the fuck up. Your mind is wandering now.

That shit would invariably happen was a fact of life, and Alistair Bibby had grown accustomed to their magnificent plans frequently going up in magnificent flames.

The surgical removal of one Mr. Tohir Khodjiev from this blue orb called earth required much forethought. The first thing you did when preparing to take out such a man was to, ahem, make sure you could positively identify him.

Fortunately, the Uzbek military had published many reports regarding Mr. Khodjiev. These reports included his movements, motives, dozens of photographs, and they noted other distinguishing characteristics, including physical marks like scars or tattoos or even a piece of jewelry worn by the wanted.

Unfortunately, Mr. Khodjiev had no scars, no tattoos, and was about as nondescript as they came. If Pope claimed to have captured TK, then, well, maybe he had.

Of course, all of them were thinking the same thing: too easy—unless, for some reason, TK wanted to be captured as part of a diversion he had planned.

Or perhaps another party had planned the diversion, the one that sent Bibby's fingers dancing over his keyboard.

He took one look at the message and cursed.

* * *

Nikolai Tikhon and his man Ivanov were hunkered down on the roof of the mausoleum. Tikhon wrenched the night vision goggles away from the heavier, stubbier man and had a look for himself, focusing on the madrassah opposite them.

"There he is, Mr. Michael Hertzog himself, our American cowboy, come to claim his prize."

The well-muscled man wearing the ball cap entered the room where Tikhon's men had been waiting. A shorter, darker man followed.

"You know this will not last long," said Ivanov. "They won't believe that Sergey is Khodjiev. They will not have a false sense of security like Petrov said. They will see through this charade. It's a waste of time."

"Don't be so sure. Sergey is a perfect match. It took months for Moscow Center to find him."

"But what if he breaks? He talks?"

"Oh, he will. He's a weak-minded fool. But by then it will be too late."

"So the Americans are diverted, leaving TK to accomplish his mission. But we still don't know where that bastard is."

"Oh, he's here." Tikhon panned around the ledges, probing the corners, the deep pockets of gloom along the balconies.

Ivanov's voice cracked: "I think he killed our men. I think he figured out who they were, and he killed them. And now he's hunting Atayev—and us."

Suddenly, gunfire erupted below, and Tikhon panned down, breathing a deep sigh of relief. It was just the actors again. He lowered the goggles and turned to Ivanov—

But the pudgy little man was hunched over, blood pouring from the back of his head.

Tikhon rolled away, came up on his knees, sweeping with his pistol. A series of low walls, no more than a meter high, cut across the rooftop, creating a stone maze. A gunman could be hiding behind any wall, and worse, the film crew had dimmed the lights below. The gloom descended upon the roof like a rain cloud. Tikhon squinted, his hand trembling.

"He has no idea," Maruf said softly in TK's ear. "He's like a scared child."

"I'm going to let this one live. Let him dangle for a while. He's older than the others, probably the leader. We should've killed him first. But maybe we'll use him as the messenger. Kill his entire group, and leave him to run home to Moscow Center."

The Russian ducked out of sight before TK could change his mind.

He turned away from the rifle's night vision scope and smiled at his brother. They were on the roof of the madrassah, but they needed to move soon.

"Atayev is down there now, with Steinberg. Why don't you take the shot, brother?"

TK adjusted his position, tried to take aim at Atayev, but the monitors were in the way. "It's no good from here. Besides, we're going to do a lot more than just kill the president, brother. We're going to kill everyone down there."

"You never said—"

"The Americans are in bed with Atayev. We will send a message to them as well."

"But—"

TK held his brother's hands in his own. "He that obeys God and His apostle shall dwell forever in gardens watered by running streams. That is the supreme triumph."

"The Koran again?"

"Maybe you need to hear it more often."

Maruf froze. "We should kill Atayev. For the money. For our people."

"And the Americans, too."

"If we do that, they will come here, as they did in Iraq and Afghanistan. We might be dead, but our children will be at their mercy. Do you want that, brother?"

"I'm sorry, Maruf. But it's too late to change anything."

"Why didn't you tell? Why did you wait until now?"

"Because I know you too well."

"You are my older brother. But Tohir, you are making a mistake."

"No. Our men are in place, the order has already been given, and they simply await my signal. The Americans are already dead. Come on, now. Help me get changed . . . "

"Blackhound One, this is Two," called Bibby over the radio.

"Not now," Mad Dog told the Brit. He had his hands wrapped around the wiry-looking man's neck while blood dripped from the hem of the prisoner's pants.

"He's begging for a doctor," said Doolittle.

Mad Dog shoved the guy down, onto the dusty floor. "This ain't him."

"You fucking kidding me, bossman?" cried Pope. "Look at the goddamn picture!"

Pope shoved the photo into Mad Dog's hand. The guy looked a hell of a lot like TK. He really did.

"It ain't him," said Mad Dog. "Our guy wouldn't beg for anything, trust me. Ask him who he is, who he works for . . . "

While Doolittle did that, Mad Dog called Bibby. "All right, Two. What do you have for me?"

"My contacts at MI6 have paid us a courtesy call. They have in custody a Russian NKVD colonel, a political officer at the Russian embassy in London. He's trying to defect. He's got an interesting story about a daughter sent to America by Moscow Center. He wants MI6 to rescue her from the Americans."

"Name of the daughter?" Mad Dog asked, hoping it wasn't the name he expected.

"Boris Sinitsyna is the colonel's name. The daughter is Galina Sinitsyna . . . or . . . Galina Saratova, our client."

Mad Dog shook his head. "Shit."

"MI6 is still trying to confirm this, but if Saratova is an agent working for Moscow Center, then the CIA has had a mole running its Asia desk for the past eight years, a mole who hired us to kill TK."

"Have they contacted anyone in Langley about this?"

"No, they're not ready to call across the pond. This was just a courtesy call from an old friend who understands our current needs and situation."

"Jesus, I had second thoughts about working for the CIA . . . so what now? We're working for Moscow Center?"

"We might be. Perhaps Saratova's father learned what she was doing, thought she was in too deep, and is trying to somehow save her."

"Who gives a shit about her! What about us? How the fuck could we let this happen?"

"The five million dollar question."

"All right, so if we're working for them, they want TK dead and Atayev to remain in office?"

"I don't know. But I ran Kat's photo through the database, and I just got the results. Positive match with a guy named Nikolai Tikhon, retired intelligence officer with the Soviet army. He was in A'stan the first time around. And more recently—and probably unbeknownst to him—he's made it onto of list of known mercenaries operating in Central Asia."

"So what now? We got a Russian merc on the set? Who's he working for? Saratova? Shit, we need to shut him down."

"He's probably not working alone, either. But more importantly, do we have TK?"

"Hold on." Mad Dog went over to Doolittle, who was still speaking with the bleeding man. "I need to know right now."

"He says his name is Sergey. He is just an auto mechanic from St. Petersburg. He says he was hired by a man named Petrov. He was to come here with another man named Tikhon, who would give him orders. Tikhon placed him here, told him to keep watch. He says that's everything he knows."

"Do you believe him?"

Doolittle threw up his hands.

"Do you fucking believe him?"

"Sergeant, please."

"Two, the guy we got here? He's working for the Russians. He looks just like TK."

"So the Russians have brought along a decoy. Why would they do that if they want TK killed?"

Mad Dog wasn't listening to Bibby anymore. He told Pope and Sapper to gag and tie up the decoy, leave him there, and get back to their posts up on the roof. Then he and Doolittle dashed out of the room, bound for the set.

If his gut was right, Tohir Khodjiev was about to seize the day—or the night, as it were—and President Atayev was about to star in his own action film, one in which he did his own stunts.

The years Drac had spent as an Air Force combat controller, deploying into forward operating locations and conducting complex reconnaissance missions, had well prepared him for sneaking around a few buildings and gathering intel on a bunch of trigger happy monkeys.

And if they were monkeys, then old Cap'n Drac was a hawk, spying them from afar, contemplating their next moves and his own. He'd even been accused of having birdlike features: long, narrow nose and thin, angular chin.

Chicks dug him—especially when the drinks were on him.

At the moment, he and Boo Boo were still clearing rooms inside the mausoleum. They found all kinds of framed wood carvings and old ceramics that looked as fragile as they were priceless. All of the complex's main rooms were faced with painted majolica tiles. The wooden doors were carved and inlaid with copper and ivory. He had remarked to Boo Boo that the place looked like a museum.

"Yeah, the Soviets really cleaned up this place," the medic had said. "Turned it into one big tourist trap instead of leaving it alone, letting it be a real city with real people instead of this Disney bullshit."

"I like Disney."

Holding his breath, Drac pressed the radar scope to the next door. Nothing. He shook his head at Boo Boo, and they moved on to the next.

At the next door, the scope immediately registered movement on the other side. One man. Strong signal.

He raised his hand to Boo Boo, then took a few steps back, about to kick in the door, his pistol at the ready.

The door swung inward, and a man appeared, looking flushed and surprised.

He demanded something in Uzbek, probably wanted to know who they were.

"We're security for the film set," said Boo Boo. "Who the fuck are you?"

The man uttered something again. He was graying at the temples, his hair closely cropped. He wore local garb, looked like a merchant, or maybe he was an extra in the movie. Despite his forceful tone, he was twitchy.

They all just looked at each for an awkward moment.

"Movie, ah, yes," the man finally said. "Me, too . . . " He tugged at his tunic. "Must go!" He walked quickly away, and as he did, he neared a row of candles burning from sconces along one wall—

And then Drac noticed the bloodstains across the back of his shirt.

"Hey, wait!" Drac cried.

The man glanced back, eyes wide. Then he sprinted away.

"Boo, come on!" cried Drac.

They charged after the guy, even as Boo Boo called Mad Dog to let him know they were in pursuit of, as Boo Boo, put it, "Some fucking guy with blood on him!"

"Is he a local?"

"Could be. Looks like a merchant. Said he was in the film!"

"I want him. You hear me?"

"We'll bring him back on a fucking platter!" shouted Boo Boo, the poet.

Drac raced to the stairwell door, slammed it open, heard the footfalls of their prey as he pounded down the stone steps. He leaned over the wooden railing, tried to spot the guy, but it was too dark, only a dim bulb hanging somewhere above them. Shit.

Down he went, his basketball sneakers, the ones everyone on the film crew liked to wear, slipping on the stone. He slowed, grabbed the railing, kept slamming down, down.

A door squeaked open. That scumbag was already outside. He took the last flight even faster, leapt from about four steps up and dropped before the door, which hadn't finished closing. With a fist, he slammed it open, rushed out.

To the right was a long alley, narrow, a half-dozen alcoves set into a long wall. No movement.

To the left, another alley. There he was, the bastard. Drac raised his silenced pistol, aimed for the guy's ass, range just twenty meters or so. He fired, then lowered his arm.

The asshole kept running.

Drac gasped. "Are you kidding me?"

Boo Boo reached him, saw what had happened. "Shit, bonnet boy, you missed!"

"No way did I miss!"

"Then he's got Kevlar underwear! Let's go!"

* * *

Mad Dog spotted Kat standing near the film crew's sound guy. He navigated over and around the jungle of wires, then slipped in beside her, just as Steinberg began shouting orders that they were about to film the next scene.

"Have you been listening?" he muttered.

"To every word."

"I think Bibby's right."

"About what?"

"About us being set up by the Russians. We're not here to take out TK. We're here to take the blame for the president's death—and I can't stand here and watch this happen."

"Neither can I."

She nudged him. "What then?"

"We're just going to march up to Atayev and let him know he's in danger."

Mad Dog was already pushing his way forward, heading directly for the big security team leader with a hand to his ear. They just needed to make it past him and—

Steinberg shouted, "Action."

But the explosions that followed were so powerful, so loud, that Mad Dog immediately knew what was happening.

The first boom sent him to his knees.

The second drove him flat onto his gut.

"Oh my God!" Kat cried as she collapsed next to him.

"Blackhounds, this is One! Everyone to the set! Now!" Mad Dog scrambled to his feet.

The area was utter chaos, crew members rushing everywhere, two huge fires burning, one of the cameras destroyed, body parts lying in the dust. The security team guys were rushing toward Atayev and Steinberg, as well as several uniformed guardsmen who protected the president. Amazingly, the bombs had not struck them. Or perhaps not so amazing.

Mad Dog probed every face, saw one of those guardsman heading toward Atayev, focused on his face.

"Oh, shit," he groaned. "That's our boy, TK. Right there!"

Chapter 8

City of Khiva
Uzbekistan
1955 Hours Local Time

Holding his breath, Mad Dog reached down to his calf holster, tugged free his pistol, then shoved past two crew members to get near TK and Atayev.

"I got a bead on him!" cried Kat.

"Wait!" ordered Mad Dog.

Chad Schmidt, unlit cigarette dangling from his mouth, had moved into the line of fire. "Jesus Christ, how unprofessional is this?" the idiot screamed. "Donny said the charges wouldn't go off this close! And my squibs didn't! Goddamn extras running around! I can't work under these conditions! This is *my* movie, for God's sake! My movie! What the fuck is this?"

Mad Dog was dumbfounded.

And Schmidt was either blind or on drugs. How could he miss the carnage around him—or did he attribute the blood and body parts to special effects?

"Get out of the way!" Mad Dog hollered to Mr. Movie Star.

"Wait!" called Kat. "Let me get him!"

Mad Dog ignored her and pushed past yet another extra until he caught sight of TK, just over Schmidt's shoulder. The notorious leader of the J-U2 had just raised his pistol to Atayev's head.

And, like a surreal image from the film itself, TK fired, blood jetting from the back of Atayev's head, Steinberg turning his own head, seeing the blast, screaming as the president's guardsmen moved in to seize Atayev.

TK whirled around, grabbed Steinberg by the neck, put his pistol to the director's head and began to drag him away from the TV monitors and cameras as the set's big security team leader yelled for him to stop—

Even as gunfire cut loose from the rooftops behind them.

"Got him!" screamed Kat.

Mad Dog glanced to her—

Just as she fired!

TK's head lolled back, revealing a dark red gunshot wound on his forehead, a large piece of skin hanging half off. He shrank to the dirt, releasing Steinberg, who was quickly whisked toward the wall behind him by the security team leader.

Under a second spate of gunfire, Mad Dog signaled to Kat and Doolittle, who were hunched over and jogging toward him. "We're out of here!"

One of Atayev's guardsmen spotted them, pointed, shouted orders, and two more soldiers broke off from the group and brought their rifles to bare.

"Oh, shit," grunted Kat.

Then shots echoed from above, and the guardsmen

dropped hard to the deck, both groaning and clutching their wounds.

Mad Dog turned in the direction of the gunfire. Pope and his men were up there, somewhere along the parapet.

"Sergeant, I recorded everything," said Doolittle as he shoved his camera into a backpack.

"Good, but I don't know how that can help us now." Mad Dog keyed his mike, wincing over the stench of sulfur and burned flesh carried on the breeze. "Blackhounds this is One. The president is dead, and so is our target. This fucking job has gone south. We are out of here. Rally back on the birds, out!"

"Wait a second, One," cried Pope over the radio. "We got more guys up here, shooting at us! Who the fuck are they? TK's guys? Movie set?"

"I don't know," answered Mad Dog. "Fuck 'em. Time to go!"

Drac drew within a few meters of the guy who had posed as a movie set extra, the one with the bloodstains on his clothes. They were charging down a dark alley between buildings, keeping tight to the wall, Boo Boo just behind them.

"Forget this guy," cried the medic. "You heard the boss. Time to evac!"

But Drac wasn't listening. He had fired his weapon and somehow missed the asshole. No way was he letting this meathead go. Besides, his identity might be valuable to the mission.

As he ran, he raised his pistol, tried to get another bead, but it was no good.

So he stopped dead. Took aim.

And fucking Boo Boo ran right into him, nearly knocked him over.

"Jesus, what?" hollered the medic. "You're letting him go!"

Drac cursed, took aim again, just as their man was about to round the corner about fifteen meters ahead.

The silenced weapon thumped, and the silhouette of their prey suddenly grew smaller, as though dematerializing into the ground.

But Drac knew better. "Got him that fucking time."

They sprinted ahead and reached the fallen man, who'd taken a round in the back, left side, near his heart. They rolled him over, his eyes growing vague, but he was still breathing. Boo Boo removed the pistol from their mystery man's grip.

"He ain't got long," said Drac.

"Who are you, motherfucker?" Boo Boo demanded.

The guy gasped, then his lips curled into a grin. "Fuck you, American cowboy. You are all doomed. I am your worst nightmare."

"Listen to fuckin' Rambo over here," grunted Boo Boo.

"Who you, uh, working for? Russians? You a fucking terrorist?" asked Drac.

Nikolai Tikhon grinned even more broadly at the Americans hovering over him. His mission had been accomplished. Yes, the call had come in. President Atayev was dead. TK was dead.

Yes, it would've been nice to live, collect his money from Petrov, spit in the man's face, then walk away. He could already hear Petrov calling after him, "We have another job for you! You can't leave!"

And he would curse the man who, like the military, had not fully appreciated his experience and talent.

Of course, two days later Petrov's men would force him at gunpoint to the office, and he would cut a deal for his next mission. Being reluctant often drove up the price, and once he understood the importance of the job—as he had with this one—his fee could double, even triple. Such was the way of the mercenary.

But no such luck now, shot up by the cowboys. No fucking justice, as they would say. But he would never show them his pain. He would smile until he couldn't.

"Forget this guy," said the shorter one, who pointed the pistol at his head.

"Leave no witnesses," said the taller one. "Then see if he's got an ID, maybe a phone."

Instead of waiting for the bullet, Tikhon imagined himself already in the afterlife, where his ex-wife waited, told him she forgave him for killing her, that it was all her fault.

But then she smiled, teeth like daggers, a silenced pistol held awkwardly in her hands.

She cursed him. He glanced down at the muzzle, saw a flash.

Drac tucked the cell phone into his pocket, along with the wallet. Assumedly, the ID was fake, but it would be of interest to Bibby.

"Should we go for the rifles?" Boo Boo asked, referring to the sniper rifles they'd hidden in the mausoleum before clearing the building.

"Boss'll have to write 'em off on his taxes," said Drac.

"All right, I'll call the boss while we boogie."

He and Boo Boo charged back down the alley, turned left, and nearly ran straight into one of the movie set's security guys, a kid no more than twenty-five.

"Shit, dude, we got one of them," Drac quickly told the guy, who was holding a Beretta.

Boo Boo was still on the phone talking with Mad Dog but reflexively raised his pistol at the crew guy. Drac slapped his hand down.

"You got one? Really? Where?" the kid asked.

"Right back there," said Drac. "Go!"

The kid nodded and charged off.

Drac and Boo Boo headed in the opposite direction, wary of the ledges and rooftops, of the shadows that gathered everywhere. Drac reached an alcove, ducked into it and paused.

"The boss sounds pissed," said Boo Boo, fighting for breath.

"Yeah. Hey, which way back to the chopper?"

"Fuck, I thought you knew."

"This place is a maze. You got the map?"

Boo Boo's expression soured. "You're kidding me. I thought you had it."

"Shit, I left mine back with the rifles." Drac stepped out of the alcove, looked up, whirled, spotted the towering minaret. "Wait. I think I know where we are. Come on."

Pope appreciated the order to get the hell out of Dodge, but the damn shooters who emerged on the roof of the mausoleum—the building Boo Boo and Drac had cleared—made the getting out part a real fucking pain in the ass.

They were taking all kinds of automatic and semiautomatic fire from three, maybe four shooters as they scooted along the roof, exploiting the parapet and balustrade for cover. If they didn't waste these assholes, Pope thought, then once he and Sapper got on the ground the two of them would be picked off at will.

Trouble was, Sapper was busy targeting the president's guardsmen, who were still down on the movie set, exchanging fire with both them and the other bad guys atop the mausoleum. Everyone was shooting at everyone. He almost smiled at the absurdity and irony of it all.

Pope dropped down behind a half-moon of stone, raised his H&K PSG1 and sighted one of the boneheads across the way. Damn, easy shot. *Boom!* But that sent the other guys scrambling for cover.

Shit, he and Sapper were running out of time. "Buddy, let's move!" he said, and they charged to the back of the madrassah, wrenched open an old wooden door, and ducked into the stairwell.

No doubt their rooftop friends would be waiting for them to emerge down below.

Sapper, who was hustling down the stairs just ahead, suddenly froze. A metallic noise, like metal thumping on stone, echoed from somewhere below. Then the burly black man came rushing back up like a mental patient whose gown had just been set on fire. "Go back!" he cried. "Fucking grenade!"

Pope turned and began taking the steps two at a time, but he'd only gone a few meters before the deafening explosion shook the entire stairwell.

Maruf had watched his brother, Tohir, die at the hands of the Americans. He balled his hands into fists and wanted to kill. Now.

He should not have acted like a coward, he told himself. TK had given his life for the cause, and what had he done? He had questioned everything, even accused his brother of making a mistake.

Tohir was dead. Maruf could hardly believe that. Only yesterday they had been playing as children in the fields, hiding from each other, making slingshots, shooting birds.

I'm sorry, my brother. I was wrong about you. I was wrong!

He would make sure that their remaining men would exact vengeance upon the Americans, upon anyone who got in their way. He had already moved his last two men toward the madrassah, with the mission of trapping the Americans on top.

Now, he would take on the old man, the woman, and the little man who had been holding the camera. They were keeping close to the walls, heading for the gate. He was only a few meters behind them. He pulled the pin on his last grenade, was about to throw it—

When a sharp pain ripped into his arm, the grenade tumbling from his grip.

Two realizations struck almost at once: He'd been shot . . . and the grenade at his feet was about to go off. With a loud gasp, he sprinted for the gate, winced as he waited for the explosion, but none came. *What?*

He was about to turn back when he spotted the trio ahead, dashing toward an idling helicopter. Despite his bleeding arm, he reached into his belt, withdrew his .45 and took aim.

"I can't see much through all the dust," Pope told Sapper as he edged back into the stairwell. "But it looks like we ain't getting out this way."

"Smart fuckers trapped us," said Sapper, who hunkered down near the door. "And it sucks for us that we got no ropes or carabiners. What you get for packing light."

Pope moved down several more stairs, drawing closer to the area where the metal railing began to twist at an improbable angle. Footfalls sounded from somewhere below, and in the distance people on the movie set were still shouting, crying, talking rapidly on cell phones, screaming for medics.

He squinted, searching for some path, finding only an empty patch of darkness where stairs should be. The air was clogged and reeking from the explosion, and his next breath made him cough—

Drawing gunfire from below, the shots ricocheting off the wall to his right.

He cursed, turned, shoved himself back, past the door and outside, where Sapper rose, darted to the ledge, looked down, spotted someone. Pope shouted a curse, fired, ducked back. "They're down there, all right."

"Funny thing is, they can't get up here."

"Wait a minute," said Pope. "This is about to get a whole lot worse. Fuck. We need Night to pick us up right here." He got on the radio.

Mad Dog couldn't hear much above the helicopter's thrumming turbine and whirring main rotor.

But he did hear something else. High-pitched. His name? Wait. He turned back from the helo's side door. It was Kat, screaming for him. Why? Maybe the adrenaline rush had blinded him for a moment.

Or maybe it was just the sand in his eyes—because it took another two seconds for him to spot Doolittle lying facedown in the dust.

Kat was already grabbing one of Doolittle's arms, trying to lift him.

Mad Dog thought of helping her, but instead looked up, his gaze burning through the rotor wash to find a lean young man dressed like one of the merchant extras. The man ran toward them, pistol in hand. Whether he worked for TK, the Russians, or the movie people hardly mattered.

The motherfucker was dead.

Dropping onto his belly then propping up on his elbow, Mad Dog raised his pistol and fired, his first round striking the man in the hip and knocking him down to the dirt.

But the kid wasn't finished. He crawled forward, raised his pistol, his mouth forming a scream as Mad Dog fired once more, hitting him the shoulder.

More gunfire resounded behind Mad Dog. He knew that was Kat, putting two more bullets in the guy's head before she resumed dragging Doolittle toward the chopper. Damn, her aim was even better than he realized.

Cursing through a groan, he burst to his feet, just as one of Atayev's guardsmen came bounding through the gate.

At the same time, Pope and Night Stalker were trading reports over the radio, something about Pope needing quick evac from the madrassah.

Ignoring that banter for now, Mad Dog fired a few rounds at the oncoming guardsman. He didn't hang back to see if he'd struck the guy but instead neared Kat and Doolittle, grabbed the translator's legs, and helped Kat carry their fallen comrade up and into the helo.

He must have missed the guardsman, he realized, because a round pinged off the bird's egg-shaped fuselage, and suddenly Bibby, pistol in hand, was firing past the door he had just swung open. The Brit was all fire and teeth and screaming for them to hurry.

"We have to check the wound!" cried Kat as she dragged the limp Doolittle onto a seat.

"He got a pulse?"

"I don't know yet!"

Bibby leaned over, slammed the side door shut. "Hang on!" The chopper left the ground, rose a few meters, then abruptly pitched forward.

"Jesus!" yelled Kat. "You're a pilot?"

"Bloody hell! I've got it!" Bibby throttled up, banked hard left and got them out of there.

Mad Dog glanced out the window, saw the guardsman lying in the dust, not far from the other guy, both men quickly swallowed in the swirling dust and gloom. Beyond them the movie set's powerful lights stood out even more prominently from the air, moths gathering near and flickering through the beams.

Then it was back to the moment, back to frantically removing Doolittle's shirt. No evidence of a gunshot wound on his chest. "Roll him over," ordered Mad Dog.

It was difficult maneuvering him in the narrow confines, but they managed, exposing two gunshot wounds on Doolittle's back. Kat checked his neck for a pulse, while Mad Dog grabbed his wrist.

"Anything?" she asked.

"Not yet."

"Hey, back there," called Bibby. "Not sure if you've been listening to the radio, but Pope and Sapper have been cut off."

Mad Dog tensed. "Say what?"

"They're trapped on the roof. Night Stalker's moving in to pick them up."

Mad Dog keyed his mike, called to Night Stalker, but the pilot cut him off with a curt, "Stand by!"

Then Mad Dog called to Pope, who couldn't talk, either: "Little busy right now, One! Waiting to fly the fuck out of here!"

"Hey, boss?" called Kat. Her voice grew tentative. "Lots of internal bleeding. We've, uh, we've lost him."

Mad Dog dug his hand behind Doolittle's head, held the man, wanted to say something, even just a word, but his mouth felt screwed shut, his stomach heaving, his heart stopped.

Kat looked at him. "I'm sorry."

He began shaking his head because he didn't want to believe that the lean Brazilian who had called him "Sergeant" all these years, the man who had been to hell and back with him, who had recently challenged him and who spoke to the animals and did it oh so well, was . . . gone.

And Mad Dog shook his head because he knew there was no time to grieve, and the shaking reminded him that he wouldn't succumb. Not now.

Kat squeezed his wrist. "Are you all right?"

"Yeah. Shit . . . Yeah."

Bibby banked hard again. "There's Night Stalker, heading toward the madrassah. And Mr. Hertzog? I've more news from London as well." Bibby's tone left nothing for the imagination.

"He's leaving without us?" cried Drac as they passed through the gates, only to watch Night Stalker guide the sleek MD600N over their heads, toward the city behind them.

"Great," Boo Boo groaned. "He's picking them up first."

"If he would've waited one more minute . . . shit!" Drac swore again, keyed his mike. "Blackhound Ten, this is Blackhound Eight. We're at the fucking gates! You just flew over us."

"Roger that, Eight. Hang tight. I'll be right back for you, over."

"What kind of Mickey Mouse shit is that!" barked Boo Boo, beating his fist on a tiled wall.

"All right, we're standing by, out." Drac sighed in frustration, cocked a brow at Boo Boo. "He likes them more than us. You should be more nice to the guy, you fucker."

"Blackhound Eight, this is One," called Mad Dog. Drac stiffened, hoping the boss wasn't about to deliver more bad news. "Just confirming your position. Stay put. And FYI: We've lost Blackhound Three, out."

Boo Boo closed his eyes. "Aw, this fucking job. Jesus Christ! You know he was in A'stan with the boss? Been with us since the beginning?"

"I know that," Drac snapped, setting his jaw against the grief welling in his gut. "I fucking know that." He began to stammer. "I—I—I know all the stories."

"Christ, poor Doolittle ain't the only guy down, either. Think about it. The president of this country was just assassinated. You know what'll happen now, don't you? Every military meathead and his mother will be breathing down our necks. Fucking air boys'll hit first." Panic crept into Boo Boo's voice. "Shit, we gotta get the fuck out of here!"

"Right now? What do you want to do? Walk?"

The medic bit his lip. "I don't want to die here."

"You got reservations somewhere else?"

"Matter of fact, I do. Cat house in Nevada. Me and a hooker named Honesty are gonna hump till I croak."

Drac grinned weakly and peered around the corner, past the gates toward the long, narrow street, where he saw at least four silhouettes and flashlights shifting about. "Look back there."

Boo Boo did. "Motherfucker. We are really having a bad day."

"You mean a bad night."

"Hey, look it up in your 'Beginner's Guide to the Care and Feeding of Mercenaries,' you wiseass fuck. And it'll only get worse."

"We should've gone back for the rifles."

"Fuck the rifles. Those assholes get close, no matter who they are, movie guys or not, we take them out. I don't care. We keep this LZ clear, you hear me?"

Drac removed his ball cap, the one with the movie's logo, and returned it to his head, brim facing backward. He shoved himself closer to the stone wall, raised his pistol and took aim at the silhouettes. "How many clips you got left?"

"Plenty, three."

"I think I got four. And I like the way you say 'plenty.'"

"Yeah, for now."

"Did Doolittle ever tell you about the little girl he adopted, the one who died with his ex-wife before he went to A'stan?"

"No, I never heard that."

"I'll tell you about her sometime."

Boo Boo darted to the other side of the gate and took up a mirror position, half-hidden beside the wall. Now they would communicate via hand signals.

Drac was about to indicate that one of the figures ahead had broken off from the group—

But a distant boom, accompanied by the steady thumping of a chopper, stole his attention.

"Oh, shit! Here comes another one," Sapper screamed as he ran along the parapet, then launched himself into the air—

As the grenade exploded off to his left, thankfully along the farthest wall.

Pope witnessed it all in high-definition, real life. You didn't need a remote control to watch this show, only an ass to kiss good-bye.

A long section of the stone and tile balustrade exploded into pieces, the debris hurtling at him, knocking him onto his back, Sapper crashing down beside him.

That was grenade number two. The assholes down below had gotten all creative. They had trapped their prey on the roof and then began lobbing grenades over the parapet.

They had shitty aim but decent ordnance. And who knew how many firecrackers they were packing?

Good news was, the absolutely beautiful sound of Night Stalker's turbine was drawing near, the wash already tugging on their clothes.

"Get up, you bastards, I'm right here," the pilot barked over the radio.

Pope was about to get up and tell the guy to scream himself when gunfire from below—directed at the chopper—sparked off the landing skids. If he and Sapper didn't haul ass now, one lucky shot might take down their ride.

Night Stalker did not disappoint, living up to his Black Hawk Down fame and experience. He brought the chopper in precariously close, the rotor less than a meter from one of the south side walls, and the skids never touched the ground as Pope and Sapper piled into the bird.

Even as Pope slammed the side door closed after he fell in, a grenade detonated just below, the concussion rattling through the chopper, fragments of metal and stone pinging off the fuselage, Night Stalker and Sapper cursing, Pope yelling for the pilot to go, go, go!

"Blackhound One, this is Blackhound Ten, over," called Night Stalker.

Mad Dog replied immediately. "Go ahead, Ten."

"I have recovered Four and Five, heading back to pick up the other two meatheads. Then we'll rendezvous in Urgench, over?"

"Negative, negative, negative," Mad Dog cried.

"Fuck . . . what now?" groaned Pope.

"What now, you ask?" hollered Night Stalker. "This is where we pucker up, boys. This is it."

Drac held his breath. The chopper was growing near, but so were the men carrying those flashlights.

The roaring turbine was drawing them to the gates, but maybe that was good. They'd have their attention focused on the sound and not on the men about to burst from the shadows.

"Hey, assholes, get ready, I'm coming in," said Night Stalker.

Damn, the volume on Drac's radio had somehow

rolled way up, and he feared the approaching men might have heard the tinny voice.

Bullshit. He was getting paranoid. The chopper's racket had concealed it.

Dust and sand began swirling behind them, and miniature tornadoes whipped up as Night Stalker guided the big helo down toward the clearing behind them—

And the men ahead, four of them now, came running toward the gates.

Boo Boo gave the signal.

Drac rushed out of the shadows, directly at the men, not bothering to stare into their faces before he pulled the trigger.

Chapter 9

....

Snick, snick . . .

Wolfgang felt something hard and wet against his cheek, felt vibrations from below course through his entire body, heard familiar-sounding men shouting to each other, along with the hookers, who muttered nervously in Tagalog.

Snick, snick . . .

He opened an eye, saw only shadows, netting, something sideways, a face?

Shit, he knew where he was now: lying on his gut inside the plane, his cheek stuck to the cold metal deck. He must have passed out.

Damn, that snicking again!

Had he finished that entire bottle of whiskey? God, his head throbbed. The spins came on until he took a deep breath, rolled over, and abruptly sat up.

Whoa. The world turned sideways again, then he felt level, a little nauseous, but okay.

Jesus, the old farts up front—Styles, Wilcox, and Zito—were still barking technobabble to each other, doing preflight checks or something, definitely freaking out.

Wolfgang wiped the drool from his face, scratched the stubble growing across his shaved head, then looked to the hookers. He swallowed, tasted something horrible, and for a moment his voice wouldn't work. Then the words finally came out, burred and broken: "Hey, bitches? What's going on?"

Both girls gave him the finger as they strapped themselves into their mesh seats. Suddenly, the plane's engines and hydraulic systems began their low-pitched start, the tones rising as they warmed up.

"We're leaving?" Wolfgang screamed. "What's going on?"

"Hey, American asshole?" called someone from behind.

Wolfgang turned, having forgotten about Mr. Pockmarked Face, the guard whose colleagues he had killed, the ugly bastard whose satellite phone began to ring. Wolfgang raised his chin to the man. "Fuck you."

"No, fuck you, American. I answer no more calls—unless I get girl." He wriggled his brows at the hookers, then added, "I don't fucking care you shoot me. Fuck you. I don't care no more."

The ringing phone was about to drive Wolfgang insane. He rose, staggered over to the seat beside Pockmarked Face, grabbed the phone, thumbed to accept. "Bend over, assholes, because you're all about to die." He hung up.

"We all will die," mimicked the asshole.

"You fucked up," shouted one of the hookers. "You very bad man. The boss maybe fires you now!"

"Shut up!"

The hooker narrowed her gaze, then shook her head. "You alcoholic. You got problems!"

Wolfgang gave her the bird, then screamed, "Styles! I want a sitrep right now!"

Gorlach, who had been dozing off inside the hangar, felt a hand on his shoulder. He snapped awake.

Mykola hovered over him, his eyes lost behind all that hair. "Something's happening."

Grabbing his night vision goggles, Gorlach rose and went to the hangar door. The racket was obvious. The C-130 was getting ready to take off, and a glance through the goggles only confirmed that.

Moreover, the *whomp-whomp-whomp* of helicopters in the distance could mean that the Americans were returning from Khiva.

Gorlach cleared his throat. "Tikhon did not call?"

"No," answered Mykola. "I tried to reach him . . . but nothing."

"Did you try the others? Ivanov?"

"Not yet."

"Try now. Tikhon is an old fool."

"You're wrong. You should respect him."

Gorlach lowered the goggles. "He probably got himself killed. Too bad. He'll miss the show."

With one hand patting the remote in his pocket, Gorlach smiled. Then he reached for his cigarettes. There should be time for a smoke before he moved into position.

Mykola, phone to his ear, gave a loud sigh. "Ivanov does not answer, either."

"Forget them. We do our job. And we collect from Petrov ourselves."

"Only Tikhon knows how to reach him."

"No. I answer directly to Petrov."

Mykola's eyes widened. "Does Tikhon know this?"

"Of course not, you naive fool. I made my own deal, as you should have."

"Maybe I did."

Gorlach chuckled. "If you expect to be paid, you will answer to me now, understood?"

Mykola's expression darkened, then he consulted his phone. "I will try Tikhon again."

"Forget that. Let's go to the Americans, see if they need our help." Gorlach's smile grew broader.

Drac and Boo Boo had taken out the four men before getting on board the chopper. That all four had been members of the production company's security team should not have bothered him, Drac thought. Yet after shooting them and realizing in that split second that he had just killed Americans, he felt sick to his stomach. Boo Boo had been right. It was worse. Shit.

At least they'd made it back to Urgench in one piece. But then again, not all of them.

The second they hit the tarmac, Night Stalker ordered them outside to begin loading his bird with extra fuel: forty-eight old-fashioned jerry cans, each holding five gallons. The cans were sitting on a pallet near one of the fuel trucks.

He, Drac, and Boo Boo formed a fuel brigade and passed the cans up the line, while Pope and Sapper made sure they were properly stacked inside the cabin.

Styles jogged down the ramp of the C-130 and ex-changed a few words with Mad Dog, who had Doolittle's body slung over his shoulder. He followed the pilot into the plane, while the rest of them stopped what they were doing to watch.

Bibby came over and cried, "What the fuck? Back to work! Uzbek forces are on their way! Load, load, load, you bloody fools!"

Kat was topping off her chopper's fuel tanks with the help of the fuel crew, then Drac assumed they would drive the truck around to Night Stalker's.

"You think the boss has a good escape plan?" asked Boo Boo.

Drac drew in a long breath. "No plan, as they say, ever survives the first enemy contact."

"Yeah," grunted Boo Boo. "Some shit."

Mad Dog buckled Doolittle's body into a seat, then told Wolfgang to wait a moment, that he wanted to speak with Styles in private. Wolfgang made a face and backed off.

"I think I know what you have in mind," Styles began, slapping a palm on Mad Dog's shoulder. "We'll head north toward the Aral Sea, get 'em off your ass."

"And you're all right with that?"

The old pilot rolled his eyes. "No, I'm not fucking all right with that, but we got no choice. So that's the way it is. Blaze of glory time. Shit, it beats dying on the toilet. Just ask fucking Elvis."

"If they order you down, just obey. Don't fuck with them. You don't have to die."

"And you'll come back for us? Don't promise that."

"So you're thinking this is a one-way."

"Maybe I can get us over the border before they shoot us down. Maybe that would help."

Mad Dog got choked up. "Christ, Gerry, I'm sorry."

"Fuck. Get out of here." The pilot shoved him.

Mad Dog turned back for Wolfgang, who kept asking what had happened to Doolittle, what was happening now.

It was frustrating enough ordering a dear friend to fly into oblivion, but to have a screw-up with bloodshot eyes, a whiny tone, and an attitude suddenly in your face—

Mad Dog snapped.

"You? You let me down, motherfucker!" He locked fingers around Wolfgang's throat and shoved him into another seat. "You fucked up big-time. What is wrong with you?"

"I don't know."

"Should I end your pathetic fucking life right now? Huh, kid? Huh?"

"Please . . . "

After a hard squeeze, Mad Dog released the man, eyes burning, drool brimming his lips. He tanked down air. "We're done. If we make it back, you'll collect your cut, pack your bags, and go the fuck home, understood?"

"This is bullshit. You wasted me on this plane, now you're punishing me for that?"

Mad Dog raised a fist. "Dude, you're from another planet. And I don't have time for this. Now you go outside and get those bodies out of the wheel wells, dump 'em on the tarmac, then you sit in that fucking seat, shut up, and enjoy the fucking ride . . . "

"Why aren't we loading the choppers?"

"Shut the fuck up and do your job!"

Mad Dog swept himself out of the plane and back toward Kat's chopper.

He felt a pang of guilt over what he was doing, but knew he couldn't dwell on it. Wolfgang had no idea that getting fired was the least of his worries. Sure, he could have Wolfgang ride along with them, but he had to think of the rest of the team, and a liability was better left behind.

God, forgive me.

Bibby toggled through the data rippling across his computer screen. There were no surprises. They had expected a strong response from the Uzbek military, and they were getting just that: rotary and fixed-wing aircraft were lifting off from K2, and no, they weren't on some coincidentally timed training mission.

Mad Dog joined him inside the chopper. "So what's the good news?"

"Mr. Hertzog, you're fucking insane."

"Keep telling me that. One day I might believe it. So we die with smiles on our faces." He peered down at Bibby's computer. "How's it looking?"

Bibby rapped a knuckle on the laptop screen. "It's looking spectacular."

"It can't be that bad."

Brows raised, Bibby tsked. "We, sir, are fucked."

"We wouldn't want it any other way. Now you said your contacts at MI6 confirmed the old Russian colonel's story, and that Saratova is definitely a Russian mole. I assume they've contacted Langley?"

"They have. Got the deputy director himself out of bed and on his way into the office. Catfish is already on his way there for what I'm sure will be a most interesting meeting."

"Perfect. You think this will work?"

"I think we'd be fools not to try . . . "

Mad Dog's old high school buddy turned Harvard grad lawyer Bryan Johnson, aka "Catfish," knew his way around the CIA better than some agents did. And the deputy director was about to receive a new rectum, courtesy of Catfish.

At the very least their friendly neighborhood attorney would "persuade" the CIA to help with the team's exfiltration out of Uzbekistan.

At the most, Catfish would blackmail the Agency out of some serious cash so that IPG would not go public with the name of Moscow's sleeper running the Asia desk for the past eight years. Wouldn't that be fucking embarrassing for the Central *Intelligence* Agency?

Coming out of that Washington restaurant, Mad Dog thought he'd landed the big one: up front payment, a toehold into future business with the guys with the deepest pockets of all, and tons of unaccounted for cash. In fact, Saratova had been *drooling* to give him the money. She played him like a fucking balalaika. She knew—Moscow knew—that if he took the cash, he was in. The two million was to guarantee he merely showed up in Uzbekistan to put on a convincing show.

Now, according to Bibby's friends in London, Moscow Center was about to expose the J-U2 plot, the CIA's presence, and his own contract complete with documentation of deposit at IPG, London.

And worse, Bibby's sources had learned that Moscow had documentation that he, as the CIA's agent in the field, paid TK to make the hit.

That's right, he and his team were being identified as CIA field agents who hired a terrorist to kill Atayev.

Talk about a holy shit moment.

Consequently, the U.S. was about to be irreparably discredited in the region—and all because Moscow Center wanted Atayev taken out so they could maneuver their own candidate into the presidency, a candidate who was not sympathetic to the U.S., one who would not re-open K2 to American forces.

So those cunning Russkies had devised a complicated plan to accomplish this goal while simultaneously burning the U.S.—and his company—in the interim.

Mad Dog rubbed his weary eyes. "Mr. Bibby, I hope that if our dear friends at the CIA fail to make amends, your friends in London will come through."

Bibby gave a weak grin. "Only mad dogs and Englishmen go out in the midday sun."

"Who said that?"

"You don't know? You uncultured swine."

The pilot's door swung open, and Kat levered herself inside. She donned her radio headset and began conversing with Night Stalker and Styles, who was getting ready to bug out himself.

"How we doing, Kat?" Mad Dog asked, donning a headset.

"Got a full tank. Reserves are loaded. Fuel guys were a little curious, but pretty helpful. Everything else is looking good. No weather issues, though there's a rumor that air traffic could get a little dense."

"No fucking shit. Let's get out of here, sweetheart."

"Yes, Daddy."

"Blackhounds, this is Blackhound One," Mad Dog called over the team radio. "No matter what they say

about you, you guys are the fucking best. See you when
I see you. Blackhound One, out . . . "

God, that sounded like good-bye . . . forever.

Gorlach was inside the near-empty fuel truck and in position, ready to detonate the C4. He watched the two helicopters lift off first, then lit up another cigarette as the
C-130 taxied along the tarmac.

Meanwhile, Mykola, who sat beside him, was still trying
to call Tikhon or Ivanov to tell them that the Americans had
split up, that yes, they would take care of the plane, but the
two choppers were now airborne and heading south. Tikhon had no doubt assumed that the choppers would be dis-
mantled, loaded back onto the plane, and that all of the
Americans would be on board for the big party/explosion.

"You're trying to contact a dead man," Gorlach said.

"I will keep trying."

"Whatever you like."

The C-130 turned onto a runway, and its mighty turbo-
prop engines rumbled. Gorlach zoomed in with his night
vision goggles as the plane began to roar down the runway, flaps fully extended. He focused on the right wing,
where he had planted the block of C4, and imagined the
detonator making its glorious spark.

"Mykola, get off the phone and watch."

"No! And you should not smoke in here!"

Gorlach smiled and continued studying the plane. For
a moment he thought he saw something drop away from
the wing.

No, it couldn't be. Impossible.

It was just his imagination.

He removed the detonator from his pocket—

As the C-130's landing gear left the ground.

Near Rock Creek Park
Georgetown, D.C.
0620 Hours Local Time

After another sleepless night, Dr. Galina Saratova was on her way to the office in a heavy storm, the Lexus's wipers barely able to compete with the downpour. Traffic was light, the road ahead empty.

She reached to turn on the stereo, thought better of it. The silence gave her more time to reflect. Her father was safe in London. She wondered how long Moscow Center would ask her to remain in the United States. She wanted so badly to run that she could taste it, but they had been insistent. Remain in position. Her disappearance would, of course, set off alarms, but it might end her trembling.

At least she had prepared. She knew, of course, that her assets would be frozen the moment the Agency suspected her of any wrongdoing; thus, she had devised a plan.

Mr. Hertzog's Myanmar mission had not only educated her about his capabilities, but also taught her about the market and demand for gem quality jade.

I don't know what came over me, but I thought it'd be nice to have something like this. I had to go to San Francisco to buy it, but I just love it. You wouldn't believe what I paid, but really, it's the only nice piece of jewelry I own. And I thought we could talk about jade, if all else failed.

Sure, she had fed Hertzog a line, but most of it had been true, except the "I don't know what came over me" crap. Oh, yes, she'd known exactly why she had bought the necklace:

Those few grams represented a secure future for her

and her father—and an easily portable and readily convertible "emergency" cash fund should the need arise to flee the country.

The cash outlay had been enormous, but was handily offset by converting less than twenty-five percent of her vast illiquid assets. Her feeling of increased security became tangible each time she fondled the cold green orbs. She reached for her neck, wishing she'd worn the necklace, but she kept it hidden inside a cleverly concealed wall safe at home.

She sighed and turned on the radio, hoping NPR would have something interesting to report.

In fact, they did.

The president of Uzbekistan had just been assassinated.

And an American film crew led by Phillip Steinberg himself had witnessed it.

Her cell phone rang, as if on cue. She checked the ID—one of her subordinates at the office, agitated by the news, no doubt.

All right. Everything had happened according to plan, and now, she assumed, it was time for Moscow Center to pull her out.

She sent the call directly to voice mail, then squinted ahead at the bright lights piercing through the windswept showers.

As she drew closer, two pairs of lights became distinct—headlights.

Two cars blocking the road.

She gasped, slowed to a stop, then immediately threw the car in reverse, cut the wheel, drove over the grass and sidewalk, only to find two more cars blocking her path.

Before she could decide whether to plow right through

them, four men wearing balaclavas and dressed in black trench coats were outside her windows, pistols trained on her.

One rapped on the window, motioned for her to get out.

Oh my God. Who are they? Please let them be from Moscow, come to extract me.

She tensed and reached for the door.

Leaving Urgench Airport
Uzbekistan
2130 Hours Local Time

Wolfgang felt a slight vibration ripple through the plane, which resulted in a whole lot of talk coming from the cockpit. He unbuckled and dragged himself up there. Wilcox and Zito gave him dirty looks, their faces glowing dimly from the cockpit instrumentation. Styles didn't bother looking back.

"What's going on?" Wolfgang demanded. "I thought I felt something."

"Go sit down and shut up," barked the old pilot.

"Fuck you, Grandpa. I want answers."

"Tell the asshole," said Wilcox, who'd unbuckled and come up behind Wolfgang.

"Fine. We got a wing fire. Fuel line must've ruptured. Don't know if those fuel guys fucked with us or what."

"Well, put out the fucking fire!"

"Sorry, asshole, we can't," said Zito from his copilot's seat. "We can't get enough airspeed. It's only a matter of time before the fire spreads."

"So what're you saying?"

No one answered.

"Fuck this! We have to go back! Land this piece of shit!"

"Go sit down," said Styles.

Wolfgang grabbed the pilot by the back of the neck. "What are you doing?"

Zito drew his sidearm, raised it to Wolfgang's head. "We're not fucking with you anymore. Sit down. Or I'll splatter your head all over this cockpit. Boss won't give a shit, trust me."

"Kid, listen to me," Styles began, his tone softer. "We're going to fly north for as long as we can. Then we'll bail out. We're going to keep them off the boss's ass. That's our job. And by God, we'll do it."

Wolfgang's mouth fell open. Jesus Christ, it'd been a long time since he'd thrown himself out of a burning plane; in fact all of them had been perfectly good aircraft.

At least the fire made bailing out justifiable. Fuck!

"What about the hookers and that other asshole?"

Zito made a face. "That ugly bastard? Fuck him. We got chutes for the girls, but without training . . . they'll be lucky to make it."

"Shit." Something occurred to Wolfgang, something that sent him back into a rage. "The boss knew all along this'd be a one-way ride."

"No, he didn't," Styles shot back.

"Bullshit! We're drawing their air defenses north, then if they forced us down, we'd be taken prisoner."

"It wouldn't come to that, trust me."

"Get out of here," ordered Zito. "You want to don your chute, go ahead. Help the girls while you're at it."

"You guys are ready to die, aren't you?"

They didn't answer.

"Well, fuck you! I'm not!"

As stunned as he was seething, Wolfgang drifted back to the hold, but then turned and looked at Pockmarked Face, who cursed him.

But taunts from a dead man meant nothing to him. He went over to the hookers, whose attitudes had vanished. Perhaps they'd overhead the conversation.

"Something wrong with the plane?" asked one.

Wolfgang nodded. "I'm going to show you guys how to put on a parachute."

They began rattling off frantic words in Tagalog, their eyes welling with tears.

"Hey, bitches, calm down! I'll be right back." Wolfgang went off to fetch the chutes, the hold growing warmer, the stench of fuel thick in the air.

Gorlach sat in the truck, utterly devastated. The charge had fallen off! Perhaps he had created a small wing fire with the detonator, but he was supposed to blow off that entire wing and send the plane screaming toward the ground, dragging a long smoke tail filled with fire.

Instead, the C-130 had banked hard, gained attitude, and was heading . . . north?

Yes, north. A decoy, while the others escaped south, toward Afghanistan, no doubt.

"What happened?" Mykola asked.

"Shut up!"

Gorlach started the fuel truck's engine, threw it in gear, then floored it, heading back toward the hangar.

"You failed to blow up the plane. I don't believe it," said Mykola. "You failed!"

Gorlach tugged the pistol from his belt, and before his

arm was fully extended, put a bullet in Mykola's head, blood jetting across the glass.

"And now I am the only one left," Gorlach said aloud. "The only one to collect from Petrov."

What would he do with all of that money? Hookers? Drugs? Booze? All of that. And more.

He headed toward their plane, whose pilot was standing by to whisk him back to Moscow.

Kat's Chopper
Approximately 90 Miles South
Urgench Airport
2145 Hours Local Time

Mad Dog and his team were flying low, trying to make good time, but Night Stalker's chopper, loaded down with the extra fuel, kept their airspeed near or around 100 knots. Not good. He had just gotten off the radio with Styles, who now had a fucking wing fire, cutting short the amount of time he had in the air. They would fly as far as they could, then bail out.

As Mad Dog sat there, thinking about Doolittle and watching Bibby on his laptop, he realized he couldn't just abandon Styles and the rest of them like that.

"Hey, Kat? It's all desert down there, huh?"

"Yeah, some rolling hills, deep ravines cut through here and there."

"Can you find us someplace secluded, good cover, where we can put down?"

"Excuse me?" cried Bibby, glancing up from his computer.

"We still have about eight hours of darkness left."

"Exactly, which is why we need to make fucking haste for the border," said Bibby.

"Kat, you find a place to put down. Tell Night Stalker to follow your lead, you got it?"

"Yes, sir."

"Does the phrase 'acceptable losses' mean anything to you?" asked Bibby.

"Mr. Bibby, unfortunately for you, I spent most of my life as a United States Marine. We don't accept losses. We don't leave people behind."

"Then why did you order them north in the first place?"

"Because I was trying to forget. And I just fucking can't. So we put down. We wait and see what happens to them. And if we have to wait it out before we can go back, then we do. But we will try to bring them back."

"Well, if your little guilt trip doesn't get us killed, then perhaps the extra time will allow the Agency and my friends to get their resources into place."

"See, now you're looking on the bright side, old chap."

"Yes, I loathe being the prophet of doom all the time, but you don't make it any easier for me, especially when these radar images Big Booty just sent look so fucking bleak."

Mad Dog studied the computer screen. At least a dozen contacts were heading north, chasing after Styles and crew.

"All right, here we go," announced Kat, taking the chopper into a dive. "Nice ravine ahead, good cover on both sides, putting us below the horizon, too. Like lying in a ditch, I love it."

"Have you considered what this little rescue mission will cost us in fuel?" Bibby asked.

"That's why you're the math guy. Make it happen."

Just then Styles's voice broke over the radio. "Blackhound One, we can't hold out any longer. We have to bail. I'll contact you when we're on the ground, over."

"Roger that. Godspeed, Mother Dog. Godspeed."

Chapter 10

....

C-130 Hercules
Heading North Toward Nukus
2205 Hours Local Time

Wolfgang strained every muscle in his arms as he opened one of two heavy paratroop doors near the back of the plane. The door worked on a counterbalance system and had to be pinned open. Minutes ago he had consulted Styles and chosen the door on the opposite side of the burning wing, which was now fully engulfed in flames. After a significant shove, the door locked into place with a muffled clink.

Out beyond the plane lay a mottled wall of dark clouds and lavender-colored sky. Below, a billion shadows blurred by. They were goddamned low—cruising at 1,000 feet—trailing long plumes of smoke, the plane beginning to shudder violently. Styles had said the fire would quickly spread to one of the engines, which could explode.

Time to go bye-bye.

Even with his helmet on, the wind roared and chilled

Wolfgang, and suddenly his heart either skipped a beat or his chest had gone numb. "All right, this is it!" he cried. Shit, he was no jumpmaster, hardly remembered the protocol, but who the hell cared? Getting out was getting out!

Styles, Wilcox, and Zito were geared up and good to go. They had their static lines attached to the metal ring of the strop suspended from the metal cable above their heads. They had finished checking each other's chutes and made sure their static lines were correctly fitted to the strop.

Then they did likewise for the hookers, who were trembling, hands to their mouths, crying, saying they wouldn't jump.

"Do you want to die?" Wolfgang screamed. "You're going to jump. You'll be okay."

Until you hit the ground, that is.

Wolfgang hollered that he would be last out, making sure the girls didn't panic at the last second.

"Go ahead!" he told the crew.

Not one of them protested.

Farther up the hold, Pockmarked Face, still cuffed to his seat, was hollering at the top of his lungs, begging to come, his voice nearly indistinct.

And for just a few seconds Wolfgang entertained the idea of saving the man. After all, in the grand scheme, the guy was just a flunky guard who had been in the wrong place at the wrong time. But the fuck could turn into a major liability on the ground, so screw him.

After Styles, Zito, and Wilcox bailed out of the plane and their chutes unfurled, Wolfgang shoved the first hooker out of the plane. The second, the one with the long purple nails, screamed, "No!"

"Look at me!" he cried. "Look at me."

Finally, she did, her eyes swollen. God, she was so young, maybe twenty, but she looked fourteen, standing there, crying.

"What's your name?"

"I can't go. No jumping!"

"I said, *what's your name?*"

"My name is Imelda."

Wolfgang nearly smiled. Imelda, as in Marcos, as in the woman with all the shoes, wife of that big shot Ferdinand who ruled the Philippines for a while. No doubt Imelda was this poor girl's professional name. "Listen to me, sweetheart, you're going to have a nice ride!"

With that, he forced her out of the plane. Her scream echoed off into the wind as her static line snapped tight, her chute opened, and off she went.

He tossed a glance back into the plane, saw Doolittle's body strapped into a seat. Poor fucking guy. No burial now. Just a cremation.

Snick . . . snick . . .

Christ, not now!

Wolfgang staggered toward the door, glanced out, and suddenly his knees buckled and he shrank to the deck.

But he hadn't passed out. Not entirely. He still heard the engine, smelled the fuel, but he couldn't catch his breath, couldn't breathe at all. He just lay there, inert, groping for the energy to move.

He felt trapped inside the plane, as though the paratroop door had slammed shut.

And maybe for a few seconds, a minute or more, he did black out.

"*Hey, Teddy, I think Wolfy's dead! Hurry! Hurry!*"

"I'm gonna go get my mom!"

"No, stay here and help me!"

"Oh, no, he really looks dead!"

I'm not dead.

Wolfgang's eyes snapped open.

I'm in a fucking burning plane, about to crash! Bail out, motherfucker!

He checked his watch. Oh my God. Three minutes had passed since Styles and the crew had jumped.

His body wracked with chills, Wolfgang threw himself into the hands of God.

Did the chute open?

It didn't!

It did!

He glanced up—

Beautiful, billowing white waves for a second and multiple pops, then he was wrenched up and away . . . Once he settled down and had control, he checked his wrist altimeter.

Only eight hundred feet until he hit the ground, and he was floating rather gently.

So he just hung there, staring at the massive plane as she plunged harder and faster toward the dark plains in the distance.

One of her engines burst apart in a shower of flames and sparking debris, sending her into a roll and a steeper plunge, more flames whipping.

And then, just a few moments later, a huge explosion rose like an erupting volcano from the desert floor, lighting up the night sky and drawing sharp orange edges around the clouds. The light flickered as the flames swelled across the horizon, then slowly began to die.

Wolfgang looked around. Checked the altimeter. One hundred feet. He was about to land in the middle of nowhere.

Snick . . . snick . . .

Chopper Landing Site
Approximately 100 Miles South
Urgench Airport
2207 Hours Local Time

Kat and Pope carried a pair of jerry cans over to her helicopter. Night Stalker was topping off his tanks as well, while Sapper, Boo Boo, and Drac were setting up a perimeter, and Mad Dog and Bibby sat inside the chopper, hunched over the Brit's laptop, gathering more intelligence.

The temperature had dropped ten, maybe fifteen degrees, cool but not cold, but the slight wind still chilled her.

"You all right?" Pope asked as she shuddered.

"I'm not shaking because I'm scared."

"Oh, trust me, lady, I never thought that."

"Smart man."

Pope attached the nozzle to the fuel can. "So how you liking the job so far?"

"It's okay. But I think we're supposed to get a fifteen minute break every four hours. I'll have to talk to management about that. I could've sworn this was a union shop."

He cracked a slight grin. "Damn straight. And hey, you smell really good."

She narrowed her gaze. "Don't go there, big guy."

"I wasn't. I just like the smell of fuel."

She smiled. "Idiot."

He shrugged, then lowered his voice. "I wish I got to know you better."

"Why's that?"

"I'd feel worse when you die."

"Gee, thanks. And hey, despite that remark, you're okay guy—Barbie doll notwithstanding."

He frowned. "Who told you about that?"

"I already got to know you better." She winked.

"Blackhounds, this is One," Mad Dog announced over the radio. "Just got word. Mother Dog and his boys are on the ground!"

C-130 Hercules Crew
Southeast of Nukus
2210 Hours Local Time

Gerald Styles had made a perfect parachute landing fall, distributing the shock along his feet, calves, hips, and shoulders. His chin had been tucked in, and he'd grasped the risers in an arm bar, protecting his face and throat. He had executed the PLF to the right front, based upon the terrain, wind, and oscillation. Then, after the fall, he expertly detached his chute.

It had all come back to him, like the breast stroke or riding a bike. Instinct took over, and he had never felt anything better than that coarse sand spraying up into his face as he thudded onto a dune.

Too bad Zito hadn't been as lucky. His chute opened late, and he'd been unable to bleed off descent speed.

"Fuck," the copilot groaned as Styles attended to him. "I broke 'em both, didn't I?"

Styles had seen open fracture wounds before, but

the penlight made them appear all the more ghastly. He knew his basic first aid, but he'd need help. Wilcox was off trying to find the two hookers and the drunken asshole. "Just relax, buddy. Nice deep breaths. You don't want to panic. You're not bleeding too bad. Only one of them is open. We'll get you out of here. Don't worry."

Just then Wilcox came hurrying forward, one of the hookers just behind him. "Hey, Gerry? Imelda's all right, but the other girl . . . "

"Shit."

"She was all wrapped up in her chute when I found her. You want me to go back for the body?"

"I need you here. Get out your kit."

Imelda began sobbing, and Wilcox seized her by the hands. "Easy, honey. We'll be all right." He looked up at Zito. "How's he doing?"

"Broke 'em both."

"God damn, now what?" Wilcox asked as he dug the first aid kit out of his pack. "This boss coming to pick us up?"

"That's not the plan."

"Yeah, but he didn't expect us to lose the fucking plane! We had a good lead on them. We might've—"

Styles sighed heavily. "What about the asshole? You hear from him?"

"Nope?"

"But you saw his chute, right?"

Wilcox shook his head, glanced to Imelda. "Did you see another man coming down?"

She wiped off tears, shook her head.

Styles laughed under his breath. "No fucking loss there."

Wolfgang's Landing Site
150 Nautical Miles North of Choppers
2216 Hours Local Time

Though he got the wind knocked out of him, Wolfgang was happy to refamiliarize himself with solid ground. He got right to work, sloughing off his harness and pack and fishing out his satellite phone, the keypad glowing green as he placed an encrypted call to Mad Dog.

At the same time, he fired up his portable GPS so he could feed the boss his exact location.

Somewhere in the distance came the drone of jet engines, along with the drumming rhythm of rotors.

His gaze shot to the left, where the ground dipped, maybe a ditch, a little cut or something. He jogged over, dropped down what seemed a long crack in the ground, and heard Mad Dog calling him.

"Yeah, boss, it's me. Fucking plane went down—"

"Shut up. I know. Where the fuck are you?"

"Give me a second. Waiting on the GPS. So, uh, where are you guys? Still heading south?"

"Negative. We've put down."

"Shit, what happened? Oh, man, is one of the choppers—"

"Just shut up and tell me where you are."

"No problem." Wolfgang ticked off the coordinates, then Mad Dog told him to stand by.

All right. Time to do the math. He remembered the three-minute rule taught to him by a crusty old navy warrant officer he'd met a bar in the Philippines. If you know the speed (in knots) of a moving object, just tack two zeros on the back end, and that's the distance (in yards) that object travels every three minutes.

He had jumped three minutes behind the others. The plane was moving at 200 knots. Add two zeros to the 200, and that gave him 20,000 yards. Since there were 2,000 yards in each nautical mile, he was ten nautical miles farther north than the rest of the guys.

He also knew he needed to move west or east to get off the baseline between the end of the runway and where the plane went down. The Uzbeks would be searching every inch along that path.

"All right, asshole, you put down about a hundred fifty nautical miles north of us. You need to get as far away from that crash site as possible."

"Roger that. And I just figured out I'm about ten nautical miles farther north than where Styles and the rest of the crew should be, which of course makes me the farthest man from home. Some fucking luck. You hear from the other guys?"

"Zito broke his legs. Lost one of the girls. But otherwise they're all right."

"So . . . the million dollar question. When are you coming for us?" Wolfgang closed his eyes, tensed.

"Soon."

"You're not coming, are you . . . at least not for me."

"Look asshole, start walking. Right angles. Get off that fucking baseline, you know the drill."

Wolfgang swallowed, nodded. "Roger that. See you soon. And, uh, I'm sorry about—"

"Forget it. We'll talk back home at the pound. Get moving."

"But I'm still fired."

Mad Dog had already ended the call.

"Yeah, I'm still fired," Wolfgang muttered aloud, then squinted into the distance.

Mostly flat to rolling sandy desert lay beneath a mantle of brilliant stars. In fact, he could see the band of the Milky Way.

He would've smiled were it not for the *snick . . . snick . . .* in his head.

He tucked his GPS and satellite phone into his ruck, slung the pack over his shoulder, then withdrew the .45 from his hip holster. He started walking, his breath hanging in the air.

The sounds of those jets and choppers grew louder, and the thought of being captured sent a shudder up his spine.

He tensed. *Stop thinking so much, asshole.* He chanced a look back over his shoulder, toward the crash site, columns of smoke still risking from a cloud of black smoke pinpricked with light. He quickened his pace.

C-130 Hercules Crew
Southeast of Nukus
2230 Hours Local Time

Just ten minutes ago Gerald Styles had spied a single light at ground level coming from the northwest, in the general direction of Nukus. Now, as he looked again, that light was on the same bearing but obviously closer. What the fuck? Constant bearing plus decreasing range equaled collision course! He hollered to Wilcox, and they began scanning 360 degrees with their night vision goggles.

"Wait a second," said Styles, bolting to his feet. He whirled around, studied the ground more closely. Being out in the middle of nowhere, at night, had done a fine job concealing the fact that they were, holy crap, actually sitting beside a dirt road running straight through the desert.

"I can see him now," said Wilcox. "Fucking truck. Russian Tatra 805. Old piece of shit with a rag top over the bed. Only one headlight's working. They'll be here in a couple of minutes."

"And our chopper won't."

"Maybe this is our ride out," the loadmaster suggested.

"No shit, young man. I'd buy that plan for a dollar."

"Or maybe that fucking truck is full of soldiers, and we should duck out, let 'em pass on by."

"Are you trying to convince me to sit here all night, wondering what we should do?"

"I don't know."

"Then shut the fuck up. They're heading away from the crash site. They ain't military. We're taking that truck. Period."

Just behind them, Imelda was trying to comfort Zito, who was lying across a few pieces of driftwood tied together to form a makeshift stretcher. He was shivering through his breath and fading in and out of consciousness. The piece of wood between his teeth threatened to snap. Styles and Wilcox had cleaned the open wound and realigned his fractured bone the best they could. They had also immobilized both of his legs, but that's all they could do for now. He needed medical attention pronto.

"All right," Styles said. "Let's run ahead. Leave her back here, then if it gets hairy, she doesn't freak out and get herself shot."

"Good. And Gerry, I just want you to know what a pleasure it's been."

"I love you, too, asshole. Now come on. I'm having a grand old time. And it's only going to get better!"

Styles wasn't lying. Hell, if he was going to die, he might as well make his last few hours count. And if he lived, what a fucking story he'd have to tell!

After assuring Imelda that they'd be right back, they jogged about a fifty yards ahead, then Wilcox lay in the road while Styles stood over him, waving his hands as the Tatra approached and came to a squeaky halt about five yards ahead.

Styles moved toward the driver's side door, one hand reaching into his belt to withdraw the .45 tucked into the small of his back. Weapon in hand, he raised his arm as the driver hopped down—

And Wilcox sprang to his feet, pistol at the ready.

"Don't fucking move!" cried Styles, about to fire— until he got a good look at the driver.

The kid couldn't have been more than ten or twelve, dressed in jeans with holes in the knees and wearing a black, long-sleeve AC/DC concert shirt. He looked like a spike-haired punk from Boston dropped into the middle of Central Asia.

"Jesus . . . " gasped Wilcox.

"Over here," Styles told the kid, gesturing to the front of the truck and into the better light.

"Got another one inside," cried Wilcox.

"And watch the back," added Styles. Who knew how many more guys—or children, for that matter—could be hiding beneath the truck's covered bed?

"Okay, don't shoot," said the kid in a heavy accent. "Are you Americans?"

"Shut up. Over here."

"Got an old one," hollered Wilcox. "Listen to us very carefully and you won't get shot!"

Wilcox's prisoner was, in fact, about seventy or eighty, hunched back, with a long, white beard and thick spectacles. Friggin' Santa Claus was dressed in a tattered woolen coat, threadbare slacks, and wearing a genuine *ushanka*, the fur hat with upturned ear flaps often donned by the Russian military. He was grunting something to the boy, looking pissed off and trying to backhand away Wilcox's pistol as though it were a fly.

"My grandfather wants to know who you are," said the kid. "He wants to know if you came from the plane crash."

Damn, the kid's English was even better than Styles had thought. "Tell your grandfather to calm down. We ask the questions. Wilcox? Check the back for more of them . . ."

The loadmaster complied as Styles crossed to the old man, keeping both him and the kid in his sights. Grandpa kept barking at the kid, who winced under the commands.

"You tell him what I said?" Styles asked the kid.

"Yeah, he's like totally freaking out now."

"Where'd you learn to speak like that?"

"At K2. I used to have a lot of friends there, American Air Force guys. They taught me English."

"No shit."

"Hey, Gerry? Get back here. You have to see this."

Chopper Landing Site
Approximately 100 Miles South
Urgench Airport
2235 Hours Local Time

Mad Dog and Bibby had reasoned that most if not all of the air support would be coming from the south, from K2, and according to their latest intel dump, that air traffic was moving directly east of their position, headed north toward the crash site. If they let Night Stalker lift off and go after Wolfgang and the crew now, there was a good chance they'd be picked up by one or more of those aircraft.

So they would remain in the ravine for a few more minutes, maybe thirty, until most of that traffic was north of Wolfgang's position, then initiate Operation Save Our Buddies' Asses.

Mad Dog called over Pope and Kat, and, in the faintest light provided by Bibby's laptop, explained why they were sitting tight, while Drac, Sapper, Boo Boo, and Night Stalker listened in over the radio, never leaving their posts along the perimeter. Bibby, meanwhile, took a call from the States, from Catfish.

"I know we have to stay," Pope said after Mad Dog finished. "But if we wind up flying in broad daylight, well . . ."

"If we don't wait, we could get picked up anyway. Yeah, I know it's a calculated risk."

Pope nodded. "I'm not bitching. I'd do the same. Just keep your eye on the clock is all I'm saying."

"We will."

"I'll get back up to the edge, help 'em keep an eye." Pope walked off.

"You got him trained well," said Kat, wriggling her brows.

"I sent 'em all to obedience school, but most of 'em got kicked out."

"You know, sometimes you're pretty smart for a jar-head."

"Or just an old fart who gets lucky."

"You're not that old."

He shrugged. "I feel like a hundred. I feel like the longer we sit here, the older I get. Just wears on you, you know?"

She took a deep breath, pursed her lips in thought.

"Do you need something?"

She removed her hair tie, let her blond locks flow freely over her shoulders. "No. If we wind up waiting here longer, we should break out the camo netting, tuck in the birds safe and sound."

"Yeah, we will." God, in the half-light she was even more stunning. He began to lose his breath, felt like a green Marine at boot camp: young, dumb, and full of cum. "Can you stop that?"

She frowned. "What?"

"With your hair . . . just please."

"You want me to tie it back up? Do I look unprofessional?"

Was she being honest, coy, or what?

Who cared? He was about to tell her that she looked incredible, that he'd like to have her right then and there—or maybe something a little less obvious—when Bibby got off the phone and walked over, causing Kat to mutter some excuse about the chopper and hustle off.

"Mr. Hertzog, in the midst of all this, there is a glimmer of good news. It seems your old high school buddy has come through for us."

C-130 Hercules Crew
Southeast of Nukus
2238 Hours Local Time

Styles had climbed up into the truck, reached into one of the crates and withdrawn an unlabeled bottle filled with a clear liquid. No huge mystery there.

Grandpa and grandson were not in the bottled water business.

And Styles proved that by unscrewing the cap, taking a sip, and grimacing.

The old man didn't like that. Fuck him.

"We got us a couple of moonshiners," said Wilcox.

Styles replaced the cap, tossed the bottle down to Wilcox. "Give this to Imelda. Tell her to give some to Zito. We'll keep him drunk. Should help."

"You'll be all right here?"

Styles made a face. "Shit. Go!" Wilcox jogged off.

"Hey, do you guys need a ride?" asked the kid.

"What's your name, son?"

"Lerick."

"Where were you guys headed with this?"

"Down to Karshi. K2. The airport. Our family makes that vodka, and we make good money shipping it out."

"I'll tell you what, Lerick, you tell your grandfather we won't take your truck or your vodka. All we want is a ride south."

After a short but heated exchange, Lerick nodded. "He says okay."

Styles winked. "But he's not happy."

The kid smiled. "No."

Grandpa, muttering a string of words, probably curses, started back for the truck door.

"One of our guys is hurt," said Styles. "They're up ahead. You keep driving, kid. I'll squeeze in that cab with you."

"Okay," the kid said. "So why did your plane crash? Did you get shot down? Is there a war going on?"

"Hey, take it easy. Let's go."

Shisha Café, Mazar-e Sharif
Northern Afghanistan
2240 Hours Local Time

CIA Agent James Moody was leaning back in his chair, staring at the computer on the table before him and smoking peach-flavored tobacco through the long hose of an ornately designed hookah pipe, its turquoise-colored shaft gleaming in the café's dim candlelight.

He read the *Washington Post* online, perfunctorily scanning the headlines and wishing his contact would have arrived already. He was gathering intelligence on two Iranian terrorists who were operating in the city, gathering intelligence on U.S. military forces.

Just fifteen minutes ago a colleague back home had called to say he'd heard a rumor about something big going down that involved the Asia desk, but he wasn't sure what. Moody had blown off his friend. Rumors within the ranks of CIA agents ran more rampant than rats through D.C. tenements.

But there were also reports from an agent in Tashkent. Lots of military air traffic moving north. There was a big shooting in Khiva from Steinberg's movie set, and some reports of at least one aircraft going down.

Moody's satellite phone rang; it was his boss. The man spoke quickly and evenly, and when he was finished, Moody nearly fell out of his chair.

"So you want me to coordinate a rescue of Michael Hertzog and his team of scumbag mercenaries? They're a bunch of criminals!"

"You have your orders. You'll meet up with your Delta

team on the Amu Darya near the border. You will extract those men at all costs. Do you understand?"

They weren't giving him a choice. So be it.

And damn, Hertzog was still alive? Last Moody had heard, the old jarhead had colon cancer and would probably die.

So what the hell had he been doing in Uzbekistan? Shooting up movie sets and crashing planes, to start.

Moody took a long pull on his tobacco, then smiled. Hertzog had nicknamed him Jimmy Judas, and old Jimmy was not one to disappoint.

Chapter 11

....

Chopper Landing Site
Approximately 100 Miles South
Urgench Airport
2244 Hours Local Time

Sometimes—most times—when you least expected it, you got a break, and you'd best be thankful for it.

So as Mad Dog listened to Styles tell him that they had intercepted two moonshiners and were hitching a ride south in an old truck, he couldn't help but get a little religious and glance up at the stars.

He imagined Jesus—dressed in olive drab, of course, and wearing a boonie hat—floating around in his white Hummer, smoking a cigar, and barking orders.

According to their sitrep, Styles, Zito, Wilcox, and Imelda were traveling about forty miles an hour, moving southeast of their position, with more enemy air traffic headed northbound in their direction.

"Roger that, Blackhound One, confirm your report," said the pilot, as though they were on the radio. Old habits died hard. "We have visual contact. They're moving awfully quick."

"Yeah, and they'll turn around just as fast. But maybe not yet. They can't make a thorough search till dawn, so let's knock on wood and say we have some time."

"Knocking on my forehead right now."

"Me, too."

"So listen, should we head west to your position, rendezvous there?"

Mad Dog took a deep breath, considering. If they were spotted, they'd be towing a whole lot of party crashers with them. "Negative."

"Zito needs a medic. He's a good man, Michael. Don't fuck me over on this."

Shit. Mad Dog considered the request. "I'll get back to you. Just keep heading south."

"Roger that. And, boss, about Wolfgang, I just thought it'd be too dangerous to go ten miles in the wrong direction. Sorry."

"You're not sorry, Gerry. You didn't even consider it. But that's all right. We'll get him. Now give me your current GPS position."

Kat and Bibby were at Mad Dog's shoulders as he jotted down the coordinates. Bibby plotted the C-130 team's latitude and longitude on his laptop, using digital maps and overlays.

"Hey, wait," said Kat. "I can go get Wolfgang, but before that, maybe I can fly directly east and drop off Boo Boo in the truck's path. He waits there until they intercept."

"Yeah, that crossed my mind," said Mad Dog. "But that's going to burn up a whole lot of fuel, and we need every drop to even get near the border."

Kat sighed. "What else can we do?"

"Mr. Hertzog, I have a temporary solution," said Bibby. "Boo Boo can advise Styles over the phone."

"Except that they don't have Boo Boo's gear. I'm sure Zito needs fluids."

Bibby sighed in frustration. "We cannot waste the fuel."

"All right. Get Boo Boo down here to talk to them. And then tell Night Stalker to start stripping down his bird. Rip out the seats. Rip out everything. We have to lighten the load."

"Absolutely." The Brit slammed shut his computer and trotted off toward the choppers.

"Gerry, you there?" Mad Dog called.

"Unfortunately, and I heard what you said. I guess beggars can't be choosers. But how we getting home?"

"You said the old man and the kid were heading to K2? A regular run for them?"

"Yeah."

"So maybe they won't draw much attention. You stick with them, on their regular course. Don't make any changes. Once you get to the outskirts of Karshi, you find a place to wait for us. And we'll pick you up there."

"Yeah, all right. What a cluster fuck this has turned out to be . . . And, Michael, I put a lot of my own money into that plane, you know that. There's no way it was a random fuel line gone bad. I knew every inch of that plane. I'm betting it was those guys at Urgench. Those friendly cocksuckers. They must've cut a line or something. Maybe they're part of the big plan. Or maybe they just hate Americans."

Rolling his eyes over the old pilot's bitching and moaning, Mad Dog said, "It doesn't matter anymore,

Gerry. Just keep heading south and we'll meet up with you, roger that?"

"Roger that. See you in Hell to regroup."

"All right, hang on, here's Boo Boo."

Mad Dog handed the phone to the medic, who began asking about Zito: What did his pupils look like? Reactive to light? Any fluid in his ears? Could he feel his toes? Describe the fractures, and so on.

In the meantime, Night Stalker and Bibby were tearing apart Night Stalker's chopper, trying to lighten the load, while Kat began her preflight check in her own bird. Pope and Sapper manned positions on each edge of the ravine, both scanning the horizon with their night vision goggles.

Mad Dog just stood there for a few seconds, watching his team go through the motions. They were good people betrayed by one clever little bitch. Galina Saratova was quite a woman. Hopefully, she would get hers.

Rock Creek Park
Georgetown, D.C.
0807 Hours Local Time

Tom Waterson and his wife had been on their morning jog along the trail when he spotted the Lexus at the bottom of the gorge, partially submerged in the river.

He looked for signs of tire marks on the street above but found none. While his agitated wife wondered aloud if anyone else knew about the car, Waterson remained calm, his instincts kicking in. He was sixty-seven, a retired D.C. police detective, and sure, there were a million reasons why someone could have "accidentally" driven off the road and wound up dead in the river—

And every one of those reasons intrigued him.

After they called 911, the police arrived and he spoke to them, and then his wife argued that they should leave. He wouldn't, and sent her home. This was fun, and he wouldn't allow her to steal that from him. She already controlled the TV and kept eating all of his ice cream.

When the press and TV people showed up, he allowed himself to be interviewed, then watched as divers went into the water and emerged with the body of a beautiful redhead.

Another man, in his forties, impeccably groomed and dressed in a Versace suit and trench coat, had arrived a few minutes earlier, and while he seemed to be someone important, he kept his distance, speaking to just a few of the cops.

Waterson couldn't help himself. He went over to the man, did a double take. "Hey, there. I'm Tom Waterson, D.C. police, retired." Waterson extended his hand.

The man took it. "They told me you found the car."

"Yeah, I did. Do I know you?"

The man smiled and started away from the riverbank. "I doubt it. I'm just one of the investigators."

"You look familiar."

The man kept moving.

"Hey, wait. I worked with you once before. I remember. You're a federal agent."

The guy turned back. "You know, come to think of it, I remember you, too. You were the loudmouth on the Carver case. You nearly ruined our entire investigation."

Waterson had put up with his share of spooks in the past, but now he was no longer bound by protocol.

"Whoa. Slow down, asshole. You broke the law, and you know it."

The spook grinned. "Have a nice day."

Waterson gave him the bird. "And by the way, no rubber on the road up there. She didn't even hit the brake."

"Go home, Dick Tracy."

Waterson shook his head. "Not yet."

Uzbekistan Desert
147 Nautical Miles North of Choppers
2308 Hours Local Time

Wolfgang moved in a brisk walk, intent upon covering at least four, maybe even five miles per hour.

After the first thirty minutes, he had stopped thinking and was just walking and listening to his breath, the footfalls, the rustling of his pack, the wind at his back. His lips were chapped, and he repeatedly blinked sand out of his eyes. The pistol had become heavy in his hand, and now he just held it at his side, his arm sore and dangling, his shoulders stiff from the pack.

The desert had grown more uneven, the sand rising a few meters high ahead, forming a mound. He started up, boots digging in, his breath growing heavy as he reached the summit.

He stood there, catching his breath, and decided to reach back into a side pocket of his pack, figuring he'd steal a look through his night vision goggles from this higher vantage point. He thought he could see more air traffic to the east. He also wanted to shoot a new bearing, make sure he was still okay. As he undid the strap, the oddest sensation crawled up his legs.

And before he realized what was happening, the ground creaked as though it were made of metal, and then . . . it suddenly gave way.

Chopper Landing Site
Approximately 100 Miles South
Urgench Airport
2308 Hours Local Time

Kat gave Mad Dog a thumbs-up, then he and the rest of the guys moved away as she fired up her 520. Her normal cruising speed was about 154 knots, but she'd be dipping too heavily into her two fuel cells, which combined held sixty-four gallons. Speed for best endurance would be between sixty and eighty knots, translating into about three hours flight time and a range of about 255 nautical miles. She and Wolfgang would have to put down once, so she could dump some fuel in the tanks to get them back to the landing site, where they would then refuel one last time for the happy ride home.

Right. With every friggin' Uzbek and his mother on their asses.

She lifted off and thundered on into the night, flying just fifty to sixty feet off the ground. "Blackhound One, this is Blackhound Six, over."

Mad Dog replied immediately, "Six, this is One, go ahead, over."

"Just wanted to tell you how good this feels . . . "

"What?"

"All this power between my legs. Blackhound Six, out." She instantly regretted the remark, but part of her found it chilling to tease him. She even gasped.

But my God, she needed to concentrate on the job! A man's life was at stake. Mad Dog said he would call ahead and get Wolfgang's most recent GPS coordinates.

Until then she would just fly on, steady course, hoping to intercept a lone warrior stuck in the middle of nowhere.

C-130 Hercules Crew
Moving Southeast of Nukus
2310 Hours Local Time

Styles had given the satellite phone to Wilcox, who was inside the truck's bed, where Zito had been positioned on the floor. They continued giving the poor guy vodka, and Imelda was doing her best to keep the copilot's legs stable, even though the truck was bouncing around like a mechanical bull across the dirt road. There was a little window at the back of the cab that Wilcox could slide open to talk with them up front, and at the moment the loadmaster was bitching about the kid's driving.

"Leave him alone," Styles said. "He knows what he's doing."

"I don't know how much more Zito can take of this. His legs are getting beat up back here!"

"We ain't slowing down. Do what you can."

Styles reached back and slammed the window shut. The old man, who sat near the door mumbled something under his breath. "What did he say?" Styles asked the kid.

"He said we shouldn't trust you. You don't even trust each other."

"He's right."

The kid shrugged. "My father liked Americans."

"Why's that?"

"He sold a lot of vodka to them. And the men at the base were very kind to us. They gave us food and music and clothes and all kinds of things, until they had to leave."

"How come your father's not on this run with you?"

"He died."

"Sorry to hear that."

"He got very sick because he spent too much time at the base. There are chemicals there. And they killed him."

"That's really terrible, Lerick."

"My older brother is sick now, too, so only me and my grandfather can deliver the vodka."

"Are you in school?"

"I go sometimes, but there's nothing they can teach me that I need. I need to make money to help my family. The medicine for my brother is very expensive."

"Listen to me, kid. You get us near Karshi, and I'm going to help you in a big way. Do you understand?"

"You have a lot of money?"

"I have enough."

Lerick scrutinized him for a second. "Why would you want to help us?"

"Just call it a trade."

"But you have a gun. You could force us."

"You tell your grandfather that maybe I don't trust my partner in the back, but I'm going to trust you." With that Styles lowered the pistol, let it rest on his lap. Lerick translated, but Grandpa would have none of it. He just waved his hand and glowered.

Blackmore Pond
Cranston, Rhode Island
27 Years Ago

Wolfy, Teddy, and Anthony were skipping stones like they usually did, talking about school and whether they would go for a swim. The water was a sheet of glass, and the kid whose stone fell short had to buy Cokes.

Sometimes when they came down to the pond they would stop and look for pickerel hiding their long slender bodies under lily pads. Wolfy thought it was really neat the way they just stayed there, very still, their snouts and eyes barely visible as they waited for the occasional dragonfly or grasshopper to skim the surface. And then . . . splash!

Teddy, who as also known as "Blohodda" because his parents forced him take French horn lessons and his teacher always yelled at him to "blow harder," would be buying the Cokes. He cursed and told them he was going swimming.

Anthony, nicknamed "Fuzznuts" by Wolfy because, well, he was two years older, agreed that it was high time they took the plunge. They tore off their shirts, kicked off their sandals, and dove in, their baggy swimming trunks nearly falling off as they hit the water.

Wolfy loved to dive deep because people dumped all kinds of stuff in the water, and you never knew what you would find: tires, lawn mowers, car engines, you name it. He felt like a pirate of the Caribbean, searching the depths for lost treasure.

"Okay," cried Teddy. "Time for hide and seek. Who's first?"

"Me!" Wolfy shouted.

"Okay," said Anthony.

"All right." Wolfy waited a moment until he caught his breath. Then, after filling his lungs, he jackknifed down into the water, eyes wide, searching for his spot.

Within a few seconds he spotted it, looming just ahead, like an ancient pillar from Atlantis.

An old, white ice box with rounded corners and algae growing along its rusted sides. The door hung half open, like a mouth calling to him.

He kicked hard and dove deeper, bursting with excitement. They would never find him.

Kat's Chopper
Northbound Toward Nukus
2312 Hours Local Time

"Blackhound One, say again?" said Kat.

"Six, I say again, Blackhound Seven does not respond, over."

Shit. What was Wolfgang's problem now? "Roger that, One. Keep trying, I guess. In the meantime, we know he's off the baseline, but did he right angle west or east, over?"

"Unknown, but you figure he's only moved four to six miles from his last known GPS, probably within a semi-circle, so that's not a huge area to cover. Turn on your SAR receiver just in case his phone's gone bad or something, over."

"Roger that." Kat was trying to sound positive.

But the "what ifs" made it real hard.

If the guy had collapsed in the middle of the desert, at night, he could be overlooked, and it wasn't as though she could turn on high power searchlights.

And if he had collapsed or was in some other kind of trouble and couldn't talk, couldn't turn on his SAR— search and rescue—beacon, then he was going to rot out there. "Well, if you hear from him, give me a shout, Blackhound Six, out."

She double-checked her own coordinates against Wolfgang's last known position. Maybe the asshole was still walking but was delusional or something and wouldn't respond. They said he'd taken a mental turn for the worse. He'd killed the minister's guards and had been drinking. Maybe he was just hung over and had passed out?

She fought the stick as a gust struck the chopper, then throttled up, the anticipation shortening her breath. How much time would she have to find him?

Blackmore Pond
Cranston, Rhode Island
27 Years Ago

Wolfy slipped inside the ice box, reached forward, and grabbed the top lip of the door, which felt cold and slimy.

Perfect. He would finally win this game.

Ha ha! He would hide just behind the door and watch them swim on by. Sure, the possibility of being trapped had definitely crossed his mind, so he was very careful not to pull the door too hard.

But even so, he misjudged his own strength.

And the door slammed shut with a muffled *snick . . . snick . . .*

Utter darkness.

Oh, no. He drove his shoulder into more slimy metal, refusing to believe what had just happened. He wasn't locked inside. No way!

But his chest felt tighter, heavier, and the walls of the ice box seemed to cave in on him. *I can't get out! I'm going to die in here!*

Then . . . an idea. He braced himself against the rear of the ice box, lifted his knees, then placed them and his hands squarely on the door. Bearing his teeth, he pushed as hard as he could, pushed again, pushed once more.

His arms and legs shuddered under the exertion.

But the door wouldn't budge.

What now? He groped along the corners, prying, pushing again, searching for a latch, feeling only solid metal, and hearing over and over:

Snick . . . snick . . .

He exhaled very slowly, knowing he was on his last breath. Was he crying? He wasn't sure. His heart raced, drummed in his ears, in time with *snick . . . snick . . . snick . . . snick . . .*

Wolfy felt like screaming, but he had no energy left. The water seemed to carry him away, away, away—

Suddenly, cold mud pressed across his back and warm light shone down on his closed eyes.

"Hey, Teddy, I think Wolfy's dead! Hurry! Hurry!"

"I'm gonna go get my mom!"

"No, stay here and help me!"

"Oh, no, he really looks dead!"

Rocked by chills, Wolfgang snapped awake.

The pond was gone.

Uzbekistan Desert
147 Nautical Miles North of Choppers
2314 Hours Local Time

Where the hell am I?

Wolfgang could barely see, felt something stabbing at the corners of his eyes. Dust? Maybe. And then it came back to him. That sound, not the *snick . . . snick . . .* but that creaking sound, like rusted metal groaning against his weight.

And the feeling of falling straight down, then suddenly stopping, his head jerking back, his body slamming into something, one arm on fire, then nothing.

He blinked again, squinted, felt his legs dangling in midair, a heavy pressure on his chest, and even more pressure on his shoulders. He tried to reach with his right arm, found it pinned against his chest, but his left arm was free. The pistol was gone. He lowered his chin, looked down. Long, curved shadows rolled out below him. He lifted his head.

About two meters directly above, framed by a jagged hole like a puncture wound in a soda can, hung the stars. Oh, shit. He'd fallen into something.

His eyes adjusted more to the darkness.

No, it couldn't be.

But it was.

He was pinned between the bars of a staircase railing inside the hold of a stranded and forgotten fishing boat that had been lying in the sand for God knew how long. Those curved shadows were, in fact, the boat's hull. As best he could tell, she was lying on her starboard side.

So, after all these years, the boat might finally be good for something:

It could serve as his tomb.

Some irony. Some cruel joke.

After all, *he* had been the one who asked Bibby about the mounds in the sand.

Well, he'd found one all right.

He tried to move his right arm again, slide it out, but it was jammed so tightly that his hand was going numb. The arm didn't feel broken, at least he didn't think it was. His head throbbed. He must've whacked it good on the way down, and his hips began to ache. He realized his pack had caught on one rail and stopped his fall, as had the other rail. If he could pry himself sideways—

Wait. Why bother? The satellite phone was clipped to his waist. He wouldn't die here. He would call for a cab! His hand moved along his belt. *Oh my God. Gone.*

There it was, about three meters below, gleaming in the half light, lying on the hull beside his pistol. The phone's clip must have shattered on impact.

Can this get any better?

The only way to contact the boss now was the SAR beacon tucked into his pack, and that would only work if the boss sent someone to pick him up.

He lifted his arm, strained. Shit, the little beacon was in the bottom of the pack, out of reach. Time to free himself. He pushed, tried to turn. With his legs dangling, he had no leverage, and the little jerking motions only brought on more pain. He thought a string of curses.

Then he closed his eyes, saw the fireman hovering over him, asking if he was all right, saw Teddy and Anthony staring at him, wide-eyed, Teddy shouting, "I saw his bubbles coming through the holes in the ice box. That's how I found him! I saw his bubbles!"

Wolfgang's breath grew shallow.

"You should have called us right away," said the fireman.

"We were scared," answered Anthony.

The fireman shook his head, his handlebar moustache twitching. "Wolfy, can you hear me? Come on, Wolfy."

Snick . . . snick . . .

Chopper Landing Site
Approximately 100 Miles South
Urgench Airport
2315 Hours Local Time

Mad Dog stared at the pile of seats and other useless equipment the team had removed from Night Stalker's 600N, now a flying gas tank filled with the remaining jerry cans, Sapper's special mortar rounds that had gone unused, spare ammo, and not much else.

The men were unusually quiet. Bibby sat cross-legged in the sand, banging on his computer. Sapper and Pope were still on watch. Night Stalker was reading the chopper's tech manual, and Boo Boo was propped up on one of the bird's landing skids and "resting his eyes," having been relieved by Sapper. Mad Dog had grown so accustomed to his team's sarcastic chatter that at the moment he almost missed it.

He tried calling Wolfgang again. The line just rang. Then he called Kat on the radio. She was still en route, everything fine so far. She'd update him as she neared the search area. Then he rang up Gerry for another sitrep.

Strangely, the pilot's satellite phone just rang and rang.

Shaking his head, he crossed to Bibby. "Now we've lost contact with Gerry and the truck."

"Maybe the call dropped," said the Brit. "Try again."

Mad Dog did. Waited. Same bullshit.

"Maybe he's got the ring on silent for some reason."

"Or maybe they got intercepted."

Bibby frowned. "There's a reason they're not answering. They could've stopped to take a piss, for all we know. Give them more time. Try again."

"You're right." Mad Dog took a deep breath. "You know, I look around, and I think, 'My God, what have I done?'"

"We haven't failed. We're still up two million, and our friends in Langley will further sweeten the pot. Have you forgotten? Three million more from their slush fund? This is our most lucrative operation ever. We've blackmailed the C.I. fucking A. It's beautiful."

"But at the biggest cost. We lost a good man. We lost our plane. Atayev is dead, for God's sake. He would've reopened K2. I wanted that base reopened for Americans. You're forgetting the bigger picture here. So we lost. And the Russkies won."

"There was no way to beat them. They were too thoroughly entrenched in all of this. But don't you find it thrilling to screw over the CIA once and for all?"

"I don't know anymore. Maybe this is it for me. I had this big dream back in the 'Stan, thought I was going to do things my way—not be used by the fucking system. And here I am. And it's all happening again. Nothing's changed. Not a goddamned thing."

"You're not a Marine anymore."

"Oh, yes I am."

"Everybody get down!" screamed Pope.

They all dove for the chopper as the sound of twin jet engines boomed across the desert.

"He's close!" added Pope.

"Shit, they've broadened their flight path," said Bibby, lying in the sand beside Mad Dog as the jet screamed by.

"And if that's the case, we got a better chance of being spotted. That's just great."

The satellite phone rang. It was Gerry. "Where the hell were you?" said Mad Dog. "I tried calling twice."

"I know, sorry. But I think our luck's just run out."

Chapter 12

....

Styles repeated himself because the boss was dumb-founded. "That's right. That's what I said! The truck is stuck! Wilcox is under the hood right now!"

Silence. Was Mad Dog popping a cyanide pill like a captured spy or what?

"You there?"

"Yeah, I'm still here. All right, here's the deal. See if you can get back rolling. If not, you stay there and we'll come. Eventually. Shoot me your GPS."

After retrieving the unit from the truck's cab, Styles fired up the device, waited, cursed impatiently, took a reading, waited again—*God damn it!*—then fed the numbers to Mad Dog.

Meanwhile, the old man was pounding his fist on the truck fender and screaming.

"Tell him to shut up!" Styles shouted at the boy.

Lerick hollered at his grandfather in a surprisingly

stern tone. Grandpa returned verbal fire, punctuating his words with more raps on the fender.

"Give me a sitrep in say ten minutes," said Mad Dog.

"You got it." Styles got off the phone, marched over to the two. "What's he saying now?"

"He says the added weight put too much strain on the engine. That's why we broke down. He says it's your fault. He says we have never had a problem with the truck until now."

"Is that true?"

Lerick shook his head. "The engine has stopped a few times. His memory is not good."

Wilcox rushed back to the cab, tried to start the engine again. She grumbled but wouldn't kick over. "I still think the fuel line's clogged. They're putting shit gas in this thing. Let's hope that's all it is."

"Just get her started."

"God, without your leadership, I'd be lost."

"Fuck you, wiseass."

"Sorry, just having one of those nights."

Styles almost grinned.

Imelda was suddenly at his arm and tugging on his sleeve. "What?"

"He call for you inside. He call for you."

"He's three sheets to the wind. Just ignore him."

"No, no. He call for you."

Styles threw his hands in the air and trudged to the back of the truck, where Zito was sitting up, his head wobbling a little. "Lay down, buddy," said Styles.

"If it's the weight, just leave me here," said the copilot, slurring his words. "It's my time to die. I know I'm a fucking hero, so it's okay. I'm a fucking hero. A goddamned American. And it's my time to die. I should've went down with the plane. I'm already dead, and I don't know it."

"Shut up, you stupid asshole."

The words had barely escaped Styles's lips when Wilcox tried to start the engine again.

She coughed and growled.

"I'm ready to die, Gerry," said Zito.

"I'm going to kill you, you don't shut that trap!" Styles turned to Imelda. "Get back in there and keep him quiet. I don't care what you do."

She pursed her lips and nodded.

"All right," cried Wilcox. "I think this time I got it!"

Kat's Chopper
Uzbekistan Desert
146 Nautical Miles North of Landing Site
0105 Hours Local Time

"Blackhound One, I'm entering the search area, over?"

"Roger that, Six. Still no word, over."

"I figure I have about fifteen minutes of fuel to burn here. Permission to use it all, over."

"You're asking?"

Kat grinned. "Roger that. I'll make as many passes as I can, then I'll have to bug out. No SAR beacon yet, over."

"Roger. Blackhound One, out."

Kat drove the stick forward, descending to less than fifty feet, whipping up dust below. As expected, it was damn hard to see anything, save for the rolling hills and broad stretches of desert lying beyond.

Would he be stupid enough to fire off a flare? Did he

even have any? Maybe they were standard issue with a parachute pack?

She checked her watch, flicked another glance to her fuel gauge, then concentrated on the view ahead, imagining Wolfgang's silhouette breaking the smooth line of the horizon.

Wolfgang was awakened by the sound of the approaching chopper. He wasn't sure how long he had been hanging there. When had he fallen asleep?

That damn bird was close! Unconsciously, he released a deep breath, but no one would see his bubbles this time.

He glanced up. Just that small hole.

The phone still lay below. How far was the drop? Ten feet? Twelve?

Jesus, they were right on top of him! Dust blowing over the hole!

This is it! You either save yourself now or die!

All too familiar with stories of mothers lifting cars to save their children, with soldiers summoning up inhuman strength to save their brothers in arms, Wolfgang released a roar, rolled against the excruciating pain—

Freed himself.

And nearly plunged from the railing, were it not for his left hand slapping on the metal. With his right arm dangling useless and numb, his ribs throbbing, he swung to and fro, trying to get one leg latched around the rail. If he lost his grip, he would drop like a used shell casing to the hull.

The chopper's rotor wash flooded into the hole for a second, then vanished, the turbines growing fainter.

Shit!

They had been right overhead!

Now they were moving away.

He swung harder, hooked his leg around the railing, hooked the other, then let go, hanging upside down by his legs.

His pack began to slide off. He caught it with his good hand, hooked one strap onto his empty hip holster, then shoved his hand beneath the main flap, up and into the bag.

Where the fuck was it? Come on! Come on!

Kat had a few more minutes worth of fuel. She scowled at the gauge and grew angry that she had burned up so much of that precious liquid and would return without Wolfgang. Mission failed. Damn it. The old "never leave a man behind" motto could now result in all of them getting killed. But that was okay, so long as you tried to save everyone?

She and Mad Dog would debate that one later, if not in the afterlife.

Fuck it. She banked hard, came around to a new bearing: south. "Blackhound One, this is Blackhound Six. I've finished my sweep. No sign of Blackhound Seven, over."

"Roger that, Six. Come on back. Blackhound One, out."

Wolfgang found the SAR beacon all right, and was about to punch the button—when the fucking thing slipped from his hand and plunged to the sand-caked hull.

Phone, pistol, SAR beacon. Everything he needed out of reach. Yep, he had really pissed off God.

No choice now.

Screw it. Better to jump and get hurt than die here.

He pulled himself up to the railing, realized that if he could get on top, he could work his way down, along the edge of the staircase, where the jump to the side of the hull was only about six feet. Looked good.

Then he slipped right off the goddamned rail, lost his breath in midair, and hit the ground with a thud that spiked through his entire body.

He had struck on his right side, his hip taking most of the blow. He realized with a start that he'd dropped directly onto a pile of sand that had filtered down into the ship before she was entirely buried.

Jesus God his hip throbbed, but he could move his leg. Nothing felt broken.

He dove for the SAR beacon, hit the switch. Then he snatched up the satellite phone and dialed Mad Dog—

But shit, he couldn't get a clear signal while buried inside the ship. Would the SAR's signal reach outside?

He couldn't take a chance, and that chopper was moving off. He stood, squinted up at the hole in the hull and gripped the beacon a little tighter. He reared back, took aim, and let the beacon fly. The device tumbled end over end, nicked the corner of the hole, but sailed on through, landing somewhere in the sand above.

Yeah!

Beep. Beep. Beep.

Kat nearly lost control of the chopper as she began receiving Wolfgang's SAR signal.

She immediately called Mad Dog, then banked hard, heading back toward the location.

Trouble was, even with the extra fuel she'd brought,

they still wouldn't have enough to reach the landing site. Night Stalker would have to link up with her, and that would waste some serious time. Tough luck for them.

She homed in on the signal, hovered over a small mound with a ditch or hole or something on one side, maybe even a shadow ahead. She was right on top of the beacon. She put down, popped open the door and ran forward, carrying a small flashlight. "Wolfgang!"

A faint voice barely echoed above the thumping rotor, and she couldn't tell its location. She slowed, took a few more steps forward. Heard it again. "I'm down here!"

She mounted a sand dune, but strangely, her boot hit something hard. She leaned down, brushed away some sand, felt metal below. *What the hell?*

"Wolfgang?"

"I'm inside a goddamn fishing boat! I fell through the hull. I'm here!"

"I hear you!"

"Yeah, but hey, be careful! The hull's not stable up there. Wood's all dry rot, and the metal's rusted."

Kat dropped to her hands and knees, crawled forward, reached the hole in the hull and glanced down into the long shadows. She switched on the flashlight, probed the darkness. "Wolfgang?"

He shifted into the dim light. "Well, I ain't the Pope."

She glanced right, saw the flashing of his SAR beacon, which was lying on the dune just a few meters off, then shook her head at him. "You really stepped in shit this time, huh?"

"Right, yeah, whatever. Just drop me a rope."

"Are you kidding me? All I got are some gas cans. I stripped the bird before I left."

He launched into a string of curses, then looked up and said, "Just fucking go."

"Come on, asshole. You need to climb out of there. Move it!"

"How? I can't reach that railing."

"See what you got in your pack. I'll see what I can do up here. A short rope. Anything. Come on!"

C-130 Hercules Crew
Moving Southeast of Nukus
0130 Hours Local Time

Styles and his motley crew were back on the road. Wilcox's suspicions about the fuel filter were correct. The delay hadn't cost them more than thirty minutes, but when you had the entire military assets of a nation on your ass, thirty minutes was thirty too many.

The old man sitting next to him had reached his breaking point and decided to get drunk. He took small swigs on the bottle of vodka balanced on his knee, while Lerick occasionally glanced at him and scowled.

Then the kid leaned over and switched on the old radio, the voices coming faintly, Styles not understanding a word. "What're you listening to?"

"Uh, it's a news program."

"Oh, yeah?"

"It helps to keep me awake."

"What're they saying?"

The kid listened for a moment, his mouth slowly falling open in surprise. "They're saying that President Atayev has just been killed. They're saying there was a big shooting in Khiva."

"Oh my God." Styles sounded about as convincing as a B-movie actor.

"They're saying that the men responsible might have escaped."

Styles leaned over and switched off the radio. "You don't worry about that, kid. You worry about driving."

"You didn't kill our president, did you?"

Styles hesitated. "No, son, we didn't. As a matter of fact, we were hired to protect him—until everything went to hell."

"I believe you."

"Why?"

"Because I heard on the radio that Atayev was friend of America, and that made me feel good about him."

"He was. But now, who knows what'll happen here?"

Kat's Chopper
Uzbekistan Desert
5 Nautical Miles North of Landing Site
0345 Hours Local Time

Using her own belt, the seat belt straps from the chopper, and her shirtsleeves, Kat had fashioned a crude rope to help Wolfgang escape from the fishing boat's hold. He'd used that rope, along with the straps from his pack, to reach the railing, after which he found an alternate route through a small window, which he broke, allowing the sand to pour in and free up another hole, through which he climbed out.

Kat had kept her tone lighthearted, joked with him as he emerged onto the dune, where he fell onto the sand, rolled onto his back, and shut his eyes tightly. He seemed about to cry, but she couldn't be certain. And he whispered over and over, "I'm not dead . . . I'm not dead . . . "

She had given him those moments, then dragged him up and into the chopper.

He had barely spoken to her during the entire flight, even dozed off for about thirty minutes, and was now just waking up as she called Mad Dog and began to land.

She had just reported her position when Night Stalker's chopper appeared like a buzzard on the horizon and raced toward them, sweeping stealthily over the desert floor.

"All right," she began, turning to Wolfgang. "Help me get this thing refueled."

"Yeah," he said, his gaze strange. "And you know, I'm . . . okay now. I'm good. I'm really, really good."

"Uh, okay. I'm glad. Now get the fuck out and move!"

"I mean I figured out what's been bothering me. I've just been scared. That's all. It's crazy. I guess nobody wants to die, huh?"

"Go! Otherwise we *will* buy it right here!"

A fuel brigade immediately formed, cans moving up the line and reaching Kat, who began the laborious process of transferring the precious liquid from cans to tank.

Mad Dog rushed up and dropped a hand on her shoulder. "Thank you."

She glanced at the hand, which made him self-conscious, and he quickly withdrew it.

"It's all right," she said softly. "You can touch me."

He snorted. "Not like that. I've already got enough agony in my life."

"Me, too. You know, we won't have enough fuel to reach Termez."

"I know it'll be close."

"You got a plan for getting across the border on foot? And last time I checked, there was a river in our way and only one goddamn bridge."

"Bibby's working on it."

"I hope so. Because we're running out of time."

"How much longer to refuel?"

She placed an empty can on the dirt. "At this rate? Another fifteen minutes."

He nodded, handed her the next can. "Let's make it ten."

Amu Darya River
On the Afghan Border
0355 Hours Local Time

CIA agent James Moody met with his five-man Delta Force team in a clearing about twenty meters from the riverbank. They had camouflaged their UH-60 Black Hawk, but the bird could be ready to fly in a matter of minutes.

Moody stood outside the helicopter, speaking with the team leader, a haughty captain, nicknamed "Hammerhead," who was about as happy taking orders from a civilian as a man strapped to a short-circuiting electric chair.

"Uh, excuse me, sir, but they put *you* in charge?" Hammerhead asked after refusing to shake Moody's hand. "Why?"

"Because it's vital to the intelligence community that these individuals are safely extracted. And yours ain't to question why, eh, motherfucker?"

"Sir, there's no need to curse. Sir."

"Don't 'sir' me, Captain. I'm no officer."

"I didn't mistake you for one." Hammerhead narrowed his gaze. Tough guy. Moody had seen a million like him. "You don't like us soldiers, do you?"

Moody threw up his hands, feigning innocence. "What do you mean? I have the deepest respect for all men and women in the armed forces. We all want the same thing. You do it your way. I do it my way."

The captain stood there, unmoved. "What's the current location of our package?"

"No doubt they're heading south, away from Khiva, but I'll make direct contact with them now. This is going to be great."

"What you mean?"

Moody wiped the grin off his face. "It's all about payback, which in some quarters is referred to as justice."

"Mr. Moody, is there anything else about this operation that I should know about? Because, given the nature of this operation and its purported leadership, I'd like to know before I hang my men out to dry."

"Relax, Captain. There's a chance we won't be doing anything. Just sitting on our asses."

"I don't understand."

"You don't need to." Moody unclipped his satellite phone and dialed.

Kat's Chopper
Uzbekistan Desert
Heading South Toward K2
0401 Hours Local Time

Mad Dog glanced around the cabin at Wolfgang, Bibby, and Kat, wondering if they were as edgy as he was. Like him, they were experts at maintaining appearances, even while their pulses leapt, their guts twisted.

Bibby had mentioned that a couple of choppers had broken off from their squadron and were now heading back toward K2. Furthermore, his contacts said that the airport at Urgench had turned into a giant gas station, with all those military aircraft needing refueling to continue their missions. That was good and bad: good, because the refueling ops would buy the team some time; bad, because once they realized the team wasn't up north, all those fully fueled craft would turn tail and bear down on them.

Mad Dog's satellite phone rang. Frowning, he answered the call from a number he didn't recognize.

"Hello?"

"Oh, excuse me. I must've dialed the wrong number. This wouldn't be Michael Hertzog, would it?"

"Who is this?"

"It is you, Hertzog! Damn, I heard you got whacked up in Khiva."

That low, grating voice caused Mad Dog's chest to cave in. "Oh my God. How did you get this number?"

Moody's loud chuckle turned to static for a moment, then he caught his breath. "Dog, you forget who you're talking to. I'm all about information. And hey, you'll need to change my nickname. I'm not Jimmy Judas anymore. You call me Jimmy *Jesus*—because I got orders to save your sphincter. Hallelujah! Jesus saves!"

"Hold on." Mad Dog covered the receiver, glanced dumbfounded at Bibby. "They sent Moody to rescue us."

The Brit rolled his eyes. "We have no luck."

"Hey, Mad Dog? You still there, asshole?"

"Just shut up with that. Where are you now?"

"Where am I? Heaven, of course, waiting to come down and bring salvation."

"Moody . . ."

"All right, Hertzog. Listen up: I've been doing a lot of work here in A'stan. I'm over here with, let's just say, a few friends and a nice little whirly bird. You got some coordinates for me?"

"I'm supposed to trust you?"

"Come on, where's the love? Who carried you on his back out of Angola?"

"I don't believe they sent you."

"Believe it. Believe in fate. It was meant to be. Who better to bail you out than the man who's been bailing you out all of your life."

Mad Dog closed his eyes. "Shit."

"You want to live? Tell me where you are?"

Mad Dog covered the phone again, glanced at Bibby. "What if he has orders to kill us? Could be the Agency covering up its tracks."

Bibby frowned. "That wouldn't prevent Catfish from going public with the mole. And my contacts at MI6 have already promised to do that if anything happens to us or our attorney. And there's another bit of information, but suffice it to say I think Moody is here to extract us. A'stan is his area of operations."

"So I'll tell him where we are."

"Do it."

Mad Dog uncovered the receiver. "Okay, Moody, we're en route to K2 to pick up the rest of our team, then on to Termez. But we don't have enough fuel to reach the border."

"That's too bad, because I'm not authorized to cross the border, but I'll do what I can from here. We're still operating those unmanned Predators out of Tuzul, all under the CENTCOM umbrella. I know I can bring those assets to bear. Hellfire missiles and good times, know what I'm saying?"

Mad Dog took a deep breath, imagining the twinkle in Moody's eye. "Hellfire missiles? I'm already getting sticker shock."

"As you should. You think I drove all the way up here at four o'clock in the morning to do charity work?"

"You got orders."

"Come on, Dog. It's me. You know I'm happy to sit on my hands and do nothing except write twenty pages of excuses why we couldn't extract you."

"You'd really leave us out here to rot?"

"Oh, don't put it that way, my old friend. It's just business."

"How much?"

"I'll be nice this time. Let's go an even million, and I'll guarantee those Predators will blow the hell out of those monkeys on your back."

"Would a nice bottle of Jack Daniel's cover it?"

Moody snorted. "Unh-unh."

"Aw, man, you know what I want to tell you."

The agent's tone grew painfully musical. "Come on, Dog, you don't pay now, you'll be heading toward the bright light."

"Okay. I'll give you the million, but you have to do something for me besides the extraction."

"Oh, yeah, Mr. Negotiator? What's that?"

"You need to retire and come work for me."

"What?"

"I'm serious. You could retire tomorrow. We'll talk more about it later. I'll call you back at this number?"

"Yeah."

"All right. When we get to K2 and pick up the rest of my team, I'll call with a sitrep."

Mad Dog thumbed off the phone.

Bibby cleared his throat. "Mr. Hertzog, you can't be serious offering him a job."

"Oh, I am. Independent analysis, consulting, public relations, that kind of thing. No fieldwork. Every team needs one major asshole, and he'd be perfect."

"I thought you hated him more than anyone on the planet," said Bibby.

"I pretty much do."

"Uh, boss?" began Wolfgang, raising his hand as though he were in grade school. "That guy might've saved you, but he nearly got the rest of us killed in Angola. You said he was on your back when you fought in A'stan the first time around. Why the hell would you want to hire him?"

"Old cliché. Keep your friends close, your enemies closer. And I think from this point on the CIA is going to be all over us, waiting for the big fuck-up. You don't blackmail them and expect to go off on your merry way."

"Then we should hire someone high ranking who's about to retire," said Bibby.

Mad Dog raised his brows. "Yeah, like, say, someone who runs the Asia desk? I'm sure she's in for early retirement."

"More than you know. One of my contacts in London saw an article in the *Washington Post,* online. Galina Saratova was in a car accident in Rock Creek Park."

"So they whacked her, damn it. Then maybe Moody is lying!"

"No. If we went public with Saratova's identity, then her sudden death would be even more suspicious. They eliminated their security leak, but in doing so strengthened our position."

"Do me a favor. Call Catfish. Ask him if a green necklace was listed in her personal effects found at the crash site. If it wasn't, pass on Saratova's home address to Marcos Sarmiento."

"I remember him."

"Yeah. That little pig is the best second-story guy in the Philippines. If she hid it there, he'll find it. We'll make him a nice deal, and we'll call it a bonus for that bitch selling us out to the Russkies."

"I'll do it," said Bibby.

"Kat, what's our ETA?"

"We should hit K2 in a couple hours at present speed. I throttle up, we burn more fuel."

Mad Dog leaned back in his seat, glanced over at Wolfgang. "Well, seeing as how we're stuck here together, let's have a little talk . . ."

Wolfgang swallowed. "I'm much better now."

"You don't look it."

Night Stalker's Chopper
Uzbekistan Desert
Heading South Toward K2
0605 Hours Local Time

The helicopter's Rolls-Royce engine purred quietly as they streaked through the early morning, an orange peel of sun just nipping the horizon to their left.

Pope noted the long faces on Sapper, Drac, and Boo Boo, their cheeks colored blue and white by the bird's internally lit instrumentation. He couldn't see Night Stalker, who had his helmet on, but expected that the pilot, too, had had enough of Central Asia, thank you, where's the exit?

Unsurprisingly, Pope hated not being in control of a situation, and he felt even more frustrated by being cooped up inside the aft cabin of a helicopter with no seats, one incapable of getting them all the way home.

Aw, hell, he told himself, he needed to stop being such a pessimist. After all, the world was free of one terrorist leader, and IPG was already up two million and about to blackmail a nice piece of change from the CIA. They had all been deeply in the shit and come out smelling like . . . well, not like roses, but more like rose-scented deodorizer, a kind of fake victory.

Night Stalker was now on the radio with Styles, who said that he and the rest of his group were about two and a half miles north of Karshi and we're getting ready to stop.

Then suddenly Night Stalker's voice grew agitated. "Say again, Mother Dog, you broke up!"

Pause.

"Say again?"

"What's going on?" Pope cried.

"I don't know. I heard him start yelling something to the kid, and now he won't respond."

Chapter 13

. . . .

C-130 Hercules Crew
2.5 Miles North of Karshi
0608 Hours Local Time

They slowed down as the headlights from the other truck drew closer.

Lerick assured Styles that the men in that truck were two brothers who smuggled black market clothing, movies, and CDs up to Nukus and often drove the same route as they did. They were probably carrying a shipment right now.

But as Lerick hit the brake even harder, slowing them to just a few miles per hour, and the other truck was about to pass, Styles knew something was wrong. He broke off his conversation with Night Stalker.

"I'm sorry," said the boy. "I couldn't stop him. And he is my grandfather."

"What're you talking about? What did you do?"

The kid just looked at Styles—

"What did you do?"

Lerick wrenched open the door and bailed out, as did

the grandfather, leaving Styles sitting in the middle and screaming, "What did you do?"

The truck rolled on with no driver, and Styles shoved himself into the driver's seat and jammed his foot on the brake pedal. He threw the truck in park and cried, "Wilcox, get your weapon and get out!"

Styles glanced in the rearview mirror, saw the other truck stopped behind them and two men rushing up with AKs. They weren't soldiers; they might even be the two smugglers Lerick had described. Neither was more than twenty-five, dark-skinned and scruffy, torn jeans, sweatshirts. "Got two with rifles!" he told Wilcox.

As Styles knifed out of the truck, a gunshot rang out, and by the time he reached the tailgate, two more rounds boomed—

One fired by Wilcox, who was on his knees and clutching his chest.

The other coming from the nearest rifleman, who fired yet another shot in the dirt at Styles's feet.

And all the while Lerick was screaming at them, and the old man continued to wave his hands, as if to say *Shoot them all,* as he spoke on a cell phone.

A cell phone, damn it.

How had they missed that? Time to admit the obvious: They were retired pilots and weren't as sharp as the other operators. Hell, they were supposed to be sitting back at the airport, sipping cocktails and cavorting with the hookers—not involved in a goddamn gunfight.

Styles raised his pistol at the rifleman, who shouted, "No!"

"Oh, God," grunted Wilcox before dropping onto his chest.

Styles hesitated, glanced at his wounded friend, then

raised a palm, tossed the pistol into the dirt. He moved to Wilcox, rolled the man onto his back.

The loadmaster's bloody chest grew very still, his eyes vague.

"Aw, no." Styles looked up at the boy. "I was going to help with your brother, with your life. Why didn't you stop him, kid?"

Lerick lifted his chin at his grandfather, who was still talking rapidly on his phone. "He thinks you did something in Khiva. I don't know what to think. Now we go back to the airport. He says they'll pay a reward for you. We have to go."

"Damn it, son. I could've helped. You let him throw that all the way!"

Before Lerick could answer, a scream came from the truck behind them.

Imelda appeared from behind the tarpaulin, Zito's pistol in her hand. She fired at one of the rifleman, striking him in the arm before he released a salvo that pinged across the truck, missing her.

But the other guy, who was a bit shorter and heavier, fired a three-shot burst that drummed into Imelda's chest and sent her staggering back into the truck.

Styles got to his feet, turned toward the tailgate.

"No move!" cried the shorter guy. He charged past Styles, hopped up into the truck, vanished behind the tarpaulin. A moment later he emerged, dragging out Imelda's body and letting it drop like a hunk of meat to the dirt.

Lerick shouted something to both men, then the taller one started for his truck, while the shorter one approached Styles. "You come now."

"Lerick? I don't care if my friends are dead. We're

taking the bodies. We're not leaving them out here."

The boy shook his head.

"Styles?" came Zito's drunken voice from the back of the truck. "What's going on?"

Ignoring Zito, Styles hardened his voice even more. "We're taking the bodies."

The kid shrugged. "They will come back for them."

Lerick's grandfather shuffled up to Styles and, without warning, drew back a fist.

Styles caught the fist before it connected with his eye—even as Lerick pulled the old man away.

With burning eyes, Styles took hold of Wilcox's arms, lifted the man and began dragging him toward the truck.

"No!" cried the shorter rifleman.

"Then you'd better shoot me, boy. Right now." Styles took a deep breath and continued his work.

The rifleman looked to the kid.

Lerick stared at him, tears forming in his eyes.

Styles thought he heard something in the distance. No. Maybe not. Just the idling truck engines. Wait. There it was.

Rotors thumping.

Kat's Chopper
2.5 Miles North of Karshi
0615 Hours Local Time

"Still no word from Styles?" Mad Dog asked Kat.

"No, but the FLIR's picking up heat sources. Two vehicles heading south."

"Two?"

"Yeah. Night Stalker confirms the same."

"Let's go get 'em."

"Whoa, hold on, cowboy. Let's get a better look."

"There they are," cried Bibby, pointing at twin dust trails rising from the dark plain ahead.

"Two trucks," Mad Dog thought aloud. "They must see us now. Why aren't they stopping?"

But Mad Dog already knew the answer. Kat voiced it: "They're in trouble."

Mad Dog got on the radio. "Blackhound Ten, this is Blackhound One, over."

"Go ahead, One," answered Night Stalker.

"No contact with Mother Dog. I want those vehicles disabled. Bring yourself in low, see if the guys can get off some shots. You take the lead truck. We'll take the rear, over."

"Roger that, we'll take lead, you take rear, over."

"All right. Let's do it, out!"

"Shit, if we knew which truck they were in—" began Wolfgang.

"Assume they're in both."

Mad Dog reached toward one of the sniper rifle cases.

"I'm the best shot here," said Wolfgang, reaching for another case. "Let me do this."

"We'll do it together. Buckle up. When that maniac at the stick gets going, trust me, you'll be glad you did."

"Believe it," Kat added.

Mad Dog and Wolfgang quickly unpacked and assembled the rifles. They strapped in and slid open the tinted windows on the chopper's two aft doors. Though rectangular-shaped and only about twelve inches long, the windows easily permitted a gun barrel, though range of motion was severely limited. It was up to Kat to line up.

"All right," Mad Dog began. "Good to go back here!"

Kat slammed the stick, and the chopper banked hard right like a hungry falcon. Mad Dog's stomach said hello to his wisdom teeth.

"Holy shit!" hollered Wolfgang.

"Indeed!" cried Bibby, whose laptop slipped from his grip and went crashing to the floor.

"God, there's a lot of dust," Kat grunted, unaffected by her own hair-raising maneuvers.

She brought them around, leveled off, then descended and came up behind the trucks.

Night Stalker's bird dove in beside them, then pulled ahead. Sapper and Pope had climbed out onto the chopper's landing skids, brandishing their rifles, while Drac and Boo Boo took aim with their pistols from the aft door windows.

"Come down a little more," said Wolfgang, peering through his sight.

Mad Dog took aim as well, trying to float his cross hairs over the truck's driver side rear tire.

A man sprung up on the passenger side of the lead truck, sitting on the window frame and bringing his rifle around. He fired erratically at Night Stalker's bird.

Pope, Sapper, Drac, and Boo Boo didn't take kindly to that, answering the gunman's burst with multiple rounds that forced him back into the cab.

"Blackhounds, watch that fire!" Mad Dog cried over the radio.

"Kat?" Wolfgang called. "A little more."

"I'm trying." She took them down to a mere twenty feet, sweeping across the desert, the truck's dust and debris blowing into their canopy. "Take your shot!"

Mad Dog's cross hairs found the tire. He fired, his round echoed by Wolfgang's.

A blink . . . and then . . . there it was: Wolfgang's round had blown out the passenger side tire. Mad Dog's had missed.

"Hooah!" shouted Wolfgang. "Snick, snick, my fucking ass!"

"What?" asked Mad Dog.

"Nothing."

"Hey, he's still rolling," Kat pointed out. "All you did was slow him down. Get that other tire!"

Styles was sitting in the back of the truck, next to Zito, who was hung over, wincing, babbling to himself.

The bodies of Wilcox and Imelda lay on the floor beside the crates of vodka. The old man stood at the back, near the tarpaulin flap, gripping a strap affixed to the rail. One of the punks had given him Styles's pistol, which he kept trained on his prisoners. He turned and stole another peek through the flap as more gunfire thundered.

Lerick was at the truck's wheel, while the shorter gunman rode up front with him. More shots rattled from near the cab, and suddenly a tire blew out.

The initial boom threw Styles down, onto Zito, who screamed in agony. The truck shook more violently, and as Styles rolled to steady himself, the old man lost his balance.

In the next second Styles slammed his fingers past the old man's white beard and found his throat. He drove the tottering man back toward the flaps.

The flat tire must have caught a rut, the truck bed dropping sharply then slamming up, tossing both Styles and the old man out of the truck.

But Styles didn't realize what had happened until he

hit the dirt on his side, felt the air escape his lungs, his hands slipping from the old man's throat.

Sand and pebbles blasted into them, then a second later the helicopter roared overhead.

Styles came up onto his hands and knees, squinting, spitting dust, his back aching. His pistol sat just a few inches from the old man's hand.

He dove for it, but the old man was faster, snatching it up and rolling to aim at him, though his spectacles had been smashed and hung crookedly from his nose.

Styles reached out, mostly out of reflex, because he was about to be shot point-blank. And he knew it.

A loud crack from somewhere . . . Above?

Styles grabbed the pistol just as the old man's head snapped back, a gaping hole opening above one brow, blood spraying into Styles's eyes.

Mad Dog lowered his sniper's rifle and shouted for Kat to land.

She wheeled around once more as Night Stalker took his bird ahead of the trucks, both crippled now with multiple flat tires and limping along the road.

The second the skids touched dirt, Mad Dog was out the door and racing across the sand toward Styles. "Gerry?"

The pilot took Mad Dog's hand, groaned as he got to his feet. "Zito's still in the back," he said, eyeing the fleeing truck.

"We'll get him."

"They killed Wilcox and Imelda."

"Who did? The kid?"

"No, they called for help—a couple of smuggler buddies, I think. Kill those bastards, Michael. Kill them."

Mad Dog's breath grew shallow, his gut burning at the news. "Come on."

"If you don't kill 'em, I will!"

They hustled back to the waiting chopper, and Kat lifted off before Mad Dog could shut the door.

Pope and Sapper leaped down from the skids and ran toward the oncoming trucks, then stopped, pistols held with both hands. Four shots. Pope saw that three tires were blown out. He'd missed one, damn it. Didn't matter.

Almost in unison the trucks stopped. Out hopped the kid from one truck, hands raised. And out hopped two other guys, rifles up, ready to surrender.

"Don't move!" ordered Pope.

"Please don't shoot us!" shouted the kid.

"Stay right there!"

But the kid suddenly bolted, slipping around the trucks and running back down the road, toward his fallen grandfather.

"We'll get him," Pope told Sapper. "But these two first!"

They moved in on the gunmen, disarmed and zipper-cuffed them as Kat landed off to their right. Mad Dog got out and jogged over with Styles.

"Give me your weapon!" Styles shouted at Pope.

"Gerry?" Mad Dog warned.

"Give me that fucking rifle!" Styles rushed toward Pope, reaching for the AK he had just confiscated.

"Sapper, get him back to the chopper," Mad Dog ordered.

"Michael, kill these two fuckers!" shouted the pilot.

"You going to make it easy or hard?" Sapper asked.

The pilot glowered at Mad Dog, shot a look to Sapper. "Fuck this!" He threw up his hands and started back for the chopper.

"Leave these guys," Mad Dog told Pope. "Give me a hand with Zito."

"You two sit down," Pope told them.

They didn't understand, so he shoved one to the dirt. The other guy got the point.

"Oh, man," muttered Mad Dog.

Pope was almost afraid to ask. When he reached the back of the truck, he flinched at the sight of Wilcox lying in a blood pool, the hooker draped across his chest.

"Be real careful," Mad Dog said, his voice cracking. "His legs are pretty busted up."

Zito looked at them, his head wobbling, then he collapsed.

While they carefully unloaded the copilot, Mad Dog's face grew even more flush.

"Maybe Gerry's right," said Pope. "Kill the fuckers."

Mad Dog didn't answer.

Sapper came jogging back and took over for Mad Dog, who was pulled away by Bibby.

On the way back to Night Stalker's chopper, Pope and Sapper just looked at each other.

The morning couldn't have been any grimmer.

Pope narrowed his gaze as they moved into the deafening rotor wash, where Drac and Boo Boo waited to help them slide Zito on board. Boo Boo went right to work on his patient.

Mad Dog shook his head at Bibby's suggestion that they leave the bodies.

"The weight's an issue," the Brit reminded him.

"We'll leave the hooker. But Wilcox comes."

Mad Dog regarded the chopper. "Wolfgang?" He waved the man over.

"What about the kid and the other two?" asked Bibby. "Damned sloppy if we just leave them behind."

"I'm not killing them."

"You've gone soft on us."

"No. I just want to get out of here. And you're bitching about the weight."

Wolfgang arrived, brows raised. "What?"

"Let's pull the two trucks together. Move those two idiots and the kid away. Then grab a couple of grenades. Boom. Smoke should draw those two choppers on our ass. Let's move!"

Bibby's gaze lit up. For once he liked the plan.

As Wolfgang ran off to fetch the grenades, Mad Dog turned to look at the kid, who was still with his dead grandfather. He jogged over there. "We're leaving," he told the boy. "But help should be coming for you soon."

The teary-eyed kid barely looked at him. "Just go."

Wolfgang pulled the two trucks beside each other, and, with the two cuffed gunmen sitting in a ditch about fifty yards away, pulled the pins on two grenades and tossed them into the cabs.

He had grabbed two bottles of vodka first. You took souvenirs whenever and wherever you could, especially alcohol.

The two trucks exploded, sending showers of glass and debris across the dunes, the fires raging, and in a moment, he knew that all the vodka would ignite, whoosh!

Too bad they wouldn't be close for the show. Wolfgang ran away from the scene, ducking as he neared Kat's chopper, then hoisted himself on board.

They left the two burning trucks behind, the gunmen clambering to their feet and screaming at the kid, who sat cross-legged beside his grandfather.

Deep, black smoke now split the horizon, which he knew would be visible for several miles. Hopefully, Mad Dog's plan to delay their pursuers would work.

Another flash from below. Much more smoke. Yes, the vodka was going up now.

Wolfgang unscrewed the cap on one of the bottles between his legs, toasted his handiwork, then took a tentative sip.

Oh, the burn, the sweet, sweet burn. He threw his head back and marveled over the silence in his head.

Strangest thing. All he'd had to do was remember.

Nellis Air Force Base
15th Reconnaissance Squadron
Outside Las Vegas
1745 Hours Local Time

Air Force Major Rick Groom, an experienced fighter pilot, would put in a little overtime today.

Typically, he kissed his wife and two young daughters good-bye in the morning, then returned home at five P.M. with weary eyes, no one the wiser that he and his sensor operator were actually fighting wars on multiple fronts from the comfortable confines of their grounded cockpit not far the brothels and hotels and casinos of sin city.

Indeed, what happened in Vegas stayed in Vegas.

Groom's "plane," technically known as a UAV—Unmanned Aerial Vehicle—but usually called a Predator, was thousands of miles away in Central Asia. The dull gray monoplane with slender fuselage was already in flight, its windowless cockpit and inverted V-tails making it appear more like a Boy Scout's unfinished model plane than a robotic killer.

Only moments ago the call had come in to help extract some individuals from Uzbekistan, and he and his partner were happy to oblige. It had been a slow day.

They sat in their big armchairs, studying the banks of flat panels displaying video images from the camera mounted on the drone's belly. Those images were also being sent to a ground force stationed along the Amu Darya River, to officials within the CIA, and to the Pentagon.

Groom's job was to fly the drone and launch its Hellfire missiles. His sensor operator controlled the camera and laser targeting device. They communicated with the troops and commanders through instant-messaging systems as well as radio transmission routed through a mission controller who sat in the command center at Nellis and would issue them orders.

And a new set of such orders had just come in. The drone was within five miles of two burning trucks sitting just north of Karshi. Two Russian made Mi-8 helicopters equipped with 7.62mm machine guns and external weapons racks loaded down with S-5 rockets capable of covering 300 meters in 1.1 seconds were nearing the area, one chopper descending to land.

That was their target. The other helicopter wheeling overhead presented a greater challenge and would be targeted after they destroyed the first.

Groom's sensor operator had lased the helicopter and was ready. Groom relayed the information to his mission controller.

Although only three, maybe four seconds passed, Groom might tell his friends later that he waited a lifetime. The anticipation of taking out the chopper gave him a bad case of the "trembles," and saliva gathered in his mouth.

Finally, the mission controller's voice came through his headset: "Permission to fire."

He squeezed the trigger.

The missile streaked away from the drone, and before Groom could take another breath, the Mi-8 exploded in a shower of debris, its rotors boomeranging off the craft as it tipped onto its side, ravaged by secondary explosions and flames. Damn, the Hellfire had struck a direct hit, center of mass. You couldn't do better.

Groom and his operator let out a whoop, the adrenaline pumping hard. Their controller tempered the celebration, ordering them to lock on to the next target.

Night Stalker's Chopper
Uzbekistan Desert
Ten Miles North of Termez
0710 Hours Local Time

Night Stalker wished he were flying one of his old Black Hawks—or better, a Cobra or Apache. At least then he might have better eyes on the battlefield ahead.

Mad Dog had just told him that Moody's buddies had a Predator in the air and had taken out one of the choppers on their asses but that the other one moved out before they could lock on.

The Soviets still had a few surface-to-air missile sites left over from their war with Afghanistan, way back when. And there was no telling whether the Uzbeks had called ahead. At least that chopper wouldn't catch up with them.

"Blackhound Ten, be advised we have multiple rotary wing craft taking off from K2, over," said Mad Dog.

Forget the SAM sites. They were about to have more meatheads breathing down their necks.

Suddenly, two rockets streaked by the chopper, trailing white plumes and vanishing toward the jagged mountains looming in the haze.

"He's on us!" shouted Pope. "Looks like an Mi-8 lining up for another shot!"

"Where the fuck did he come from?" asked Night Stalker. "We had a good lead on those assholes!"

"He must be from K2," answered Pope. "His buddy radioed ahead."

"And now he's firing his machine guns, shit!" hollered Sapper. "Get us out of here, buddy!"

Night Stalker throttled up and pulled back on the stick, banking as he gained altitude, the engine wailing, Boo Boo hollering about their patient.

He knew he couldn't outrun the larger, faster chopper—and even if the engine had been capable of such a feat, he didn't have the fuel to spare.

Gunfire tore across the fuselage once more, and it was all Night Stalker could do to evade the onslaught. He cut the stick again, fighting it all the way as they dove at a forty-five degree angle back toward the desert.

"Sapper! Sapper!" cried Pope.

"Oh, shit, he's been hit," said Drac.

Night Stalker didn't dare glance backward. He pulled

up once more, leveled out—just as another wave of fire came in—confirming that the asshole was still back there, wasn't giving up, and that it was just a matter of time.

The fuel gauge warning light was already flashing, and a hydraulics malfunction sent a tremor through his shoulders. The smell of fuel permeated the cockpit.

He cursed and dragged them up again, climbing higher, higher, the sun blinding, something acrid wafting into his nose.

"Night Stalker, look!" Boo Boo shouted.

He stole a glance over his shoulder.

There it was: smoke billowing from the direct jet thruster at the end of the chopper's tail boom. Some of those rounds had penetrated the fuselage and struck the engine.

"You got control?" asked Pope.

"Yeah, but not for long!" He keyed his mike. "Black-hound One, this is Ten, we're taking heavy machine gun and missile fire from a chopper on our six. We're losing power and going down!"

Kat's Chopper
Uzbekistan Desert
Ten Miles North of Termez
0710 Hours Local Time

Mad Dog couldn't see what was happening behind them—they had about a mile lead on Night Stalker—but his imagination ran wild with images of the 600N spiraling out of control and exploding across the sand, leaving a wall of fire in its wake, his men, blackened and still burning, hobbling forward from the wreckage.

"Ten, hold on for as long as you can! We have to get closer, over!"

"Doing the best I can. Still losing power. I'll need to autorotate to get us on the ground. Can we get this asshole off my tail, over?"

Bibby was already instant messaging Moody's Delta team and conveying the information. The Brit paused and said, "Predator crew has destroyed the second helicopter. First drone only carries two Hellfires, but a second one is en route, ETA fifteen minutes."

Mad Dog swore through clenched teeth.

"If they're going down, how're we going to get them?" asked Wolfgang.

"We'll walk," said Kat. "'Cause we'll all be on foot in a few minutes. Gentlemen, we're flying on fumes."

"How far are we from Termez?" asked Mad Dog.

"About three miles."

"Shit. Bibby?"

"I'll see if I can get us a ride."

"Try your MI6 friends first. Moody says he can't cross the border."

Bibby punched a button on the satellite phone.

"All right. I'm getting ready to autorotate myself," announced Kat. "Prepare for landing. It won't be pretty."

Wolfgang opened his bottle of vodka, took a swing. Mad Dog snatched the bottle out of his hands and downed a gulp himself. The burn left him groaning—just as Kat shut down the engine and began their descent.

Chapter 14

····························

Amu Darya River
On the Afghan Border
0714 Hours Local Time

M oody was about to light up another cigarette when
Hammerhead, who was leaning over his radio operator, shifted away and crossed to the back of chopper,
toward the designated smoking area established by the
captain.

The other Delta guys had taken up positions along the
river, and Moody had lost sight of them in the mud and
brush.

Hammerhead's face was unreadable, his tone equally
absent of emotion. "Mr. Moody, both choppers are going
down."

"Well ain't that fucking fabulous."

"One still has a bogie on his tail. And more choppers
are launching from K2."

"What about the drones?"

"Predator took out two bogies. Second's en route,
won't reach them in time."

"Then, Captain, gather up your monkeys and fire up your bird. Let's get out there and help 'em."

"I thought that was made clear to both of us. We're not authorized to do that."

"Do you call your mom and ask for permission every time you want to hump a girl?"

"Mr. Moody, do not test me."

"My orders are to extract those men at all costs. Fire up the fucking bird. We're going!"

"We can't enter their airspace. If they fire upon us, this could turn into an international incident."

"Jesus, Captain, it already is."

"Sir, I say again, we are *not* authorized to go into—"

"Captain . . . " Moody lit up his cigarette, blew smoke in the man's face. "You know you want to go. Just like me. They can't be that far off."

Hammerhead called out to his radio operator. "You got GPS on them?"

"Yeah, they're about three miles out now, sir."

"Shit, that ain't nothing." The captain thought it over, raised his chin at Moody. "Saddle up, asshole."

Moody took a long drag on his cigarette and smiled.

Night Stalker's Chopper
Uzbekistan Desert
Three Miles North of Termez
0715 Hours Local Time

Night Stalker had managed to regain control and squeeze another seven miles out of his wounded bird, but now he couldn't get her goddamn nose up.

Yes, he'd lowered the collective all the way down and trimmed with the antitorque pedals, but getting those parts right didn't matter if he couldn't get the girl look-ing up. She literally needed an attitude adjustment, but she just wouldn't budge, the bitch. His throat lumped. The ground was coming up way too fast. He always told the nervous guys he was transporting, "You know you're in real trouble when the pilot himself tells you he's about to throw up. Just remember that."

Night Stalker gagged and swallowed hard.

"Sapper's gone," called Boo Boo. "He's gone."

Pope said something, even as Drac made a few com-ments, their voices lost in the white noise of alarms, wailing engine, and the pounding of Night Stalker's heart.

No, she wouldn't look up. Shy bitch. Demure. Wouldn't stick out her tits. Wouldn't give him the time of day.

Why weren't the others screaming?

Or maybe they were. Gerry Styles was trying to give him flying advice—or crashing advice, Night Stalker couldn't be sure. He couldn't hear much—

Just that damned voice in his head, that crazy little voice that in one moment reminded him he was a failure . . . and in the next of how exciting it all was, that he wasn't sitting around like a cab driver waiting for a fare, that he was up to his ears in the shit, that after all these years he was back in Somalia—but God damn it, he wasn't getting any payback. It was all happening again. They were going down.

Three seconds. Two . . .

The rotors struck first, digging in for a few seconds as a terrible screech echoed from above.

Glass broke, then came another boom as the ground rushed up at him.

Reflexively, he threw up his hands and was about to scream, but the voice in his head beat him to the punch.

Kat's Chopper
Uzbekistan Desert
Three Miles North of Termez
0718 Hours Local Time

Kat didn't remember to breathe until after the skids touched ground. They bumped hard, but Jesus, she had just performed the best autorotation of her entire flying career—and she'd pulled it off when it really counted.

She should be proud of herself, but she had better catch her breath first.

Wolfgang, Mad Dog, and Bibby rushed from the helicopter, rifles slung over their shoulders, Bibby loading his computer into his pack.

But Kat just sat there, frozen, gripping the stick.

And trembling.

A muffled voice came from outside. "Kat? Come on!"

She gazed through the canopy at Mad Dog, his eyes wide as he raised the satellite phone to his ear.

Suddenly, her door clicked open and a hand locked around her wrist. Wolfgang.

He winked. "Hey, this ain't valet parking."

She sighed. "Yeah, coming . . . " She climbed out, turned to the desert behind them, where gray smoke swirled in several columns, and off to the right something glinted: another chopper.

"It's hot back there," said Wolfgang. "We'd better haul it!"

Mad Dog waved them over. "Moody's got a chopper. He's going for Night Stalker's team first. They'll grab us on the way back. But it won't hurt to put more distance between us and them."

The four of them took off running toward the city, adobe roofs and a pair of minarets visible below the cracked peaks and mottled brown ridgelines of the mountains ahead.

Kat couldn't help but hazard another look over her shoulder. More smoke. Reflections.

And the chilling reminder that they were out in the middle of nowhere in broad daylight, running like pathetic ants.

She wanted to reach out, hold Mad Dog's hand, feel some kind of reassurance that she wasn't about to die.

But there wasn't time.

And he was back on his satellite phone, talking to Moody, screaming that they still didn't see his chopper, getting updated GPS numbers from Bibby, waving off Wolfgang, who kept wanting to interrupt him.

"What is it?" asked Kat.

Wolfgang cocked a thumb over his shoulder. "It's that."

An Mi-8 chopper was barreling toward them, just a hundred or so feet above the sand.

U.S. Army Black Hawk
Uzbekistan Desert
Crossing Border into Uzbekistan
0722 Hours Local Time

Moody sat toward the back of the chopper's cabin, watching as two of Hammerhead's men manned the

7.62mm machine guns mounted at each door.

One of the guys, a tall blond with an icy expression, made a jerking motion at his crotch, then smiled darkly at Moody, who simply flipped the man the bird.

These men were professionals and rarely behaved this way, Moody knew; he just brought out the worst in people, especially U.S. military personnel.

In a way, he didn't blame them. They were as territorial as wolves and were ready to sink their teeth into anyone—especially a civilian—who peed on their sacred ground.

Moody turned away, let the chopper's pair of turboshaft engines lull him into a false sense of security.

Suddenly, the men at the guns perked up, and Moody leaned forward, stole a glance through the open doors. "Oh, don't even fucking tell me," he grunted.

"He's fired a rocket!" one of the men screamed.

The Black Hawk suddenly dove as though a giant had taken a swat at it, and Moody's harness dug into his shoulders.

"Missed us!" reported the same man.

"He's going for our guys on the ground now," said the blond gunner. "We got four down there."

"Return fire!" cried Hammerhead.

Both gunners opened up as the Black Hawk wheeled around in pursuit.

Moody felt the blood drain from his veins.

Hammerhead looked at him with great amusement, then hollered to his men, "Watch those muzzles! You get 'em too hot, you'll melt 'em off!"

* * *

Night Stalker's Chopper
Uzbekistan Desert
Three Miles North of Termez
0723 Hours Local Time

Drac and Boo Boo had pulled themselves from the wreckage, but when the first Mi-8 arrived, the pilot had come in low and opened up with machine guns.

Pope had been lying there, bleeding, half hidden behind the shattered tail boom. He didn't blink. He just stared as though it were all happening on TV, the rounds punching gaping holes in his friends before the fire ceased and the chopper flew off.

Night Stalker was still inside the cockpit, presumably dead. Zito, too, was still inside, asphyxiated for sure from all the smoke and fumes. At least Sapper had bought it quick, Pope thought. That's how he himself would've preferred it.

How had he escaped? There was the horrible impact, then the disorientation, the dizziness, all that smoke.

Then he was outside and awake.

Gerry Styles lay beside him, taking in his last few breaths, a huge piece of metal jutting from the man's side. Styles must've dragged him out of the cabin, away from the smoke and back toward the tail boom. Crazy old man.

"Gerry?"

The old pilot gazed absently at him, his lips twitching, as though he wanted to smile, then he grew very still. His chest was still rising and falling.

Pope grabbed his hand, barely noticing the rocket launcher slung over Styles's shoulder.

"I just thought the end would be different, Gerry. I bet you did, too, huh?"

The pilot was no longer breathing.

"You were a good man, buddy. A good man."

At the sound of another chopper, Pope sat up, removed the launcher from Styles's body. The old man had been trying to tell him something: Fight till the fucking end. And he would. He got to work, and when he was finished, crouched behind the tail boom, not caring if the chopper was about to explode. He needed the cover. He had no choice.

The AT4, with its shaped charge warhead—the good old HEAT round—was balanced on his right shoulder. He peered through the rear sight, his pulse thumping hard.

The Barbie doll that belonged to his dead sister sat on the tail boom. For good luck.

No lasing the target. No fancy ballistics computers. Just make sure the target was within 250 meters.

And the target in question was another Mi-8 landing directly ahead, to check for survivors, no doubt.

Ten seconds to touchdown.

He would wait until they were on the ground and completely vulnerable.

The deep gash in Pope's right thigh was bleeding again, but he was relieved that at least the other one across his forehead had stopped. The blood had poured into his eyes, momentarily blinding him. He might've broken a rib or two. It hurt to breathe.

But God damn it, he was strong enough to launch this round, and maybe, somehow, save his ragged ass.

He thought aloud to calm his nerves, remind himself

that gorillas could fire this weapon; the manufacturer had even added a little picture on the launcher that showed how to do it, with the words FIRE LIKE THIS etched below.

"Just wait a minute, Billy. Just a few more seconds. There they are, right there. Just a hundred meters or so. Perfect. Perfect." He took in a long breath, held it. Asked his sister for help.

And fired!

One one thousand . . .

His shoulders were warmed by the weapon's massive back fire—

Boom! The warhead's nose cone impacted with the chopper and caved in, triggering the impact sensor to activate the fuse.

The piezoelectric fuse element activated the electric detonator. The booster detonated, initiating the main charge, which fired and forced the warhead body liner into a directional gas jet that penetrated the chopper's armor plates.

Finally, the projectile fragments and incendiary effects produced blinding light and blasted through the interior of the helicopter.

That was the science of it all. The reality was that within two seconds, he had cremated every human being inside and turned the chopper into an inferno whose flames were further whipped up by the slowing rotors.

Pope let the launcher slip from his shoulder and fell back onto the tail boom. He grabbed the Barbie doll, clutched it tightly, and closed his eyes as the *whomp-whomp* of more helicopters continued in the distance.

And then a noise strangely out of place broke the

whooshing of flames: His satellite phone began to ring.
He answered.

"That you, Pope?" asked Mad Dog.

"Yeah?"

"I've been trying to reach Night Stalker."

"They're all dead. I'm the only one left."

Silence.

"Did you hear me?" Pope asked.

"Yeah, just hang tough, SEAL. There's a Black Hawk
on the way. Look for it."

Pope's voice cracked. "I will."

"Billy?"

"I'm with you. I'm just . . . I'm cut up pretty bad, but I
can move. I'm good to go."

"That's what I want to hear. That's what you do."

"Yes, Sergeant."

"Now you sound like Doolittle."

"Sorry. I'll see you in a little while."

Pope hung up. He knew Mad Dog was blown away,
and he knew the boss couldn't show it. Not now. Neither could he. But if they lived, the nights would be
harder than ever, the faces even more distinct. What had
they accomplished, other than getting some good men
killed?

U.S. Army Black Hawk
Uzbekistan Desert
Crossing Border into Uzbekistan
0728 Hours Local Time

Hammerhead's men were still firing at the enemy chopper when one released his trigger and announced that

they'd gotten him, that he was going down. The men whooped and hollered.

The Black Hawk's pilot broke off from the engagement, then came around, returning to their northbound heading.

Behind them, the smoking helicopter plummeted, and Moody leaned forward to watch it shatter across the dirt, multiple fireballs filled with tumbling debris.

Mad Dog called to say that he had made contact with one of his men, that there was only one survivor at the first helicopter's crash site but they should recover all of the bodies.

Moody passed that on to Hammerhead, who nodded, consulted his watch, and said, "At least the drones should be back up there and provide us a little cover." He hunkered down near his radio operator, who was nodding confirmation and speaking with the mission controller at Nellis.

Within three minutes they were wheeling over the still smoking debris.

"Man, they got fucked," he said under his breath, squinting at the bodies, the pieces of chopper, the deep furrows in the sand.

Once they were on the ground, Moody hopped down and jogged over to the tail boom, where a familiar-looking man sat, clutching his leg and . . . holding a kid's doll.

"Hey, Billy Pope," called Moody. "Didn't I almost slit your throat?"

Moody wasn't lying. Back in Angola he had held a knife to Pope's tender flesh, but that was strictly business, nothing personal.

"I heard you were here," Pope said weakly. "And I thought you were a spook, not a stalker."

"Big Billy, A'stan is my playground. And old Jimmy Jesus is here to give you the grand fucking tour, once we get out of this ass-backward dump." Moody proffered his hand and helped Pope to his feet. "The medic will look at you once we're on board. How's your doll? She hurt?"

Pope self-consciously stuffed the doll into his pants pocket. "Fuck you, asshole."

"No, really. You all right?"

"You care?"

Moody flashed a broad grin. "I got a million little reasons."

An explosion tore into the sky farther north, and Moody shielded his eyes for a better look. "The Agency's spending a lot of money to save your ass. Forty-five grand every time that drone fires a missile."

"It'll cost them a whole lot more if we go public with what we know."

Moody looked confused. "What're you talking about?"

"Nothing."

"Come on. I'm sure it's something, and we'll have plenty of time to chat." He led Pope back toward the chopper, while the other men collected the bodies.

As they reached the hold, Moody grimaced at the sight of the corpses. He only recognized three of the seven, even remembered their names: Sapper, Boo Boo, and Drac. He raised his voice over the rotor wash. "Hey, man. Sorry about your buddies. Who were these other guys?"

"Chopper pilot. C-130 crew." Pope blinked hard, fighting the obvious burn in his eyes.

Even Moody was rendered speechless. He'd seen a lot of death in his day; it never got any easier, at least not for him . . .

Hammerhead ordered everyone on board, then they lifted off, the Black Hawk tipping its nose toward the south as Moody and Pope clambered for seats.

Mad Dog's Party
Uzbekistan Desert
1.5 Miles North of Termez
0745 Hours Local Time

It's never easy, is it? thought Mad Dog.

The commotion out in the desert had drawn the attention of local police, who sent out a van along a dirt road that he and the others had found just a quarter mile east of the chopper.

Wolfgang had stopped, used his binoculars to ID their company, and was now hurrying to catch up with them.

"Yeah, they're about a half mile out," Mad Dog told Moody over the satellite phone. "They'll reach us before you do."

"Wave and ambush," Moody said. "If you got something better, some old jarhead trick, be my guest."

"Just move your ass," he told the spook, then hung up.

They had kept a brutal pace and were already drenched. Kat and Bibby had pistols, he and Wolfgang their sniper rifles. Wolfgang also had about a half-dozen grenades in his pack. And that was it. The price you paid for traveling light.

The van rumbled closer, towing a train of dust, and

Mad Dog almost laughed at what these cops were forced to drive: an old Daewoo Damas that seemed squashed on both sides and would seemingly tip over if the driver cut the wheel too sharply.

"All right, stop," Mad Dog ordered. "Holster your weapons and wave at Uncle Meathead and Aunt Crotch. And don't forget to shoot your cousins, okay?"

"What do we got?" asked Kat through her forced grin. "Looks like four, one for each of us. Isn't that special—I got the driver."

"I'll get his buddy up front," said Mad Dog.

Wolfgang jogged up to them, breathless, about to raise his rifle. Mad Dog slapped it down. "Wave asshole. Soon as they stop, boom, you shoot 'em right through the glass."

"Roger that."

"You take the guy behind the driver."

"And that leaves the guy behind the passenger for me," said Bibby.

"So what do you think, governor?" Mad Dog asked. "Do we have any chance in hell?"

"Of absconding with this van? Absolutely. Of reaching the border? Well, if we can make it to the river, past the kilometer or so of fences, mine fields, watchtowers, and half-dozen checkpoints, the odds improve dramatically."

Mad Dog winced. "Good."

The van came within ten meters and slowed.

"Keep waving, now run toward 'em, and when I say so, draw your weapons."

With his pulse rumbling like a timpani drum in his ears, Mad Dog held his shit-eating grin, ran forward, then cried, "Now!"

The front passenger, a young cop no more than twenty-five in a green uniform, was just getting out when Mad Dog drew his pistol and capped him.

Glass blew out everywhere as Bibby, Kat, and Wolfgang fired at the others.

The driver slumped over the wheel, blood pouring from his head.

"Watch him in the back!" screamed Kat. "In the back!"

"I got him! I got him!" Wolfgang answered.

His man had been hit in the shoulder and was firing wildly through his shattered windshield. Wolfgang shifted right up to the window and fired two shots into his head before he could fire again.

No hesitation. Swift. Efficient.

The old Wolfgang. Though he had missed his first shot. Nice recovery, though. Nice.

"God damn," grunted Mad Dog.

Wolfgang wrenched opened the door, seized the dead guy by his shirt, and pulled him out of the van.

Mad Dog did likewise with his victim.

"Wait," said Bibby. "There's the Blackhawk."

"With two more choppers on their tail," Kat added. "They can't land and get us. Come on!"

Kat took the wheel, and Mad Dog rode shotgun. Bibby and Wolfgang piled into the back, and Bibby got a call from his MI6 contact just as Kat floored it, turned, and spun out.

They raced toward the outskirts of the 2,500-year-old city, mud huts rising beside more modern-looking buildings. Mad Dog never visited Termez during his Marine Corps days, but he'd heard a few Special Forces guys sum it up in three words: dirty, ugly, and old.

Something flashed behind them, and Mad Dog looked into the rearview mirror.

One of the helicopters pursuing the Blackhawk had exploded, assumedly struck by a Hellfire missile launched from one the Predators somewhere above.

But the remaining chopper was closing in on the Blackhawk.

Twin pinpricks of light shone from the enemy's weapons racks, and the Blackhawk banked to evade, dispersing white-hot chaff, which puzzled Mad Dog since the S-5 rockets on its tail were unguided.

Nervous pilot, no doubt, but his quick reflexes paid off. The rockets flew over him, one engine fanning out, sending the missile tumbling out of control to the deck.

The S-5s were crap, introduced in the fifties and way out of date, but they were the best the Uzbeks had.

Their machine guns, however, were not to be dismissed, and that clearly was the enemy pilot's plan. He rolled right, keeping himself behind the Blackhawk like a kite's tail, and let those machine guns blaze.

The Blackhawk's pilot yawed and pitched, but he just couldn't evade the fire fast enough. He came around, heading north momentarily, then rolled back, never shaking the Uzbeks.

"Kat, you're missing some show back there," Mad Dog said. "Some show."

"Got another one right in front of us."

Mad Dog craned his neck. "Damn it."

As they neared the first stretch of single-story buildings, seemingly strung together by telephone poles bowing under the weight of heavy wires, two more police cars came straight toward them, both with men leaning out of the windows, guns drawn. They were either in contact with the chopper pilots or had seen what happened out in the desert.

"Oh, shit!" cried Wolfgang. "Blackhawk's been hit. Tail rotor's smoking."

Mad Dog glanced back, saw the chopper, then faced forward. "Wolfgang, get up in that window. You got the guy on the right. I got left. Kat? Stop the van!"

"What?"

"I said stop!"

"You want me to stop dead right here?"

"Sweetheart, do I have spell it? S-T-O-fucking-P!"

U.S. Army Black Hawk
Uzbekistan Desert
Crossing Border into Uzbekistan
0755 Hours Local Time

Pope's leg and forehead were throbbing, and the immediate pain bothered him more than the fact that the chopper was going down. He could only handle so much at a time. Only way to keep sane. It didn't dawn on him that he'd been shot out of the sky twice in one day—

Until Moody looked at him with that pale yellow light in his eyes: *I think I'm going to die.*

Pope had seen that light before. Too many times.

He grabbed Moody by the shoulders. "We're going to make it! Just hang tight."

"Yeah, just give me a fixed-wing aircraft over one of these fucking egg beaters!" He shivered through his words.

The Black Hawk began spinning as they lost altitude, the wind howling through the open cabin, smoke whipping as somewhere above came a massive thunderclap that shook the helicopter.

Some of the men cursed. Pope added his collection of four letter words to the cache.

A gasp later, pieces of debris began pinging off the fuselage, and Pope wasn't sure, but he thought another Predator had taken out the asshole on their tail.

"He's got it now!" shouted Hammerhead as the helicopter came out of the spin and suddenly gained altitude.

Swallowing against the nausea, Pope leaned forward, squinted past the open door at the narrow streets and alleys of Termez.

"He says he can get us to the city," reported Hammerhead, one hand covering his radio's earpiece. "But not much farther. He'll put us down near the river, near the first LZ. I'll see if I can get another bird or boat to pick us up from there. But it don't look good! Not in broad daylight."

Pope dialed up Mad Dog on his satellite phone, but it rang and rang.

Out beyond the chopper, a lone van sat in the middle of the dirt road, two cars barreling toward it.

"That's them," said Moody.

"Why'd they stop?"

Moody shrugged. "Maybe they ran out of gas."

Mad Dog's Party
Uzbekistan Desert
.3 Miles North of Termez
0757 Hours Local Time

Wolfgang was a man who'd been held by the heel and dipped in the river Styx by his mother.

He felt fully alive, invincible. He could not recall feeling as good. Damn, he'd have to fall inside buried fishing boats more often.

As he targeted the driver of the police car, he remembered Angola: the trembling, the rain, the rebels who vanished because he had hesitated.

He remembered his jittery hand, the one that had belonged to someone else.

The moment that had belonged to someone else.

Not this moment.

So what had happened? Was curing himself that simple? He just told himself it was okay to brush up against death. He'd been doing it all his life. There was no reason to be scared.

And what the hell, it worked. At least for now.

Bibby cleared his throat. "Mr. Wolfgang? Mr. Hertzog? Our fate is, unfortunately, in your greasy paws."

"I'm the dog, and this is my day!" cried Mad Dog.

Kat revved the engine. "I hear two shots, and we're out of here."

"All right," said Mad Dog. "I got a bead."

"So do I," Wolfgang reported.

"Fire!"

Wolfgang wasn't sure if he pulled the trigger first or if the boss was a nanosecond quicker.

Both drivers took head shots in a feat of marksmanship that you had to witness to believe.

And then, as though they had been cut off from "central control," both vehicles veered wildly off the road and slowed.

Kat punched it, and the van coughed, leapt forward, as Bibby joined them in his window.

All three hung off the van, firing at the two cars as they streaked between them.

Mad Dog didn't need to order it: They went for the tires first, multiple booms sounding as rubber popped and hissed.

The van's back window shattered after a round struck somewhere, the corner, maybe. Wolfgang shuddered, wondering if he'd been hit. No pain yet.

They roared into a dense cloud of dust that chewed into Wolfgang's eyes. He ducked back into the van, carefully sliding his rifle in after him.

Not a full second later, a muffled boom came from just outside his window. His seat shook as though an earthquake had just struck or Kat had driven them into a pool of quicksand.

"We lost a tire!" said Kat, straining at the wheel. "Come on, you piece of shit!"

They reached the first row of buildings and mud huts directly opposite a church or mosque of some kind.

"Turn left," said Bibby, studying a map on his computer. "We'll follow along the west side—more obstacles here."

"That's a good idea," said Wolfgang, cocking a thumb over his shoulder. "Because we got another meathead on our ass."

He glared at the Mi-8 whomping toward them. They were so close now that he could see all three crew members behind the canopy, microphones to their lips, helmet visors down as they opened fire with machine guns, blasting apart the wall of the building just behind them.

Their next salvo took out the other back tire, and Kat screamed, "We're riding on rims!"

"Wait," said Bibby. "Look at that."

An old school bus painted red and white and emblazoned with the logo A BRIGHTER DAY MOBILE HEALTH CLINIC, along with a pair of American flags, was parked in an alley, a line of old women and young mothers with their kids waiting to get inside.

"We're taking that bus," said Mad Dog.

"What about them?" asked Kat, lifting her chin at the civilians.

"We take them hostage," said Bibby. "Perhaps those chopper pilots will think twice about shooting us."

"They won't," said Mad Dog. "No hostages. We take the bus and go."

Bibby's expression went sour, but he didn't argue the point.

Kat brought them to the corner near the bus, and at once they bailed out, yelling for the civilians to clear the area, even as the chopper launched a rocket at their abandoned van. The explosion sent Mad Dog diving to the dirt, the flames warming his neck and fanned by heavy rotor wash.

Suddenly, he was being hauled to his feet.

"You okay?"

He looked at Kat, dirty, strung-out, as beautiful as ever. "Thanks."

Then they stole off toward the bus.

Chapter 15

"**O**h, man, he's missing the riverbank," said Moody.

Pope didn't want to look, but couldn't help himself. The chopper drifted over the bank and, with a thud and splash, touched down in the middle of the river.

Water rushed into the cabin as the Delta guys shouted for everyone to get out.

Pope wrenched off his harness and dragged himself forward into the greasy water. Was that raw sewage he smelled? The odor was enough to make him gag.

Thankfully, the pilot had shut down the engine only seconds before they landed, so the rotors were beating more slowly as the chopper began to sink.

But then the vehicle touched bottom, submerged to about a foot above the forward landing gear.

Pope cleared the cabin and tried to stand, but the cut

on his leg throbbed and stung. Putting any weight on it sent needles through his back. Seeing that, Moody grabbed his arm, slung it behind his head, started carrying him away.

"I don't know how many of you mercs I've saved, but this is getting a little ridiculous now."

"You mean when you're not trying to kill us," said Pope. "And we ain't saved yet."

Another helicopter's turbines sounded somewhere behind them, the thumping louder.

Hammerhead waved them over to the opposite shoreline, toward throngs of shrubs, weeds, and a few stands of trees.

Damn, that enemy helicopter was nearly on top of them now, and Pope wished he hadn't tossed a look back.

"Come on!" screamed Hammerhead.

Suddenly the water erupted, parallel lines of machine gun fire kicking up a fierce spray.

Moody splashed even harder, grunting and swearing that he would never, ever help Mad Dog and his fucking cronies ever again, no matter the order, the situation, no matter if Jesus himself willed it.

The helicopter finished its pass, then came around as though riding on rails, lining up to strafe them once more.

Just as the machine guns rattled again, one of the Deltas latched onto Pope's free arm, and all three of them burst forward, out of the water, up the muddy the bank, and toward the first row of thick shrubs, the brambles snagging on their pants as they came around and got out of sight.

Moody and the Delta guy set him down, and he was already back on the phone to Mad Dog. This time someone answered, though it wasn't the bossman.

"Wolfgang, that you?" he asked.

"Yeah, man, where are you?"

"We're east of your position, right on the river. We set down in the water. Where are you?"

"Listen, I can't talk. We commandeered an old school bus now. Believe that shit?"

"What?"

"Dude, I'll call you back."

Just as Wolfgang cut the line, a nearby whoosh and boom had Pope whipping his head around.

One of Deltas was on his knees, the Command Launch Unit of a Javelin missile system balanced on his shoulder. He'd sighted the chopper and had just fired.

The Javelin was a fire-and-forget system with lock-on before launch and automatic self-guidance. The warhead had two shaped charges to better penetrate armor.

In the span of two seconds the missile flew toward the chopper, arcing high then dropping like an eagle with talons flexed.

And right there, just on the other side of the river, a second sun was born, a fiery orange orb that had once been a Russian-made helicopter.

Flaming debris burst from that sun, arced across the brilliant blue sky, and began splashing into the water. At the same time, the rotors flew off, then a huge section of the tail boom appeared from the flames, tumbling end over end like a solar flare extending from the explosion, breaking off, then crashing into the trees and mud.

The sun consumed itself in black smoke that painted a smear across the horizon.

And at the point Pope and the rest of them remembered to breathe, and someone cried, "Yeah!"

Mad Dog's Party
Streets of Termez, Uzbekistan
0808 Hours Local Time

Their only saving grace, thought Kat, was that the narrow streets had originally been designed for oxen and goat carts, and all of the stone balustrades, parapets, rooftops, antennae, and telephone poles kept the chopper's pilot from getting too close.

However, his machine guns had a ceaseless appetite for stone, plaster, and anything else in the way. Pieces of the stuff crashed onto the bus's roof, sending chills down Kat's spine, and with all the banging, she couldn't tell if they were getting hit by debris or gunfire.

Two American doctors and a nurse had been on the bus and were treating three sisters, all younger than ten. Wolfgang had ordered them off at gunpoint but allowed them to take some of their medical gear. One doc had shouted, "I don't know who you assholes are, but these people need us!"

"Don't worry, Doc," said Mad Dog. "If we scratch your ride, I'll buy you a new one."

And with that, they rumbled off.

"Oh, hell," said Bibby from the seat behind Kat. He was studying real-time satellite images and talking with his contacts. "The Uzbeks are moving up some LAVs from the border."

"LAVs, as in what?"

"Maybe a few BRDMs, BMPs, light tanks."

Kat rolled her eyes. "They all sound bad."

"Just get us to the river."

"It'll be that easy?"

"My contacts will be in position. They'll get us across the border."

"If you say so. What are we, ten klicks out?"

"About that."

"I hope they have air support."

A rocket streaked overhead and exploded no more than fifty feet in front of the bus.

Kat cut the wheel hard, turning into an alley so narrow there was only a foot of clearance on each side.

Several merchants behind carts loaded with pottery and clothing dove for cover as she flattened their displays and tore awnings from doorways before she turned hard left, down another street, this one wider, only to find yet another police car coming straight for them.

Wolfgang shoved himself into the window and began firing, taking out one tire and sending the car caroming off to their left. Kat turned, but not in time, and they sideswiped the vehicle as Wolfgang fired at the driver.

Meanwhile, Mad Dog was shouting into his satellite phone at Moody: "We're heading down to the river. Do you or do you not have transport out? I need to know! And I got another chopper on my ass! Where the hell is that Predator?"

"Hey, where'd he come from?" shouted Wolfgang.

Kat checked her rearview mirror. One of the cops was hanging off the back of the bus, angular eyes widening as he reached for one of the open windows, took hold, then shoved his pistol inside.

Mad Dog broke off from his conversation, turned back

and fired two rounds from his pistol, striking the man in the arm. The cop lost his grip and fell away.

"Shit," gasped Kat.

"Turn left now," ordered Bibby. "Right there!"

Kat rolled the wheel, taking them down a much wider dirt road, past a row of single-story buildings.

Just ahead rose a ten or so story modern structure, gray with blue windows, that Bibby said was one of the main hotels, the Meridian.

A half-dozen subcompact cars converted into taxis were parked out front, and just as Kat was about to ask Mad Dog if they should switch vehicles again, the Mi-8 swooped over them, broke into a long, lazy turn, then prepared to strafe.

"He's got us now," muttered Wolfgang.

Kat tensed. "The hell he does."

With nowhere else to go, she did the only logical thing:

She drove the bus straight under the hotel's covered entranceway, up the short flight of stairs, and right through the glass entrance doors, the sound like a hundred chandeliers crashing to the concrete.

Mad Dog, Bibby, and Wolfgang yelled nearly in unison, the former two protesting, the latter getting off on Ms. Kat's wild ride.

The bus bulldozed farther into the lobby, sending a bell captain and two bellhops scrambling for their lives as concrete, more glass, and twisted steel arced through the air. Kat wondered if she'd run some people over—she wasn't sure because the windshield had shattered all over her—as she hit the brakes, threw it in park, then reached for the lever to open the school bus door.

She burst outside, waving her pistol at the concierge, a gray-haired man dressed in black, along with two more women, either guests or employees, who couldn't believe what they were watching.

Bibby, Wolfgang, and Mad Dog hopped out, crunching over the shattered glass as they picked their way through the dust clouds and back outside, toward the taxis.

The helicopter was still up there, damn it, but as they crossed beneath the entranceway, drawing stares of disbelief from two young valets, Bibby, who had just answered a phone call, cried, "Hold up."

"What now?" asked Mad Dog.

The Brit held up a finger. "Listen."

Mad Dog started for the taxis. "Come on, man."

"Wait!"

A curious hiss sounded from the distance, followed by a thunderclap so loud it sent Kat to her knees and covering her ears.

The explosion echoed off the building, shattering more glass, and glancing up, she realized what was happening. She opened her mouth. No voice for a second, then: "Go! Go! Go!"

She waved them all on, toward one of the cabs, even as the chopper fell from the sky and crashed onto the covered entranceway behind them.

The weight of that bird was too much for the concrete and steel, which gave way, the blazing cockpit appearing within a cloud of dust and twisted metal just thirty feet away.

Kat came around the taxi, ripped the wiry and stunned driver out of the seat, and jumped in. Wolfgang, Mad Dog, and Bibby were a couple of breaths behind her.

She hit the gas as Wolfgang slammed his door—
And the chopper burst into flames in their wake.

"Oh my God," Wolfgang said. "Are we still alive?"

No one answered.

Bibby was panting as he flipped open his computer, scanned the map. "Take this road all the way to the end, then turn right. We're almost there."

"Your friends shoot down that chopper?" Wolfgang asked Bibby.

"No," answered the Brit. "But they're monitoring the Predators. However, they've launched their last Hellfire."

"They coming back?" asked Mad Dog.

"It'll be twenty minutes or more before they can get another drone within range. But it's not the choppers we should worry about right now. It's those LAVs."

"How many?" asked Mad Dog.

"Not sure. Maybe four. Lots of firepower."

Pope, Moody, and Delta Team
Amu Darya River
Termez, Uzbekistan
0820 Hours Local Time

Pope had one arm draped over the shoulder of the Delta team's medic, a hard-faced black man nicknamed Huff, and they moved east along the shoreline, putting more distance between themselves and the crash site. Unfortunately, the best cover remained near and around the riverbank, so the group could not stray very far without being spotted.

Behind them, about a half a klick away, the Afghanistan-Uzbekistan Friendship Bridge spanned the Amu

Darya, connecting Termez with the city of Jeyretan in northern Afghanistan. The bridge had been built by the Soviet Army in 1982 to supply its troops during the war. The sub- and superstructures were no visual thrill—the basic erector set of girders and stanchions atop the requisite concrete pylons.

Hammerhead told them that he'd observed several LAVs moving away from the bridge entrance, bound for the city. He had reported those findings to his CO while making the urgent request for immediate extraction.

He had also learned that another Black Hawk was on its way, but its ETA was over thirty minutes. He had called for some Apache support but couldn't get it. Pope wasn't surprised.

As they hustled on, weaving through the shrubs and trees, Moody kept close and muttered to himself about how they were almost home and he'd collect the big bucks.

"Lost it already?" Pope asked.

"Probably. But I ain't the one carrying around a doll."

Pope ground his teeth. "My sister drowned when I was a kid. It was my fault. The doll was hers."

"That's sad."

"Yeah."

"I mean you carrying a fucking doll because you can't get over your sister's death. That's just fucking stupid. Move on, asshole."

"Jesus Christ!" Pope wrenched his arm away from the medic and hobbled after Moody, who increased his pace.

"That's what I'm talking about," said the spook, glancing back to wriggle his brows. "Keep moving."

"Hold up!" cried Hammerhead from somewhere up front.

Pope, Moody, and the medic reached the captain, who squatted down near two bushes.

"What?" asked Pope.

Hammerhead pushed away the fronds to reveal a Russian BRDM-2 rolling toward the river, about thirty meters ahead. The BRDM was a four-wheel-drive armored amphibious vehicle with a wedge-shaped nose and 14.5mm and 7.62mm machine guns. There would be a crew of two inside, with as many as six infantry ready to pop out the back and raise hell. The vehicle was also armed with some missiles, either surface-to-air or antitank.

"Shit, they're trying to cut us off," Moody said.

"We'll take 'em out and keep moving," said Hammerhead.

Moody shook his head. "Predators can't help now."

"Don't need 'em." The captain called for his man with the Javelin missile system to come forward.

Barely two seconds later another Delta guy rushed up to say that a squad-size force of Uzbek Army infantry had reached the crash site and were heading their way.

Hammerhead tugged his .45 free and handed it to Pope. "You stick with my guys to the rear. Hold 'em off while we clear us a path."

"Yes, sir."

"So you really like this shit, huh?"

"What shit is that?"

"Being a merc."

Pope chuckled under his breath. "Most days."

Hammerhead grinned. "Just not today."

Pope realized that he and this guy were no doubt cut from the same cloth, and as Moody looked on, scowling, Hammerhead returned the look and said, "Mr. Moody, we're going to kill the enemy, if that's all right with you."

"You ain't asking, Captain. So start killing."

Mad Dog's Party
Nearing the Amu Darya River
South of Termez, Uzbekistan
0822 Hours Local Time

A long white railing separated the loading docks' entrance with the serviceway, and those who weren't fleeing from Uzbek's military would take the service road running parallel with the railing, then turn left to enter the docking area proper.

But those who were would crash through the railing and come to a squealing halt not more than two meters from the edge of one such dock.

It wasn't great driving, but then again, Kat thought, she had just driven a bus into a hotel lobby. What did Mad Dog expect?

She must've cracked the radiator, too, because the thing was smoking as they knifed out of the cab and ran with Bibby along a narrow boardwalk, toward an approaching riverboat, a PBR with twin .50 caliber machine guns (aka "forward fifties") and one M60 7.62mm machine gun, all manned by military personnel, their uniforms as yet indistinct.

Another man was positioned on the deck, a rocket launcher of some type held high on his shoulder.

Mad Dog did a double take as they came into better view. The men on board wore Uzbek Army uniforms.

And asshole Bibby was running straight toward them.

But then he abruptly stopped and whirled back, as Kat ran forward, ahead of the rest, her pistol raised.

"What did you do?" she cried, facing Bibby, jamming her pistol into his head. "You screwed us over!"

"Please, Ms. Kugelkerl. Lower your weapon."

Mad Dog dove for cover behind a row of empty shipping crates, took aim at the approaching boat.

"Mr. Hertzog? Her majesty takes great umbrage when hostile fire is directed at one of her vessels."

Suddenly, the man on board holding the rocket launcher fired, and the missile screamed over their heads.

Mad Dog craned his neck and watched as an Uzbek BMP-1, a tracked infantry combat vehicle that resembled a small tank, blew twenty feet into the air and was swallowed in a ball of fire. The BMP had, without their knowledge, been rolling up on their tail.

"Lower your weapon, Ms. Kugelkerl."

"What is it with you?" asked Kat, holstering her pistol. "Always the secrets."

Bibby just looked at her with an expression Mad Dog had seen before, which said, *Isn't it obvious?* As though Bibby were a genius trying to explain quantum mechanics to a chimpanzee.

The PBR pulled up smartly alongside the doc, and a lean man with bright blue eyes came forward. "Hello, Mr. Bibby. Your colleagues Albert and Patrice from Vauxhall Cross send their regards."

"Thank you, Captain. This is Ms. Kugelkerl, Mr. Hertzog, and Mr. Wolfgang. We'll be heading west downriver to pick up that Delta Force team, a CIA agent, and one more of our men."

"Very good, sir. We'll contact our extraction team and have them pick us up from there."

"Excellent. Best possible speed, sir."

"Indeed." The captain hollered to his men, and the PBR whirred away from the dock.

Mad Dog turned to Kat, who looked at him and suddenly collapsed into his arms.

"Kat!"

Without warning, rounds pinged along the PBR's sides as yet another BMP-1 drove beside the fiery remains of the first and opened fire. About ten soldiers were already on the dock and firing as well.

The PBR's crew returned fire, along with Wolfgang and Bibby.

Mad Dog shrank to the deck with Kat, whose eyes flickered opened. She looked at him. Smiled. "Fuck."

Pope, Moody, and Delta Team
Amu Darya River
Termez, Uzbekistan
0828 Hours Local Time

"Here they come," whispered Moody.

Pope smirked.

The other Deltas were in position. Pope counted seven infantrymen moving toward them, wearing camouflage uniforms and heavily armed with grenades, AK-47s, lots of spare ammo.

"Pick a guy and kill him," Pope muttered to Moody. "I don't care which."

Moody raised his pistol at Pope, who grinned crookedly.

Multiple cracks of gunfire broke the calm, and three of the Uzbek infantrymen staggered back or turned or clutched their chests and hit the muck.

Pope targeted the fallen and systematically put an insurance round in each man, while the Deltas went after the rest.

Moody was firing, though Pope couldn't see a target.

Then all of the Deltas came running past them, and the medic, Huff, cried, "They shot Hammerhead! Come on!"

Huff helped Pope to his feet, and they charged after the others, threading through the undergrowth until they reached a small clearing, where they found two men: Hammerhead, clutching a wound on his neck, and his missile guy, lying dead, shot in the chest, the launcher on the ground beside him.

"They dismounted before we could get off the missile," gasped the captain.

Although he didn't know their names, Pope immediately barked orders: "You and you, out front. You take up the Javelin, go right up over to the side. They're moving up on us now."

The Deltas looked to Hammerhead, who widened his eyes. "Do it, now!"

"Call Mad Dog," Pope told Moody. "Give him our GPS, tell 'em we're in deep shit."

Moody moved off, hunkered down near a bush, and worked his satellite phone.

Pope figured they had about five minutes, maybe less. While Huff treated the captain, he removed three smoke grenades from the medic's pack.

Then he limped forward, spotted the BRDM parked near the riverbank.

Though the dismounts had scattered to find them, there were still at least two soldiers manning the vehicle—one guy behind the wheel inside, another at the machine gun, the muzzle sweeping for the next target.

Pope pulled the pin on his first grenade and let it fly. He did likewise with the second, and the thick, purple smoke began obscuring the riverbank—

As the BRDM's gunner opened fire.

Moody didn't have much breath left. His nerves were pulled taught. He had to take a piss. But he ignored all that, ignored the automatic fire razoring through the trees overhead, and waited for Mad Dog to pick up the fucking phone.

Finally, Wolfgang answered.

"We got infantry and an LAV pinning us down," he said. "Our chopper's still twenty or so minutes out. Where are you?"

"We got a patrol boat, and we're on our way. Just hang on. You got GPS?"

"Coming up."

Men shouted ahead, and Moody couldn't tell if the voice belonged to the Deltas or the Uzbeks. Rifles rattled. Was that a grenade? He fed the coordinates to Wolfgang, then asked, "Why isn't Mad Dog talking?"

"Look, we'll be there in a minute." Wolfgang hung up.

Another explosion blew dirt all over Moody. He hit the deck, gasping, trembling violently.

"Mr. Moody?" called one of the Deltas, who'd come running from the brush. "Time to move!"

Mi-6 Patrol Boat, Riverine (PBR)
Amu Darya River
South of Termez, Uzbekistan
0833 Hours Local Time

Kat had been shot in the shoulder and was fading in and out of consciousness. The Brits had a medic on board who took her below and was treating her.

Mad Dog had to tear himself away, get back up top, and keep low to the gunwales as the boat raced down-river, toward the leaning towers of purple smoke risking about a half kilometer in the distance.

Well off to the right, something gleamed in the sky. He shielded his eyes, spotted the long, broad fuselage of a tandem rotored helicopter—a Royal Air Force Chinook, to be exact—streaking in from the south, and farther back, yet another chopper, still indistinct.

"Cavalry has arrived!" he shouted.

Bibby was on the satellite phone, talking with his contacts again, confirming the chopper's arrival.

The PBR's engines roared louder as the skipper took them into a wide arc, then abruptly rolled the wheel right, directly toward the riverbank. "Hang on," he ordered.

And the boat raced forward, scratching like sandpaper on metal as it ran aground, its bow sweeping up and onto the riverbank.

"Let's go!" hollered Bibby.

"I'll take her," said Mad Dog, after heading back below. He hoisted Kat over his shoulder and carried her back onto the deck. Wolfgang helped him down to the mud just as a massive explosion rose beyond the treeline to their west.

Pope, Moody, and Delta Team
Amu Darya River
South of Termez, Uzbekistan
0836 Hours Local Time

Pope balled his hand into a fist as the BRDM flipped onto its side and fire licked and spat across its undercarriage. The Javelin had struck a direct hit, and he shouted for the Deltas to fall back after learning from Moody that the PBR had arrived and the approaching Chinook was going to put down just behind them.

The medic had remained with Hammerhead, and hopefully they could move the captain without causing further injury. Pope knew he could use a hand moving himself, but the others were too busy trying to suppress a wave of fire from the remaining Uzbek dismounts who'd been part of the BRDM's crew.

He estimated that maybe three or four were left and had taken up firing positions along a little cut just south of the vehicle. If he didn't put an end to that shooting, those soldiers would have an obstructed bead on the chopper.

He still had one more smoke grenade, so he rose, lurched out of the shrubs, and squinted in search of muzzle flashes.

There they were.

Holding his breath, he pulled the pin on the grenade and lobbed it directly in front of the men.

Something stung his arm, stung his leg, and he collapsed in the weeds and mud.

Damn it. He hadn't even heard or seen the fire. He rolled onto his side, glanced toward the Chinook as it touched down, the surrounding grass and shrubs shivering.

He tried to lift himself. The pain made his eyes burn, and he dropped down again. He was low, thoroughly concealed, and reaching for his satellite phone when he passed out.

Chapter 16

....

Royal Air Force Chinook
Amu Darya River
Termez, Uzbekistan
0838 Hours Local Time

Mad Dog, knees buckling, struggled toward the waiting chopper. Kat lay across his shoulders and was chillingly silent. A few glib or wiseass remarks about the way he carried her would have been welcome, but she only gasped and moaned at every boot slip.

The chopper's crew, a collection of pale and stern-looking Brits, accepted Kat, moved her up the rear loading ramp and onto a well-padded rescue stretcher, just as Moody and his Delta team fled across the field.

"Shit," Mad Dog muttered as the spook came toward him. Old James Moody, aka "Jimmy Judas," or, as the meathead now preferred, "Jimmy Jesus," hadn't changed a bit—still the awkward caveman whose hand had never gripped a toothbrush.

Mad Dog gave the spook a poison smile. "You were supposed to save *us*, asshole."

"You didn't say how many I had to save." The spook whirled back, studying the trees and shrubs. "Pope? Come on, let's go! Pope! Move out!"

A wave of small arms fire ricocheted off the fuselage, sending both of them to the dirt.

The rest of the Deltas were coming forward, one of them toting another in the fireman's carry. The other two returned fire as the medic, Mad Dog assumed, hauled their injured comrade toward the back of the Chinook.

"Pope!" Moody screamed again.

Wolfgang dove to the ground beside Mad Dog. "I'm going for him."

Mad Dog glanced sidelong, about to nix the plan, but Wolfgang's eyes shimmered the same way they had on the day he'd hired him. There was no mistaking the man's intensity. "You're going for him?"

"I am." Wolfgang widened those eyes. He was back in the saddle, all right.

Mad Dog nodded, then lifted his head to the men inside the chopper. "I need covering fire, right now!"

Like a Doberman who'd broken his leash, Wolfgang sprang to his feet, leaped over a small mound, then beat a serpentine path for the river.

He had opted for two pistols, and felt the salvia gathering in his mouth.

Right now, at this moment, in this place, he was no longer a man and existed somewhere on the periphery of the mortal world. He believed that with every ounce of his being. Nothing could touch him.

And he was no longer afraid.

The remaining shooters had shifted position upwind

of the smoke grenades, so Wolfgang chose to keep close to the riverbank, work his way in their direction, then dart toward the water and circle around to catch them from behind.

As the chopper crew, along with PBR crew and the Deltas, joined forces to unleash their second barrage of gunfire, Wolfgang blasted through the tall grass, gripping his pistols tighter, letting the rhythm of his breath dictate his pace.

All was right. All was clear.

You will fear me.

Sweat dripped off his face as he reached another stretch of yellowing grass that rose to his chin. Using his pistol, he ducked and slashed his way forward for several meters until he arrived between two rows of bushes and a pair of trees. He continued on, gaze sweeping, the gunfire resounding. He suppressed the urge to call Pope's name, but a faint beeping noise came between the cracks of rifles.

A phone.

He threaded through the bushes, came into another path of tall grass, homing in on the sound—

And found Pope lying there on the ground, bleeding, the phone still clipped to his waist.

Wolfgang dropped to his knees, placed his fingers on Pope's neck. "Come on, bro. Come on." There it was. Good pulse.

Someone shouted at Wolfgang. He looked up.

An Uzbek solider stood there, his AK pointed at Wolfgang's head.

The son of a bitch had heard the phone, too.

Wolfgang had set down one of his pistols to check for

Pope's pulse, but he still had the other clenched in his left hand.

However, the Uzbek need only pull his trigger, and he had to raise his arm then fire.

The guy screamed again, then added in English, "Stop! Pistol!" He motioned for Wolfgang to drop his weapon.

Pope's phone kept ringing.

Ironically, the sound irritated the soldier as much as it did Wolfgang. He glared at the device.

Suddenly, Wolfgang didn't feel immortal after all. No Superman leotards for him. And worse, the solider was no kid, probably thirty, a man with a family. He had a lot to live for and wouldn't make mistakes.

Wolfgang set down the pistol, extended his fingers, then motioned with one hand toward the phone, saying, "Okay? Okay?"

Mad Dog let Pope's phone ring. The rest of the PBR guys and the Deltas were piling into the chopper. The pilot had no intention of sticking around much longer. Mad Dog couldn't fault him. The Uzbeks had reinforcements on the way.

And Bibby kept reminding him of that: "Enemy aircraft inbound. We're out of time."

"No shit."

"I can't convince them to stay any longer. You have no idea what it took to organize this."

"Yeah, I do," said Mad Dog. "Just tell them to give me two more minutes." Mad Dog pressed the receiver to his ear, and realized with a start that someone had answered and left the line open. "Bibby? Wait!"

*   *   *

The soldier motioned for Wolfgang to stand, and as he did, he calculated the distance between them, considered how long it would take for him to push forward and clutch the rifle away before the guy shot him.

He half expected to hear a *snick*, but hallelujah, it didn't come.

He took a deep breath and—

Boom! A crack of gunfire sent a bolt through him. Had he been shot? His hands groped along his chest.

The Uzbek soldier fell forward.

But how? Wolfgang looked to the chopper, visible in the distance. A sharpshooter from there?

Then he glanced down at Pope, who was holding his pistol. The big guy with shaved head grinned weakly. "Little help, please?"

"Holy shit . . . holy shit . . . " Wolfgang could barely breathe.

"Hey, shitbird? Rescue me."

"Uh, yeah." Wolfgang glanced to the dead solider. "Thanks."

"I won't tell the boss I saved your ass—if you save mine."

"That's a deal." Wolfgang hauled the man up and onto his shoulders, nearly breaking his own back in the process.

With his boots sinking deep into the dirt, he grimaced and walked hard toward the chopper, flooding with relief as Mad Dog and Bibby rushed out to help.

The Black Hawk that had been called in by the Delta team provided suppressing fire against the LAVs as the

Chinook lifted off and aimed for Afghanistan. Bibby said another Black Hawk would join it to recover the bodies from the Delta team's downed chopper. Moody had arranged it, and all ball-busting aside, Mad Dog sincerely thanked the spook for helping to bring back all of their men.

Leaning against the seat, Mad Dog craned his neck to stare out one of the windows, watching as the Friendship Bridge shrank behind them. They flew over the mine fields, barbed-wire fences, and the watchtowers. Within minutes they would be in good old A'stan, land of opportunity. No, he wasn't being sarcastic. The country had given him the chance to soldier on his own terms. Now it gave him freedom. While in many ways it might be hell on earth, for him it was still a sacred ground where men had lived, fought, and died.

Kat was on the stretcher near his boots, and he gripped her hand tightly. She looked up at him, her expression sober, as if to say, *I said you'd be lucky if half of us come back alive. But I didn't want to be right. God, I didn't.*

Mad Dog glanced away, then massaged his aching eyes.

"Hey." Moody had shifted across the cabin to sit next to him.

Mad Dog frowned at him. "Yeah?"

"We're heading to Camp Cunningham at Bagram Air Base. Pope and your friend here will see the docs."

"Good."

Moody hesitated and seemed to grope for words.

"What?"

"The Agency wants you back in Langley."

"Bullshit. I'm going home to Cebu."

"You need to meet them first. Debrief. Hand over any and all intel. They'll have you arrested if you don't."

"I'll give 'em what they want, but you tell them they can come to me, have a nice little vacation in the Philippines while they're at it."

"I'll let you tell them that yourself. Hey, you okay?"

Mad Dog glanced suspiciously at the spook. "You're supposed to be gloating, not asking how I am."

"Well, I'm asking."

"I'm not very good, if you want the truth."

"It seems to me there's a lot more to your little escapade in Khiva then you're letting on—and I'm betting there's some major cash involved."

"You'll get your fucking money, if that's what you mean."

"You're going to throw me a million, just like that?"

"Fuck the money. Fuck it all. I don't even know what I'm doing here."

"That job offer still good, or are you quitting the business?"

Mad Dog frowned. "You want to come work for me?"

"Fuck no. It's just nice to be wanted."

"Go away, asshole."

Moody raised his palms. "I'll get with Bibby to make sure the transfer goes okay."

Mad Dog gave him a lopsided grin. Then he sat back, closed his eyes. Felt Kat squeeze his hand. He squeezed back.

"You can't quit," she said softly. "I won't let you."

* * *

Camp Cunningham
Bagram Air Base
Afghanistan
1920 Hours Local Time

Wolfgang sat in the makeshift coffeehouse, watching the big screen TV with a trio of enlisted Air Force personnel. Reporters from CNN were discussing Moscow Center's claim that the CIA hired terrorist Tohir Khodjiev to assassinate the president of Uzbekistan. Reports of President Atayev's death were still not confirmed since the Uzbeks kept tight reins on their news media. A couple of the men who were watching with him glanced at each other, and one nerdish looking dude with bad acne said, "I think the CIA did it. I think the CIA has been in bed with terrorists from the very beginning."

"I don't," snapped Wolfgang, drawing their stares. He took a deep breath and threw his hands behind his head as the anchors went live to the White House Press Room.

Was it just a coincidence or something more powerful? He didn't know, but he watched as an old friend from twenty-seven years ago got behind the podium. He'd forgotten that while he had gone into the army to become a master gunner, Teddy went to college, became a lawyer, was lured into politics, and worked his way up the ranks. Now old "Blohodda" was the White House press secretary, God bless him. And he'd best start blowing some hot air, some very hot air.

Teddy issued a curt statement denouncing Moscow Center's claims and assuring everyone that the CIA had absolutely nothing to do with the purported events taking place in Uzbekistan.

When he was finished, he began fielding questions, the first from a CNN reporter. "Ted, our London office is reviewing some pretty convincing video of the alleged assassination as it took place in the old city of Khiva."

"I'm sorry, Eddy, but if there's a question there, I missed it. I do know your competition over at Fox sent over some footage labeled 'daily rushes' from an action film called *The Perfect Target* they're shooting at the same locale. Phillip Steinberg's directing, and I think Chad Schmidt is in it, along with Tina Rosalie. Is this the video you're referring to, Eddy?"

A few chuckles echoed through the room as the reporter winced and replied, "I don't think so. But I have no way of verifying that at this time."

"Well, Eddy, the White House can't comment on your footage without seeing it. Yes, Lisa?"

A hard-faced blonde with narrow eyes and a pen and notebook in hand cleared her throat. She was from the Associated Press, according to a caption. "As I assume you're aware, Galina Saratova, head of the CIA's Asia desk, was just killed in a terrible car accident. Does the White House believe there is any relationship between Saratova's death and the accusations coming out of Moscow Center?"

"Lisa, local authorities have already ruled Ms. Saratova's death as accidental, and at this time the White House has no reason to believe there is any connection between the accident and the accusations from Moscow. The Agency was deeply saddened to learn of Ms. Saratova's death and will do everything in its power to assist her family." Teddy dodged two more questions about the president's strained relationship with the Russian president, then decided his time was up. "On that note let me conclude by stating that the president would be deeply saddened if, God forbid, the rumors about President Atayev turned out to be true. We need to wait until the Uzbekistan government clarifies the situation."

One of the enlisted guys thumbed down the TV's volume. "I bet we whacked him because the bastard kicked us out of K2."

"He didn't kick us out," said Wolfgang. "Guy before him did. Atayev was a good guy."

"How the fuck do you know?" asked the nerd. "And who the hell are you?"

Wolfgang rose, put a finger to his lips. "You didn't see me. I was never here." He blew the knuckleheads a kiss.

"The Dog Pound"
Talisay City
Cebu, the Philippines
Ten Days Later
0922 Hours Local Time

It was Sunday, and Mad Dog stood on the back porch of the main house, watching Wolfgang put the finishing touches on a row of soldiers' crosses he had set up in memory of their fallen comrades. Small piles of sandbags kept the rifles erect. Helmets hung from the rifle stocks. The boots of each man sat in front of the bags.

Doolittle, Drac, Boo Boo, Sapper, Night Stalker, Styles, Wilcox, and Zito.

Eight brave individuals. Operators par excellence, full of esprit de corps, warriors who happened to be mercenaries, but men cut from the most sacred of cloth.

Sacred.

Old Dan came up beside him. "It'll be a real nice ceremony today. Got over a hundred people coming."

"That many?"

"You know, Michael, you've done so much for this island, single-handedly revitalized tourism, that you're going to see an outpouring that will shock you."

"Maybe so. But I think we're done, Dan. The only thing we got out of this was money blackmailed out of the CIA and an agreement to shut our mouths or else. Five million won't bring back our men. Eight men. Jesus."

"What about the necklace?"

"Not sure yet. We wound up paying our little thief half a million for his part. I figured he'd grab it and run. But the son of a bitch can be trusted, after all. Probably wants more work from us. Anyway, it's too soon to sell it. We'll see."

"Hey, Michael, just remember something: You couldn't have anticipated a mole in the CIA, for God's sake. Your men knew the risks. You got a right to feel bad about losing them, but don't feel sorry for yourself."

"How's it look?" asked Wolfgang, heading up onto the porch. He was wearing white cargo shorts and a loud print shirt.

"The crosses look good. Why don't you go put something on to respect the dead?"

Wolfgang glanced at his duds, frowned. "What? You

want me to go put on a black suit? I thought this was a memorial service. Like Dan said, it's a chance to tell people about our friends. It ain't a funeral. It's a party."

Mad Dog wasn't sure how to respond. One minute he wanted to celebrate their lives, the next he wanted to burn down the whole fucking pound and ask God for forgiveness. He just shook his head. "You do want you want."

"All right." Wolfgang made a face and headed off. "I'll see if Pope's ready to get up."

After Wolfgang was out of earshot, Dan called, "Michael?"

Mad Dog just waved him off and started into the house, toward his room. He mounted the stairs and found Kat waiting for him at the top. At least one thing felt right: her. "How're you feeling today?"

"Even better." She gently touched her gunshot wound. "Even better."

"Good." He shifted past her.

"Hey, thanks for the flowers. They even match the décor in that room. I didn't know you were so anal."

"I'm not. But I figured you might be."

"No, but that's sweet. And hey, I just have to know . . . last night . . . why didn't you come? I was waiting for you."

"Kat, I'm sorry."

"For what?"

"I don't know. You're just . . . you're still part ghost."

"What does that mean?"

"I need to change. I'll talk to you later." He headed into his room, shut the door and collapsed onto his bed. He balled his hands into fists, then rolled over. God, he needed to vent. He grabbed his notebook computer, fired it up, loaded the file ACCOUNT #A011, CODENAME: THUNDERKILL.

God, the balance sheet looked abysmal.

They'd lost the C-130, which cost about $68 million to replace, given all of the upgrades Styles had made to the craft. They'd lost Kat's chopper, which the company was responsible to replace at a cost of nearly two million with upgrades for a new one. The MD600N would go for nearly four million, but maybe they could find a used one in good condition for about half that.

So they'd lost over seventy million in aircraft alone, not to mention weapons and ammo, fuel costs, salaries, etc. IPG only had about $32 million in the bank, thrusting its net liquid assets deeply into the red. His dream was crumbling before his eyes. Would he watch that happen? Or would he do something about it?

He clicked on his journal to where he had left off, remembering his first encounters with each of the men he'd lost, and realized it was time to write about the living, about her. He began:

She told me in no uncertain terms that she wanted me to spend the night, but even that I couldn't give her. Even that.

Funny thing yesterday. I called up my cancer doctor. Just wanted to hear her voice. Just wanted to tell her that she was a survivor like me. Just wanted to remind myself of that. I could tell she thought I was out of my mind, but I didn't care. She started her chemo, and she's going to be okay. I'm going to be okay.

But back to Kat. Every time I look at her now, all I see

are the faces of the dead. And when I look at Pope, I feel the same way.

Oddly enough, I don't get that from Wolfgang. He's a renewed spirit, found his mojo or something. I wish I didn't have this much time on my hands. I wish I was too busy to feel any of this bullshit. Bibby provided me with a list of grief counselors, some employed by his friends in the UK and Middle East, but I'll work it out on my own. I always have. Yeah, but in doing so I'll probably alienate everyone around me, but that's how it goes in the beginning.

Mad Dog slapped the computer shut, then reached into his nightstand and withdrew the jade necklace. He ran his fingers over the stones and thought back to his lunch with Saratova. She didn't seem the cunning bitch she turned out to be, and there had to be more to her story, much more. He rose and thought about what he'd wear. Five minutes later he left his room wearing blue cargo shorts and a floral print shirt.

Wolfgang showed up to the memorial service in a black suit and looked daggers at him for the first fifteen minutes until he found a chance to slip off and change.

Pope hated being wheeled around in a damn chair, especially when his driver was none other than Wolfgang, who had decided that he would practice for a stint as a NASCAR driver by first racing Pope around the backyard.

When they reached their table, they settled down to a few beers, and he finally got a chance to ask Wolfgang how the hell he'd come out of his funk.

"I don't know," the guy said. "I just remembered when I almost drowned as a kid."

Pope felt as though he'd been shot. Again.

"Jesus . . . I forgot about your sister. Sorry."

"It's okay. It happened a long time ago."

Wolfgang nodded. "Well, I finally remembered the whole thing. And I guess that same feeling was repressed or something. Fucking brain. Who knows how it works? But I didn't die. And I'm not scared to die anymore."

"Bullshit."

"Maybe what I'm trying to say is that I'm not scared to be scared. They always told us that in the service, right? I guess it's easy to forget."

Pope nodded. "I hope you didn't forget about the girls for tonight?"

Wolfgang's mouth fell open. "Wait till you see them."

Old Dan had been right about the locals. The love shown was beyond words, and lots of tears were shed. By mid-afternoon the booze flowed freely, as did the stories and the laughs. The "party" lasted until nearly midnight, and when it was over, Kat and Mad Dog sat in rocking chairs on the back porch, while everyone else had stumbled back to their rooms, girls and half-empty bottles in tow.

"This is it, Kat," Mad Dog said after a long silence. "This is it. That's what Eddy and Doc would've wanted, especially Doc. He always said we pushed it too far."

"Who are you talking about?"

"Damn, I thought I told you that story."

He went on about Afghanistan, about the cave containing that warlord's gold and cash, about how he and his old Marine Corps pals Eddy and Doc had smuggled the money out of A'stan and into Switzerland, thoroughly pissing off one James Moody, who had been bribing the warlord.

And when he was finished, Kat shook her head. "That's amazing. So what happened to Eddy and Doc?" She lowered her voice. "Or shouldn't I ask?"

"Land mine got 'em both. Took 'em fast. But they've always been around."

"So you have a habit of conferring with ghosts."

"Got more friends who are ghosts now. And that's some depressing math."

"So you're thinking they'd want you to quit?"

"Yeah, I am. Doc's telling me we can't afford to keep the door open. Better to get out while we can."

"Well, fuck Doc."

"Excuse me?"

"Michael, you have the means and the talent. And you still have a lot to do. We should get more into training and let those other poor bastards die for their country."

"With five people? Wolfgang, Bibby, Pope, you, and me?"

"So now we're a squad. Who cares, right? You want to recruit new guys, go for it. Hard to find people you can trust, though, huh? Maybe we stay lean and mean."

"Maybe I should let you run the show."

"I already do. No need to make it formal."

He grinned. "Is that right?"

"For example, if I ordered you to kiss me right now, you would, because you—"

"Yeah, yeah," he said, cutting her off, grabbing her wrist and pulling her from the chair. "Come here."

He took her in his arms. Damn, he'd been wrong. She wasn't part ghost. She was all woman.

Hornsea on Bridlington Bay
England
Two Weeks Later
1130 Hours Local Time

A man named Allyn Gulthewaite, one of the "transition team" members, led Bibby up the bungalow's stone walkway, toward the side entrance door. A pang of nervousness struck Bibby, and he ordered himself to remain calm. Despite the terrible, terrible guilt, he would do what he must. There was no longer any choice. He took a deep breath and stepped inside.

Gulthewaite, who spoke perfect Russian, introduced him to Boris Sinitsyna, the NKVD colonel and political officer who had been assigned to the Russian embassy in London. Sinitsyna was tall, bald, clean-shaven, and had a slight paunch. He wore a T-shirt and pair of slacks, and was smoking a cigarette while drinking a cup of tea. He had military written all over him, and for man over sixty, he had remained spry. He eyed Bibby as though about to interrogate him.

Which of course he did, via Gulthewaite, who translated. "He wants to know who you are."

Bibby removed his glasses, stared directly into the colonel's eyes. "Sir, can we speak alone?"

Gulthewaite straightened his tie. "I'm not sure that's a good idea."

Bibby glanced at the rafters. "The room is clean, correct?"

"Yes. Surveillance outside only."

"Excellent. Leave us."

Gulthewaite shrugged. "I hope you've brushed up on your Russian—because he refuses to speak to anyone in English."

Bibby just glowered at the man until he wandered outside.

Once the door closed, the colonel moved up to Bibby, stared him down. Then, in perfect English, he said, "You have the time it takes for me to finish this cigarette, and then you're gone."

Bibby opened his long trench coat, reached into one of the interior pockets, and produced an eight-by-ten-inch dark blue box. He set it down on the wooden table between them.

The colonel raised his chin at Bibby for an explanation.

"Open it," instructed Bibby.

Frowning, the man took a seat at the table, lifted the box, and slowly peeled back the lid—

To reveal a perfect circle of translucent, emerald green beads nestled in yellow silk. The colonel ran his finger over the beads. "Are they real?"

"Indeed. That necklace was your daughter's. The American government confiscated all of her possessions—except that. Conservative estimates value it at over ten million U.S. dollars."

"How did you get it?"

Bibby sighed. "I stole it from my employer."

"Why?"

"That's unimportant."

"Do you know what's important to me? The names of the men responsible for killing my daughter."

"I'm not here for that."

The man smote his fist on the table, rattling the necklace. "Then why are you here?"

"Colonel, I have a serious problem, and you're part of the solution." Bibby pointed to the beads. "See that jade? That's your retirement in luxury. Your daughter wanted that for you."

"And I know what you want from me," the colonel said through his teeth. "God help you, I do."

Bibby grinned darkly. "Welcome to the world of mercenaries, Colonel. I trust you'll find it quite enlightening."

SEALS

THE WARRIOR BREED

by H. Jay Riker

SILVER STAR
978-0-380-76967-4/$6.99 US/$8.99 Can

PURPLE HEART
978-0-380-76969-8/$6.99 US/$9.99 Can

BRONZE STAR
978-0-380-76970-4/$6.99 US/$9.99 Can

NAVY CROSS
978-0-380-78555-1/$5.99 US/$7.99 Can

MEDAL OF HONOR
978-0-380-78556-8/$7.99 US/$10.99 Can

MARKS OF VALOR
978-0-380-78557-5/$6.99 US/$9.99 Can

IN HARM'S WAY
978-0-380-79507-9/$7.99 US/$10.99 Can

DUTY'S CALL
978-0-380-79508-6/$6.99 US/$9.99 Can

CASUALTIES OF WAR
978-0-380-79510-9/$6.99 US/$9.99 Can

ENDURING FREEDOM
978-0-06-058597-6/$7.99 US/$10.99 Can

IRAQI FREEDOM
978-0-06-058607-2/$7.99 US/$10.99 Can